how to
make
a
wish

# how to make a wish

ASHLEY HERRING BLAKE

HOUGHTON MIFFLIN HARCOURT
BOSTON  NEW YORK

Copyright © 2017 by Ashley Herring Blake

Also by Ashley Herring Blake

*Suffer Love*

www.hmhco.com

The text was set in Adobe Garamond Pro.

Library of Congress Cataloging-in-Publication Data
Names: Blake, Ashley Herring, author.
Title: How to make a wish / by Ashley Herring Blake.
Description: Boston ; New York : Houghton Mifflin Harcourt, [2017] | Summary "A small town pianist ponders a new life away from her embarassing mother when a beautiful girl shows up and changes everything"— Provided by publisher. Identifiers: LCCN 2016015270 | ISBN 9780544815193 (hardback) Subjects: | CYAC: Pianists—Fiction. | Friendship—Fiction. | Mothers and daughters—Fiction. | Self-actualization (Psychology)—Fiction. Classification: LCC PZ7.1.B58 Ho 2017 | DDC [Fic]—dc23 LC record available at https://lccn.loc.gov/2016015270

Manufactured in the United States of America
DOC 10 9 8 7 6 5 4 3 2 1
4500649408

*For Dahlia, Ami, Tehlor, Sara, Jenn, and Tristina,*
*who helped me see myself a little clearer*

There are two tragedies in life.
One is to lose your heart's desire.
The other is to gain it.

—GEORGE BERNARD SHAW

# chapter one

S HE WAITS UNTIL WE'RE DRIVING OVER THE BRIDGE TO tell me. This is a strategic move. Wait until your temperamental daughter is suspended over the Atlantic Ocean to drop the bomb, thereby decreasing the chance that she'll fling open the car door and hurl herself over the edge.

My mother is many things. Beautiful. Annoyingly affectionate after a few drinks and mean as a starving snake after several. Quick-witted and hilarious when her latest boyfriend isn't turning her into some sycophantic sorority girl. But a fool?

No.

My mother is no fool.

She swerves to pass a car that's already going at least ten over the speed limit. The ocean, a dark sapphire blue, swings out of my vision and back in. I grip the handle above the window, shifting my gaze over to Mom to make sure her *I forgot this silly thing again* seat belt is securely fastened.

"What did you say?" I ask. Because I must have misheard her.

Surely, my subconscious anticipated returning home to some catastrophe after leaving Mom on her own for the past two weeks, and it conjured up something totally absurd to lessen the blow.

"Grace, don't make a big deal out of this. It's just an address," Mom says, and I bite back a bitter laugh. She loves that word. *Just.* Everything is *just. It's just one drink, Grace. A birthday is just a day, Grace. It's just sex, Grace.* My entire life is one gigantic *just.*

*Well, I'm* just *about lose my shit if you're serious, Mom.*

How's that for a freaking *just?*

She steers with her knee for a few terrifying seconds while she digs a cigarette out of her purse and sparks it up. She blows out a silver stream of smoke through the open window, and I watch her fingers. Long and elegant, her short nails perfectly manicured and glossed eggplant purple, like always. She used to press our fingers together, kissing the joined tips and making a silly wish on each one. I would measure my hand against hers, eagerly waiting for the day when mine was the same size. I thought that the older I got, the older she would get and the less I'd have to worry about her.

"Pete's place is really nice," Mom says. "It's so unique. Wait till you see it."

"Pete. Who the hell is Pete?"

She glances at me and frowns, flicking ash out the window as we exit the bridge and drive onto the road that leads into town. "I started seeing him before you left for Boston. I told you about him, right? I'm sure I . . ." She trails off, like not being able to finish a sentence automatically releases her from any obligations.

"You're serious, aren't you?" I ask, struggling to keep my voice even.

She laughs. "Of course, baby. This is a good thing. Our lease was up and that dickhead of a landlord wouldn't renew it because he claimed I still owed him three months' rent for that dump he called a beach house. And things with Pete were going so well. He'd just moved and needed a woman's touch." She giggles and snicks the cigarette butt out the window. "That's what he said. A woman's touch. Such a gentleman."

Oh Jesus. I recognize that tone, that girly giggle, that glassy look in her eyes. I can almost mouth the next words along with her, reciting the lines of a painfully familiar play. I've been off-book for this shit show for a long time.

Cue Mom's dreamy sigh.

*Three . . . two . . . one . . .*

"He might be the one, baby."

My fingers curl into fists on my bare legs, leaving red nail marks along my skin. When I left a couple weeks ago, I swear to hell Mom didn't have a boyfriend. I would've remembered. I always remember, because half the time, I'm the one who reminds her of the asshole-of-the-month's name. Okay, maybe that's a stretch, but I really thought she'd run out of options.

Cape Katherine — Cape Katie to locals — is a tiny spit of land jutting into the Atlantic with about three thousand residents, a quaint downtown with lots of local shops and restaurants, and an ancient lighthouse on the north end that's still maintained by a real-life lighthouse keeper. We moved here when I was three, and in the fourteen years since, I've lost count of how many guys Mom has "dated."

And the whole lot of them has had the honor of being *The One* for about ten minutes.

Mom turns onto Cape Katherine Road. The Atlantic rises up on our left, flanked by rocks and gravelly beach. Early-afternoon sun spills coppery sparkles on its surface, and I take a few deep breaths. I'd like nothing better than to jump ship, streak down the beach, and throw myself under its waves, letting it roll over me. Let it have me for a few minutes, curling my body this way and that, transforming me into something free and weightless.

But I can't do that.

For one, it's cold as hell this early in the summer.

And whatever knot my mother's woven herself into with He-Might-Be-The-One-Pete, I'm the only one here to untangle it.

"Okay," I say, pushing my hair out of my face. "Let me make sure I've got this straight. In the twelve days since I've been in Boston, you moved everything we own into a new house I've never seen to live with some guy I've never met?"

"Oh, for god's sake. You make it sound like I'm dragging you into some disease-ridden jungle. I'm telling you, you will *love* Pete's house."

I don't really give two shits about Pete's house.

I'm more concerned about Pete.

Mom flips on the radio while I try to decide if I want to vomit, scream, or cry. I think it's some awful combination of all three.

"Mom, can we please talk about—"

"Oh, baby, hang on." She turns up the volume on Cape Katie's one and only radio show, hosted by Cape Katie's one and only radio host, Bethany Butler. It's on every morning and evening, and people call in and tell Bethany sob stories about their missing cat or how their coffee burned their taste buds off or something equally inane and irrelevant. Mom freaking loves it. She's a total sucker for anything potentially tragic and unrelated to her own life.

*"You heard it here first, Cape Katians, so keep an eye out for Penny. She was last seen on East Beach . . ."*

"Who the hell is Penny?" I ask.

"The Taylor family's corgi!" Mom says, a hand pressed to her heart. "She got loose from Tamara while she was walking her on the beach, poor thing."

*". . . And remember, Penny is very skittish around men with red hair and—"*

I flip off the radio. "Seriously, Mom? A corgi?"

"It's sad, that's all I'm saying. They've had her for a decade. She's older than Tamara."

"Yeah, cry me an effing river," I mutter, looking out the window, the familiar sights of my town flashing past me in a blue-and-gray blur. "So do we still live on the cape, or are you just swinging by our old place for one last haul?"

"Of course we live here, baby. Do you really think I'd take you away from your school and all your friends right before your senior year?"

I choke down a derisive laugh. I'm not sure which is funnier: her comment about *all my friends* or the fact that my brain can't possibly conjure up half the crap in my life that comes from being Maggie Glasser's daughter. I would never *think* any of it. But it all seems to happen anyway.

# chapter two

T EN MINUTES LATER, MOM PULLS INTO A FAMILIAR
gravel driveway. It's one I've seen a million times before.
As kids, my best friend, Luca, and I used to fly over this
winding, rocky path on our bikes until the trees split and revealed a
little sliver of adventure right there at the edge of the world.

"Mom, what are we doing here?" But she just grins as she
throws the car in park and opens her door. "Mom."

"Stop being such a stick-in-the-mud, Gracie. Come on."

She climbs out and I follow, craning my neck up, up, up to the
top of Cape Katie's whitewashed lighthouse. A red-roofed bunga-
low sits below it, tucked into its side like a little secret.

Mom comes to my side and slides her arm around my shoulder.
The wind tangles her dirty-blond hair.

"This is going to be so great," she says.

"What is going to be so great?"

She giggles and gives my arm one more squeeze before

practically skipping up the drive toward the house. I gulp briny air, willing the crashing ocean to swallow me whole.

I shoulder my duffle and follow her to a small detached garage next to the side entrance of the house. The yawning door reveals stacks of open cardboard boxes, some of the contents draped over the sides. Glass beads, scraps of metal, and a soldering iron from Mom's handcrafted jewelry business are spread over a large plastic table. I spot a pair of my sleep shorts—black with neon-pink skulls—puddled on the dirty cement floor, along with a few piano books.

"I've done a bit, but we still have a lot of unpacking to do, baby," Mom says, heaving a box overflowing with our decade-old towels into her arms. She chin-nods toward another box, but I fold my arms.

"Are you for real? Mom, the last I heard, the lighthouse keeper was about a hundred and ten years old. Please tell me you're not shacking up with Freddie Iker. His best friend is his parakeet."

She breaks into laughter, dropping the box in the process. Her tank-top strap slides off her shoulder as she guffaws, really throwing all she's got into it. My mother's laugh has always been infectious, clear, and light. I hate to crack even a hint of a smile at the stuff my mother finds funny, but most of the time I can't help it.

"Good lord. I'm not that old." She pulls her hair into a sloppy bun on top of her head and picks up the box again. "Or that desperate."

My smile morphs into a massive eye roll. Over the years,

Mom's traipsed guys as young as twenty-one and as old as fifty-four through our many homes, so I'm not sure how to even begin to respond to that one.

"Freddie retired and Pete took over last week. He's got an electrical background and has some really innovative ideas for the museum. He even wants to incorporate some of my jewelry in time for next tourist season. Isn't that something?"

"It sure is." I grab my sleep shorts and music books from the floor and tuck them under my arm. Not sure which is better. An old geezer who can't even get it up or some starry-eyed electrician with *ideas*. Ideas are dangerous around my mother.

I shade my eyes from the sun hanging just over the tree line and take in my surroundings. My new home. An SUV with peeling black paint on the hood is parked on the other side of the garage. It looks vaguely familiar, but considering there are dozens of these kinds of cars on the cape, that's not too surprising.

"Pete's at some budget meeting in town, but I think Julian's home," Mom says, heading toward the main house. She sticks a key in the side door, and the hinges squeak as she nudges it open with her hip. Cool air rushes out to meet me.

"Julian?"

"Pete's son. He's a nice boy. I think he's about your age."

And with that, she disappears into the house, leaving me open-mouthed in the doorway. This just keeps getting better and better. What's next? Sharing a room with Pete's mother? Maybe a lunatic ex-wife is bunking in the lighthouse tower who screams like a banshee at night and has to be chained to her bed. Hell, at this point, I'm waiting for Mom to tell me Pete's actually a polygamist and she's been chosen as a sister wife. I comb through the roster of my high school for a *Julian,* but I've got nothing.

I follow Mom into a shabby-chic-styled kitchen with chrome-rimmed white appliances, white cabinets, and navy-blue curtains with red lobsters all over them framing the window above the sink. The living room is a mixture of our old leather recliner and scarred coffee table and a bunch of junk that looks like it just got dragged out of a frat house. There's a plaid couch sporting a busted spring and duct tape, along with a TV the size of a car mounted over the fireplace. The only redeeming thing about the whole weird scene is the wall of windows revealing the sprawling blue ocean sparkling under the sun.

We head down a narrow hallway. At the end, Mom opens a door next to the bathroom and gestures me inside with a flourish of her hand.

"This is you. Isn't it nice? So much natural light."

I enter the room, and it's like walking into one of those dreams where everything seems familiar and foreign all at once. The space is square and small and white. My twin bed is shoved into the far corner under the wide window that's also facing the ocean. White furniture, mine since I was four, is arranged smartly around the room. Mom has already spread my plum-colored sateen comforter that she found for half-price over the bed and filled my closet with my hanging clothes. The few books I own are stacked neatly on my little desk, and framed photos are displayed on the dresser. Sheer white curtains sway in the breeze from the open window. My eyes drift to the wall above my bed, taking in the framed print of a beautiful grand piano on the stage at Carnegie Hall, an empty auditorium lit by golden light and waiting to be filled with an audience, a pianist, music. Luca gave it to me for my birthday two years ago. Mom's actually managed to hang it straight, no cracks in the glass or chips in the black wooden frame or anything.

Aside from the stray things in the garage, Mom has *worked* on my room. My eyes burn a little, imagining her organizing my space before she even unpacked her own things.

"So, Pete's and my room is at the other end of the house, and Julian's just across the hall," she says. She peers anxiously at me, no doubt searching for signs of an impending explosion.

And, oh, do I feel it brewing. Despite the homey feel, this is still a room I didn't choose and never planned for. My throat feels tight from holding back all the eff-bombs I want to drop right now. Not that I usually rein them in too much in Mom's presence, but she looks so damn hopeful. She's trying really hard to make this a good thing.

"Okay," I say, as usual.

"It's going to be so lovely, baby," she says. "I mean, it's the lighthouse! I know you love this place and have always wanted to live right on the beach."

I nod, looking out my window at the rocks dotting the shore, angry waves spitting white foam all over their surfaces. She's right.

I used to love this lighthouse. It always seemed so magical when I was six or seven, but you can only hold your own mother's hair back while she pukes up vodka so many times before you get a little disenchanted.

"Oh!" Mom says so loudly, I startle. "With the move, I almost forgot." She grins at me and digs into her back pocket, retrieving a folded rectangle of paper. She opens it up, her smile growing wider as she holds it out to me. "This is for you."

I take the wrinkled paper, almost scared to look at it. Because what now? As usual, when it comes to my mother, curiosity and hope nearly smother me. My eyes devour the writing.

When the content registers, my head snaps up, gaze locking with Mom's. "For real?"

She nods. "For your audition. We can drive there pretty cheap and stay at that hostel, tour the Big Apple during the day, eat off the street carts. We need to plan ahead if we want show tickets. I've picked up a few shifts at Reinhardt's Deli, and with some help from Pete, I'm saving a little. You need to do more than audition when you go, baby. You need to see where you'll be living next year, and I want to be part of that. I'm so proud of you."

I stare back down at the paper, which tells me there are two beds at a New York City hostel reserved under Mom's name for July thirtieth through August second. Underneath that is Mom's chicken-scratch handwriting, listing all the things we've always talked about doing in the city. It's got the usual stuff, like visiting the Empire State Building and Times Square, Central Park and

Ellis Island. But it's also got the Grace stuff—auditioning and touring Manhattan School of Music. Seeing *Hedwig* on Broadway. Finding a way to get a backstage tour of Carnegie Hall and standing on the stage, maybe even sliding my fingers over one of their piano's keys.

"Thank you," I manage to whisper. Part of me knows she timed telling me about this trip to perfectly coincide with this move to the lighthouse, a little peace offering. The bigger part of me doesn't care.

"Of course, baby. It'll be the perfect weekend. Just wait." She pulls me into her arms, crushing the already-crinkled paper between us, and presses a kiss to my forehead.

"Well, I know you're tired from your bus ride," she says, releasing me. "Get settled in. You can meet Julian later and . . ." Mom must see all the roiling emotions mirrored on my face, because she pats my shoulder and is out the door without finishing her sentence.

I drop my stuff and sink onto the bed, finally overwhelmed. To clear my head, I close my eyes and mentally go through the beginning of Schumann's *Fantasie* in C major, Opus 17. The piece plagued me at the piano workshop I just completed in Boston, the complicated, rapid fingering and the ethereal, dreamlike quality of a first movement a pleasing sort of torture. The music is pretty kick-ass, all chaotic and angsty. And it kicked *my* ass, which I have to appreciate.

Now I play it on my bed. I imagine myself on an auditorium

stage or in a practice room at some college. Manhattan School of Music. Indiana University. Belmont in Nashville. Though Manhattan is my white whale, my dream, and the thought of going far away and staying in dorms that I can actually *live* in for longer than three months makes me giddy, it also freaks me the hell out. I can't imagine actually moving away. Leaving Mom alone to flit from one house to the next, one guy to the next, one skipped meal to the next bottle of beer.

My fingers fly over the wrinkled comforter, the music alive and real in my mind. Nerves coil in my stomach—but whether from auditioning and laying my whole future on the piano keys in front of a few judges or leaving Mom, I'm not sure. Either way, I keep pressing into the soft cotton until my left hand collides with a box. My eyes flick open and absorb the room again.

*My* room.

I unzip my duffle and dump its contents onto the bed, sorting through dirty clothes and the ones clean enough to wear again, even though they smell like the inside of my bag. I rearrange a few things around the room, moving my composition paper from my desk to my nightstand—when I can't sleep, I make up dumb little songs in bed—and find a picture of Luca and me that Mom had tossed on a shelf in the closet and place it on my dresser. Luca looks predictably happy, grinning through his curly mop of hair with his arm slung around my shoulder at the beach last summer.

Halfheartedly, I order my little universe. No matter how many times I tell myself it doesn't matter—that I'll have to pack it all up in a matter of months anyway—I can't resist trying to make a place my own. This lighthouse that I used to love and now suddenly hate is no exception.

I grab my toiletry bag and venture into the hallway to check out the bathroom. It's clean; a clawfooted tub with one of those wraparound shower curtains sits against the wall under a frosted-paned window. The tiled sink is cobalt blue, and an antique-looking light fixture sends an amber glow through the room. It smells like wet towel mixed in with some crisp, boyish scent. Aftershave, maybe. A navy-blue toothbrush sits in a holder by the sink. I throw mine into an empty drawer. Call me unreasonable, but sharing toothbrush space with a guy I've never met just seems weird.

I unpack my face wash and deodorant and then stuff my empty bag under the vanity before flicking off the light. As I enter the hallway, the door to my left swings open and my eyes dart over.

I swallow a few colorful words and press my back against the wall.

He's tall. I mean, of course, I knew he was, but he looks gigantic in the tiny hallway. Intentionally messy light-brown hair. Hair I used to yank to get his lips back on mine whenever he started sucking on my neck too hard.

"Oh my god," I choke out. "What are you . . . How did you . . . Why are you . . . ?" I swallow, trying to get my breath back as his mouth—a mouth I know way too damn well—bends into a smirk. It pisses me off to no end.

"What the hell are you doing here?" I finally spit out.

Jay Lanier pops his hands up on the door frame and leans toward me. Leather cuffs circle each wrist, and ropy muscles in his forearms ripple with tension. His smirk morphs into something so self-indulgent that I wish I had long fingernails so I could claw it right off his face. His gaze trails up my body, pausing at every possible spot that I never planned on letting Jay Lanier glimpse ever again, even through a tank top and shorts. I glare at him, but my hands are trembling and my stomach heaves, my mouth watery.

He laughs softly—demonically, if you ask me—and leans closer.

"Did I ever tell you that Jay is my nickname?"

My mouth drops open.

He smiles, a maddeningly slow spread of his mouth like the fucking Grinch. "No. I don't think I did."

I try to conjure some insult, anything to put me on equal ground here, but only incoherent combinations of four-letter words come to mind.

"Welcome home, Grace," he says.

And then he slams the door in my face.

# chapter three

I STARE AT THE BRIGHT WHITE DOOR. BEHIND IT, THE guy I planned to avoid all summer bashes around. Something heavy—I'd think it was a book if Jay Lanier had ever been spotted with one—*thwacks* onto the floor. Music clicks on and some sugar-shocked, overly eager male voice filters under the crack in the door.

Son of a bitch.

And son-of-a-every-other-swear-word-in-existence.

"Grace!" Mom bellows from the kitchen. "You hungry? I have some sandwich stuff here!"

Her voice grates on me like an oboe just a nick out of tune. Every affectionate feeling I had toward her a few minutes ago about New York, about my cozy little room, vanishes. I stalk down the hallway, pausing by the dining room window to toss back the curtains and eye what I now recognize as Jay's Jeep. Not that I've ever been inside it. He got it after we broke up last fall, but I've seen it in the school parking lot and around town enough times to realize why it looked so familiar on first glance.

I find Mom rummaging through the vintage one-doored refrigerator. Her shorts are so low on her hips, I catch an unwanted glimpse of red thong. Straightening, she tilts her head at the muted TV on CNN, mouth open a little as it flashes live shots of some tornado that ripped through Nebraska last night. Mom sighs and I grit my teeth.

"Pete's last name is *Lanier?*" I ask.

She startles and drops a few squares of American cheese. "Yes. Honestly, Grace, I know I told you about him."

"You didn't. You told me nothing, as usual. You also failed to mention Jay."

"Jay?"

"JAY!" I whisper-yell, flinging my hand behind me toward the bedrooms.

"You mean Julian?" She picks up the cheese and tosses it onto the counter next to a package of turkey and opens a bag of bread. "Did you meet him?"

I can only stare at her. Is it possible that she's really this clueless? Well, yeah, of course it is. I know this about my mother. She can't remember what grade I'm in half the time. Still, I sort of expected her to remember the name of the boy I dated for six months who then made my life a living hell after I dumped him. I thought our breakup was going to be pretty quiet. I mean, it was clearly time. I was bored. He was bored. But he went ballistic. Right there in the school cafeteria. Knocked his tray full of tacos off the table and stormed out. The next day, a screenshot of every text message we'd ever exchanged that mentioned body parts ended up on his Tumblr page.

I told Mom all of this. Unlike her, I *do* tell her things about my life, stuff other girls would never tell their own khaki-clad mothers. I guess it's my pathetic-as-hell attempt to bond or something. As usual, it's backfiring bigtime.

"He's a sweet boy," she says. "Helped me move in all your furniture when Pete was busy learning the ropes here."

Yep. She really is that clueless.

"Mom."

She stops spreading mayonnaise on a piece of bread and looks at me pointedly.

"Jay. Lanier." I enunciate every syllable, making my eyes as wide as they'll go.

Her penciled brows press together for a few seconds before popping up into her hair. "Oh my god."

"Yeah."

She points the mayo-covered knife toward the hallway. "*That's* Jay?"

"Yes."

She's nodding now, probably remembering the few times I brought Jay home for about ten minutes. I mean, yeah, I made sure the two of them spent very little time together when we were dating, but still.

"Oh my god," she says again. "Well, this is a surprise."

"Clearly."

Mom cranes her neck around me and eyes the hallway. Her shiny lips spread into a flirty grin. "I think what's clear is that you have excellent taste in men, baby."

"Mom. Ew."

Mom laughs and slaps greasy turkey slices onto her bread. "Do I need to pick up some condoms? I wish you'd go on the Pill, because you don't want—"

"God, Mother! He's a total dick, remember? Can you just . . ." I flap my hands around, trying to grab the right words out of the air. "Can you act like a parent for five damn minutes?" She flinches and I rub at my temples, my head suddenly aching.

"Gracie," she says, coming to my side. She wraps an arm around my shoulders, and I lean into her for a minute. "I'm sorry, baby. You know how I get when I'm excited." She smooths her hand over my hair. "You're right, I wasn't thinking. I know Julian—*Jay*—gave you a hard time a while ago—"

"'A *hard* time'?" She's making it sound like he got mad and drew devil horns on my yearbook picture or something. The guy posted our sexts for the entire world to see, for christ's sake. Consequently, everyone at school hoisted him onto their shoulders, and I got a bunch of averted gazes in the hallway. Not that I really wanted their gazes, but it's the principle of the thing. "Mom, you can't be serious. There's no way this is going to work."

"I'm sure Julian is over it. You'll see. It'll be fine. He's a sweet boy."

"Mom. He's an asshole, and now I'm living across from a guy who's seen my boobs—"

"So have I."

"—and I'm supposed to sister up to him for however many months you and Pete live in la-la land? Can't you see how messed up this is? You should've seen the way he just looked at me in the hall. I mean, 'It'll be fine'? Really?"

She bites her lower lip as her eyes search my face. "God, you're right. I'm sorry, baby. I see how this might be weird for you."

*Weird* isn't exactly the word for it, but still, it's something. I feel my shoulders relax a little, prepare myself for more packing and moving.

Then she removes her arm from around me and twists her fingers together into a little knot. "But—"

I press my eyes closed for a few seconds. *But. Just.* Round and round we go.

"—Pete makes me happy," she says. "Maybe you and Julian can work it out, talk it through. Please, baby. This is my chance. Will you just try? And then, before you know it, we'll be off to New York for a nice break."

A dull, familiar disappointment fills me up. Whenever I find myself in some awkward situation, I always, always hope. And she never, ever surprises me.

"I'm going out," I say, moving away from her.

She perks up at that, taking my action as a sign of acceptance. "Good idea. Get some air. Just be back in time for dinner. We're going to eat as a family; won't that be great?"

I grab my messenger bag back from the barstool where Mom dropped it earlier and head for the door. With my hand on the doorknob, I turn back and meet my mother's desperate gaze. I fight the urge to stay, to help her unpack, to make sure she eats that sandwich she's making, to say, "Yeah, that'll be swell."

Instead, I leave without a word.

# chapter four

I CALL LUCA AS SOON AS I'M OUTSIDE.

"Gray-Gray!" he shouts into the phone. I'm so wound up, I don't even have the energy to give him crap about his ridiculous nickname for me. It's a play on *cray-cray* that arose after my legendary leap from Colin McCormick's second-story balcony and into the pool at his Memorial Day party last year. Luca thinks the name is freaking hilarious. He also thinks my jump was inspired by a multitude of lime-green Jell-O shots. It wasn't. It was only fueled by one. I jumped because I goddamn wanted to. I had recently spent the better part of a Saturday on the phone with the electric company trying to figure out our bill — and by *figure out,* I mean asking them how long they'd give us to scrounge up some more pennies before leaving us in the dark. I was so pissed off. For weeks. Colin's party rolled around and I just wanted to feel like a damn teenager, stupid and carefree. So I jumped.

"Are you back?" Luca asks. "Tell me you're back."

"If you'd call it that." I walk over to the garage and peer inside, searching to make sure my beach cruiser is still in one piece. It's my only mode of transportation around the cape.

"What does that mean?"

"Typically, in order to *come back* you have to return home." I wade through more boxes, shove aside golf clubs, and edge around a rusting lawn mower before pulling my bike from a corner by one handlebar.

"What the hell are you talking about?" He yells it, but only because he's at LuMac's, his family's diner, and a blender starts whirring in the background.

"We moved."

There's a beat of quasi-silence. I can almost feel Luca wincing through the phone. I push on my bike's dingy white tires, amazed Mom managed to keep them intact during the move.

"Are you serious?" Luca finally asks.

"Yes. To the lighthouse."

"Okay, Virginia Woolf. Wait . . . Peter Lanier is the new lighthouse manager—"

"Yeah, no shit."

"So . . . you're *living* with Jay?"

"Again, no shit."

"Damn."

"Do you have anything helpful to offer, or should I try to hit up my mother again for a little comfort?"

"I've got pizza fries."

"That'll do. But you know I can't leave Mom here by herself for too long when she's unpacking. She'll probably start a fire trying to store pillows in the oven or something. Or she'll channel-surf until she finds the most depressing UNICEF commercial in existence, and then she'll really be useless." I think about my neat little room and swallow a lump in my throat. Mom can be damn focused when she wants to be. Key word *want*.

"Gray, she's a big girl. You're allowed to do something for yourself."

"I did. I went to Boston for two weeks and look what happened."

He doesn't say anything to that. In the background, I hear his mother, Emmy, calling out orders. "Blue Burger up for table ten!"

Luca clears his throat, then laughs a little. "If anything, she'd burn the place down with her hot glue gun. Remember that time she left it on in the bathroom of that crappy duplex you lived in a couple years ago?"

"And melted my toothbrush — yeah, I remember."

When things get heavy, Luca likes to whip out a story or two and hardy-har-har over it. From anyone else, I'd rip them a new one, but I know he only does it to keep me from using Mom's legendary hot glue gun for much more sinister purposes. Either that, or he legit has no idea what to say to all this insanity, which is highly likely. Still, no matter how many times this happens, no matter how many times Luca smiles through it all, it's still embarrassing as hell that this is my life.

"Hey, seriously," he says. "Do you want me to talk to my mom? You could move in for a—"

"No."

"But—"

"Luca. No."

He sighs so loudly into the phone, it hurts my ears, and I know we're both thinking the same thing. When we were thirteen, my mom disappeared for a few days. Luca came over and cooked up a pretty convincing lie to tell Emmy, said he was staying over because we were helping Maggie with some huge jewelry order. Emmy has an enormously sensitive bullshit detector. She showed up an hour later at our apartment, a casserole dish for dinner in hand. When we couldn't produce Maggie, she hauled me home with her, despite my protests.

When Mom came home two days later, she went to Emmy's looking for me. They had a huge blowout, Mom screaming at her that she had no right to take her kid, and Emmy calmly—but with a firm fury to her tone that scared the shit out of me, to be honest —explaining to her that I wasn't old enough to be on my own for that long.

Mom went apoplectic. She grabbed my arm so hard, it bruised —the only time she's ever laid a less than gentle hand on me—and took me home. She didn't talk to Emmy for a year after that, and even though a sort of strained peace exists between them now, their interactions are still awkward as hell.

Luca tries to bring it up every now and then—like *now*, when he knows I'm in a situation that's less appealing to me than a Brazilian wax—but I always shut him down. I can't leave her. She's my mom; I'm her kid. We belong together. I start to tell him this, to tell him about the New York audition trip and how she organized my lighthouse room and managed not to break anything, but even in my head, it sounds like an excuse.

"Okay, fine," Luca says. "I'm training the new girl in an hour, but I'm done at six and then I'm coming over, no arguments."

"You don't have to do that—wait. What? What new girl?"

"She's—"

"Luca, dammit, I needed that job." We'd talked about this before I left for Boston. Mom's online jewelry shop and occasional waitressing jobs are spotty at best. She still gets survivor benefits from the military every month, but it's not enough. She has a little from my dad's personal life insurance too, but again it barely covers our food, much less my lessons with Mr. Wheeler, my piano instructor. Consequently, I've had some sort of job since my age hit double digits.

"Claws in, cat," Luca says. "You know you've always got a job here if you want it."

"You're sure?"

"I'm sure. You're golden. Just hide your tips in a safe place, if you catch my drift."

"Do I ever miss your drift?"

He grunts acknowledgment, knowing he's got a point. Mom's been known to . . . borrow from me, rooting through my room in whatever dump we're living in until she finds a twenty or two. Sometimes it goes toward a phone bill, a meal. Sometimes it doesn't.

"Besides," he says as I pull a loose piece of wicker off my bike's basket, "it's Eva."

"Who's Eva?"

He pauses and takes a deep breath. "Eva Brighton? She's my mom's friend's daughter. Remember?"

My stomach plummets to my feet. "Oh, crap. I'm sorry, I totally forgot."

"It's okay."

"No, it's not. God, I suck, Luca."

"Stop. You have a few things on your mind."

I nod, even though he can't see me, but dammit. Hurricane Maggie strikes again, obliterating everything in my life but *her*. About a month ago, Emmy's childhood friend Dani Brighton, who lived in Brooklyn with her daughter, died suddenly. She taught ballet at a fancy company in the city, and during a practice, her appendix ruptured. After surgery, everything seemed fine, but then she got some infection they couldn't get under control. She died a week later. Emmy was devastated. Still is, I would assume. Plus, she not only lost her friend; she gained a daughter. Emmy and Dani only talked sporadically over the past several years, so when a lawyer contacted her and reminded her that she'd agreed to be Eva's guardian years before, Emmy was thrown for a major loop.

"Dani never got married," Luca told me when it first happened. We were at LuMac's sharing a plate of pizza fries while Luca pretended to roll silverware.

"Did they contact Eva's dad, though?" I asked.

He broke a long string of cheese and wound it into his mouth. "Can't really contact a guy whose name you don't know."

"Oh."

"Actually, I think Eva knows his name, but there's nothing to legally bind them. The only thing on her birth certificate is 'father unknown.'"

"Wow."

"Yeah."

Right before I left for Boston, the Michaelsons launched into full panic mode getting ready for Eva to come, transforming what was once Macon's bedroom-turned-storage room into an inhabitable bedroom. Emmy was a total mess, reading through her old self-help books on grief and mourning and healing. It made Luca nervous as hell. Since their dad left, he and his older brother, Macon, have been super protective of Emmy.

And, of course, I forgot all about this huge change in my best friend's life, because I'm me.

"How's it going with Eva?" I ask now. "Is she . . . okay?"

"Hard to tell. She just got here last week, but so far she's pretty quiet. Stays in her room mostly."

"Weird. You, like, have a sister. Sort of."

"*You're* my sister. And Eva's kind of hot, which makes drumming up any sisterly feelings really hard."

"What the hell? Are you saying I'm not hot, Luca?" I ask, a teasing lilt to my voice.

"Gross."

I smile and walk the bike around the side of the garage before flipping out the kickstand. I look back toward the house, torn between wanting to go back inside and fix this mess with Mom—if it's even fixable—and needing to get as far away as possible.

"So I can come over when my shift's done?" Luca asks.

"You don't have to. Mom wants a 'family dinner,' god help us all."

"With Jay Lanier?"

"Will you stop saying his name?"

"He's *your* roommate."

"I swear to god, Luca Michaelson, if you laugh right now, I will shave your head with a cheese grater while you sleep."

Luca gasps dramatically, and I can picture him clutching his beloved locks. "Look, Gray, I know this sucks. Just let me come over. Your mom loves me—"

"Mom loves anyone with a generous helping of testosterone."

"—and I'll bring pizza fries and Cherry Coke."

I sigh into the phone. Normally, I wouldn't let even Luca near one of our residences right after Mom and I crash into it, especially with a Pete involved. But this time, there's a Jay thrown in for good measure, and I'd be lying if I said the thought of him existing a few feet from my bed didn't make me want to curl into an itty-bitty ball. But really, it's not only Jay. Jay is a minor annoyance. Jay is the growl of a much larger beast.

"Okay, but if it gets too weird, you can leave at any time," I say.

"Right."

"Hey, set me up with pizza fries and a Cherry Coke, and I don't really care if I ever see you again."

He laughs. "You couldn't live without me, Grace. You know it."

I laugh back and hang up, although he's sort of right on that one. I know a lot of people on this godforsaken waste of space and a lot of people know me.

But no one really knows me.

For a while I was pretty much a sugar-and-spice kind of girl. I've had a handful of friends here and there, but with the ebb and flow of my existence, it was easier to keep my world as small as possible. Less explaining. Less lying to cover up why I'd moved again. Less worrying about what totally messed-up situation I'd encounter when I brought a friend home. Sure, Mom's not always a mess. She has her good days. Good months, even. I just never know when a good day is going to turn to total crap.

# chapter five

I SHOULDER MY BAG AND HEAD TOWARD THE SHORT walkway that leads down to the beach. It's low tide and naked rocks pebble the sand on either side of me, the ocean spitting and spinning just ahead. The water is almost the exact same shade of blue as the sky, the two pressing together like a kiss. I kick off my flip-flops, leaving them near the dunes, and start walking.

The sand is cool between my toes, and the briny air opens up my lungs a little. The rolling *hush-hush* of the ocean and the yawning expanse of the sky open up something else in me too. I kick at the ground, sending puffs of off-white into the air. The wind seems just as angry as I am, flinging the sand around, and I kick at the earth again. And again and again until I'm walking through a sandstorm.

My eyes start to feel gritty and my knees wobbly, so I finally slow and sit down, folding my legs underneath me. I dig through my bag and pull out the wrinkled, torn-in-one-corner picture of my parents I always carry with me. My father is tall and handsome and refined in his uniform. My mother is smiling and bright-eyed, her perfectly purple-painted nails resting gently on her pregnant stomach. Luca's caught me staring at this photo a few times. Usually he doesn't say anything, just offers a shoulder squeeze or one of his annoying-as-hell noogies.

But I don't really stare at this picture because of my dead father. He was killed in Afghanistan when I was two, so I never really knew him. No. I pore over this picture because of the woman. Maggie Glasser. Same name as my mother. Same face. Same long fingers. But everything else is different. Her hair isn't dull and stringy-looking but shines like spun gold. Her eyes aren't ringed with lack of sleep and sadness and booze; her shirt doesn't droop on her shoulders as if from a clothes hanger.

Both people in this picture are total strangers.

And it pisses me off to no end.

I stuff the picture back in my bag and tamp down the maddening crawl of tears up my throat. I'm wrenching the zipper closed when I hear something that sounds like a sob. It takes me a few seconds to realize it's not coming from me.

About twenty feet away, there's a girl sitting in the sand. Her back is to me, but I can tell she's curled into a ball, her knees tucked to her chest as she huddles against the wind. The current laps over the shore, and her slouchy white T-shirt is dotted with salt water. Her hair is a halo of black spirals around her head, her skin a warm brown. From where I am, I can see her shoulders moving up and down—she's definitely crying—and her left arm jerks here and there like she's fiddling with something in the sand.

I stand and take a step closer to get a better view of what she's doing. There's a jar of peanut butter next to her, silver spoon jutting out from the top. Every now and then, she reaches over and scoops up a bite, sucking on the spoon through her sobs.

I watch her, totally transfixed by how the wind keeps picking up locks of her hair and tossing them around before setting them back down. She wipes her face before digging into the peanut butter again, her left hand still sweeping over whatever she's focused on in the sand.

After a couple minutes, I pick up my bag and start walking toward the lighthouse. Time to check on Mom. Time to deal with Jay. Maybe work in a little daydream about the New York trip in between all the real-life suckage.

But then I hear that sob again—deep and almost free sounding, like it's a relief to let it loose—and it makes me stop. It makes me turn back around and find the girl in the sand, who's now standing and facing the ocean with her bare feet in the freezing water, her peanut butter jar and what looks like a large square-shaped book clutched to her chest. I can see her profile now, and tears stream down her face.

That's when it hits me.

This is Eva.

Luca's Eva. Emmy's Eva. Just-lost-her-mom Eva. There's a

34

picture of Dani Brighton and her daughter on the bookshelf in Emmy's living room that I've seen at least a hundred times. In the photo, Eva's around thirteen or so, middle school lanky with a mouthful of metal, but it's definitely the same girl standing on the beach now. Same lean frame and sleek cheekbones and wild, curling hair.

I should leave. God knows, when I'm upset enough to actually let some tears leak out, I want to be left the hell alone. But something makes me hesitate and take a few steps closer to her. That something might be the fact that my best friend would stare me down with his big disappointed puppy-dog eyes if he knew I left Eva out here, alone and crying, without so much as a howdy-do.

Or that something might be that I'm curious. That I don't want to go check on Mom. That I feel miserable right now and misery loves company or whatever the hell. That something might be a lot of different somethings, but either way, my feet carve through the gravelly sand, weaving in between the sharp rocks until I'm just a couple of steps behind her.

"Hey," I say, reaching out at the same time to tap her elbow. My voice and my touch are as soft as I can make them, but she still startles, actually coming off the ground a bit as she whirls around. Everything in her arms tumbles onto the wet sand.

"Crap, sorry," I say, bending down to pick up her stuff. There's the open peanut butter jar, a spoon, a pack of colored pencils, and one of those grown-up coloring books titled *Lost Ocean,* all of which is now partially covered in the real-live ocean.

"It's okay," she says as she kneels to help me. Her voice sounds clogged, and the tears keep coming. She doesn't even fight them back, just lets them have their way.

"Were you actually trying to color out here?" I ask, handing her the book. "It's windy as hell and you were sort of sitting . . ." I gesture to the waves lapping closer as the tide rolls in.

"Yeah, it's a policy of mine to only color in really precarious places."

"Really?"

She laughs, a watery chuckle. "No, not really."

We both stand, and I see now she's a little taller than me and slender. Her T-shirt hangs off her shoulders, neon-green bra blazing through the thin cotton, and her skinny jeans are wet to the knees.

"Well, this is unfortunate," she says, peering into her jar of peanut butter. Specks of sand dot the gooey surface almost entirely.

"The hazards of a New England beach," I say. "The sand and the wind have wills of their own."

"I see that." She scoops up a spoonful and lets it hover near her mouth. "Can't be much different than the crunchy version, right?"

"Oh sure, just a little more protein."

Her light-brown, amber-flecked eyes rest on mine, grinning through a sheen of leftover tears. She opens her mouth, resting the spoon on her bottom lip. I watch her, sure she's going to pull away at any moment. There are even a few short strings of seaweed stuck in the peanut butter, for god's sake.

When she starts to close her top lip, I can't take it anymore. I yank the spoon from her mouth, and it plunks into the sand.

"Hey, now," she says firmly, but she's half laughing.

"I could not in good conscience let you eat that. There is such a thing as marine bacteria, you know."

"You could've just said *Stop*. You pretty much hit me." She rubs at her wrist, but she's still sort of smiling. There's a hint of relief underneath, like she's happy to be joking around and distracted from those tears. Or maybe that's just me.

"Desperate times," I say. "Suck it up."

"You're a little bit prickly, you know that?"

"Better prickly than infected with a tapeworm."

"I see your point. Still, one can't discount the importance of new experiences."

"Oh, god," I say, picking up the spoon and holding on to it. "You're not one of those people with *carpe diem* tattooed on your ass, are you?"

She lifts her brows. "No, but now I'm feeling inspired."

We both laugh while she wipes away the last bit of salt from her cheeks. I watch her put all of her stuff into her messenger bag, sand and all. Her slender arms flex with lean muscle, her collarbone delicate under her skin. Both ears are lined with tiny hoops and studs. Every movement graceful and intentional.

It's a good fifteen seconds before I realize she's done packing up and is watching me, too. We're pretty much staring at each other like dumbasses. I clear my throat and run both hands over my hair, which the wind has whipped into a fine frenzy. She follows my movements, then reaches out and catches one of my hands. I'm about to yank it back when her thumb smooths over the lacquered polish of my middle finger. Then my forefinger, followed by my ring finger and pinkie and thumb. Each nail is expertly painted a different shade of purple, from eggplant to lavender.

"Why different colors?" she asks, still gliding her fingers over mine.

I pull my hand back, swallowing hard. I run my own thumb over a few nails, assigning a wish to each one, before tucking my hands behind me, spoon still in my grip.

"Ah, a secret," she says, offering a tiny lopsided smile. "I get it."

"It's not a secret." I can't keep the edge from slipping into my voice. "It's just not your business."

She nods, her expression unreadable. "Right. Weirdo stranger coloring intricate ocean scenes on the beach and eating sandy peanut butter doesn't exactly inspire confidence."

"It's not that."

"Okay, well, I'm Eva. Eva Brighton. Now I'm not a stranger anymore. Weirdo, maybe, but not a stranger."

I inhale some briny air. I don't want to talk about my nails or purple or anything remotely associated with my mother.

"I know who you are," I say, tossing the focus back on her. "I'm Grace."

Her eyes widen. "Well, isn't that the icing on the proverbial cake."

"Huh?"

She laughs, but it's got an exhausted edge to it, and a few more tears trickle out of her eyes. She wipes them away, but not like she's embarrassed by them. More like they're simply in her way. "You're Luca's best friend. Great first impression, right? Unhinged new girl with her coloring books and sand fetish. Jesus."

"Don't worry about it."

She nods but continues to look everywhere but at me. "You live here?"

I follow her gaze toward the lighthouse, my breath sticking in my chest. Such a loaded word — *live*. It could simply mean existing. Heart pumping blood, lungs taking in air. Or it could mean settling into something. Being a part of what's around you. Investing.

"For now," I say.

"For now," she echoes softly. Her gaze shifts toward me, and I find myself staring again. Her face warrants it, familiar and new all at once. Pretty. I force my eyes away.

"I should go," I say.

"Me too."

I hitch my bag higher up on my shoulder and start to tell her goodbye when she reaches out and swipes a finger down my cheek. Her touch scrapes my skin, both gentle and rough. I step away from her, ready to unleash a few colorful words about her scratching me, but she holds up her finger, smudged with a tiny dollop of wet sand.

Then she sticks her finger in her mouth. My eyes widen and laughter bursts out of both of us so hard, I feel the sting of tears under my eyelids.

"Oh my god," I say, trying to breathe normally.

"Not bad, if I'm being honest," she says, patting her flat stomach dramatically.

"We should ask Emmy to put it on the menu at LuMac's."

"We'll call it Summer Surprise."

"Instant classic."

Our laughter continues for a couple more seconds before she takes several deep breaths, each exhale a little shaky. She keeps her hand on her stomach as though she's holding herself together.

"Thanks, Grace," she says. Then, before I can ask why she's thanking me, she turns away and starts off down the beach. Even plodding through the sand, she's graceful. I watch her get smaller and smaller. I keep watching, her spoon still in my hand, until she's nothing but a speck on the blue horizon.

# chapter six

P ETE IS HUGE. HIS SUN-DARKENED ARMS ARE LIKE HAM hocks, and he likes to grab my mother's ass. He's smacked, tapped, flicked, pinched, or patted it seven times since he walked in the door five minutes ago.

"So *this* is Grace! I remember you," he says, after they make out for about ten damn hours while I busy myself digging around for some olive oil. He says my name like "Grice," his lazy southern drawl warping the vowels. He and I only met once or twice while Jay and I were together—obviously, neither one of us was too keen on meeting the parents. I had totally forgotten that his first name was Pete until a few hours ago. He was always just Mr. Lanier.

Now he winks a gray eye at me and pats my shoulder. His brown close-cropped hair is speckled with sawdust. A little falls onto my forearms. "You sure do make pretty babies, sugar," he says to Mom with a butt slap. She giggles.

I grit my teeth and turn back to the chicken browning in the skillet. "I take after my father."

A charged silence fills the kitchen. I fight to keep the smile off my face and glance over my shoulder to find Pete frowning and Mom glaring at me.

"Right. Well, I'm going to hop in the shower," Pete says.

"Okay, honey. Dinner in ten, right, Grace?"

In reply, I stir the rice a little more vigorously than necessary.

Pete winks at me again and smacks a kiss onto Mom's cheek before disappearing down the hall.

"You call that trying?" Mom asks as soon as he's out of sight.

"I call that the best I can do."

"'I take after my father'? What the hell was that about?"

I whirl around to face her, rice-covered spatula in hand. "What? I *do* take after him."

She flinches, then scowls as she cracks open a Bud Light. "For god's sake, Grace. Grow up."

I can't help but laugh at that one. *Grow up?* I grew up a long time ago, the first time I walked into the living room to find her passed out on the couch, cozied up with a bottle of vodka. I was eight. It was my birthday.

A door down the hall creaks open and then slams shut. My stomach knots up. I turn off the burners, flip the chicken onto a clean plate, fluff the rice, my hands shaking through every movement.

"Julian!" Mom calls, and I cringe.

"Hey, Mrs. Glasser," he says. I hear a barstool creak as he sits.

"Oh, honey, call me Maggie. Please."

"Okay. Maggie." He drawls her name out using what he thinks is his sexy voice. She giggles. I turn around and glare at him. He winks at me. What is it with these damn Lanier men and their damn winking and my mother's damn giggling?

"Baby, I think that's enough," Mom says next to me.

"Huh?" I look down at the plate in front of me, half the pot of rice covering its surface. "Oh. Right." I scoop some back into the pan and carry two plates to the table, *accidentally* kicking Jay in the shin as I pass him. He grunts but says nothing.

Mom fills glasses with iced tea, and even Jay deigns to set out forks and knives. God, it's like something right out of a 1950s sitcom. Jay and Mom banter back and forth in a way that can really only be described as flirting. I'm about two seconds from scratching both their eyes out when the doorbell rings and then the door opens. Luca pops his head through and calls out, "Hello?"

"Luca!" Mom squeals, and runs over to him. She tackle-hugs him, and he lets out an *Oof,* nearly dropping the grease-stained paper bag in his arms.

"Well, hello to you too, Maggie." His sandy hair is longer since I last saw him, his curls sticking up everywhere. He's got on his summer uniform — ironic T-shirt, board shorts, and flip-flops.

"How's it working out with that girl Emmy took in?" Mom asks, gripping his already-tanned arms. Other than sun-deprived tourists, Luca's the only person I know who swims in the ocean this early. "What's her name? Ella?"

"Eva. She's doing okay, I guess, considering."

Mom presses a hand to her heart, and I fight an eye roll. *Here we go again,* I think. Then mentally slap myself because, Jesus, this Eva girl just lost her mother.

"So heartbreaking," Mom says. "I'm going to stop by LuMac's really soon and meet her, okay? She's our girl now, right? We'll take care of her."

Luca flicks his eyes to me and then back. "You got it, Maggie."

Mom beams and finally releases Luca. He brings the bag from LuMac's to the counter, unloading two tinfoil pans of pizza fries and a huge plate of brownies covered in Saran Wrap. Then he folds me into a hug, his arms swallowing me. He smells sort of coco-nutty, like sunscreen.

"Mom sent over some goodies," he says, my face pretty much still buried in his armpit. "A housewarming gift."

"Oh, I'll be sure and thank her when I stop by," Mom says, but her posture stiffens. She sniffs the brownies like she's expecting them to be rancid or something.

"She'd love to see you," Luca says, releasing me.

Mom nods, but it's impossible to tell what she's thinking. When Luca and I were around four years old, she and Luca's mom met at a support group that Emmy was running for people with spouses killed in action. Emmy used to be a licensed counselor, specializing in grief and family therapy, and she immediately took to Mom. She even did a couple of private sessions with her. True to form, Mom clung to her pretty tightly at first but balked once anything got too hard to deal with. Not so coincidentally, that was around the same time she started dating Rob. Or maybe it was Rick. Whatever. Point being, Mom's therapy was the definition of sporadic. Then, five years ago, Luca's dad found greener pastures in his secretary's pants—god, the man is a walking cliché—and moved to California, so Emmy decided to start over too. She quit her practice and opened LuMac's. Without the counseling, our moms interacted less and less, and any lingering affectionate feelings they once shared disintegrated when Emmy tried to "steal" me.

Now I'm the only one who's really trapped in Mom's rip tide.

But only for another year. I think. Crap, I don't know. I get chills just thinking about the whole thing, but I'm not sure if they're the good kind. On the one hand, I've only got a year to put up with Mom's messes. On the other, I've only got a year to get her to stop making them in the first place.

Luca smiles at me and I steal a pizza fry off the top pan. A long string of mozzarella cheese stretches to my mouth. I hear an annoying clicking sound and turn to find Jay watching me. No, not watching. *Leering.* He wiggles his eyebrows, clicking his tongue again. I ignore him, meeting Luca's boiling-anger expression. I shake my head and Luca nods, my nonverbal *leave it alone* received.

"Can I get one of those, Michaelson?" Jay asks, reaching for a fry.

"Sure, *Lanier.*"

I stifle a laugh. Luca hates it when guys call each other by their last names. "Hey, look at me, I'm too manly for those girly first names," he always says in an overdone booming voice with his chest puffed out.

Mom calls Pete for dinner while I watch Jay and Luca fake smile and chomp on pizza fries. They never liked each other, even when Jay and I were a thing. It was a pain in the ass then, but the whole Tumblr-sexts incident pretty much cemented their enmity and I'm just fine with that.

"I'm starving," Pete says as he comes into the room, his hair still wet. We all sit at the table, and he tucks his napkin into his collar. "Looks great, Mags."

Mom simpers. "Thanks, hon."

I bite the inside of my cheek and feel Luca's gaze shift to me. He knows Pete would be hacking at a charred lump on his plate if I hadn't intervened. But whatever. Let Mom play the adoring wife if that's what makes her happy. God knows it won't last long.

Polite conversation ensues. Mom asks Luca about the diner and his brother and when Macon's very pregnant wife, Janelle, is due. Pete asks Jay when training for fall football starts. Eventually, Luca forces me to talk by asking about the piano workshop in Boston. An instructor at Juilliard runs the whole thing. It's scholarship based, which means if you're good enough to get in, it's paid for. That also means it's basically one big sticks-up-their-asses ego fest. Mr. Wheeler says I got in because I'm just that talented, but really I got in because he went to high school with the director.

Plain and simple. All the other kids there had private tutors and their own personal piano studios. I've got an uptight high school music teacher and part-time jobs. Either way, I went and learned a ton of new techniques and got some awesome tips for my audition.

"That's wonderful, baby," Mom says after I spit out some details.

"I need to get busy on all the stuff I learned," I say, picking at my chicken. I cooked it too long. It's a weird combo of dry and rubbery. "The piano probably needs to be . . . tuned . . ." I trail off as I look around the tiny living area. "Wait a minute."

I slide back my chair and get up. I walk slowly through the house, unbelieving eyes cutting into every corner.

*No. She wouldn't.*

"Where the hell is my piano?" I ask when I circle back to the table.

Mom sits back, squirming in her seat. Pete squirms right along with her. Luca looks at me like he's waiting for me to combust, and Jay continues to shovel rice into his gaping maw.

"Gracie—" Mom starts, but I cut her off.

"Where is it?"

She visibly pales. "Baby. There . . . there just wasn't room—"

"There wasn't room?" I say, my voice a rising screech.

"Oh, crap," Luca mutters under his breath.

"We had to consider Pete's and Jay's things too. But don't worry. I got a good deal on it."

I nearly choke. "You sold it? You *sold* my piano? I have an audition in six weeks."

She folds her arms and huffs out a breath. "I'm aware of that. You still have your keyboard."

My nails cut half-moons into my palms. She can't be serious. Despite my mixed feelings on leaving next year, I submitted a pre-screening video to Manhattan School of Music back in January. You can't just apply to that school and then sit yourself down in their performance hall and play them a little ditty. You have to get *invited* to play them a little ditty and, by some miracle, I was. My audition is on July thirty-first, which is the whole reason I went to the Boston workshop. It's no small thing. It's a huge, holy-shit kind of thing for serious pianists. I thought Mom knew that. She encouraged me to submit the video. She always said I was made for big things. She talks about when I'm a fancy-schmancy pianist performing in Carnegie Hall. Of course, over the years she's said all of this with a wave of her hand, like we're discussing whether to have chicken or steak for dinner, but still. And back in April, when the letter from Manhattan came, she squealed and jumped around our duplex's kitchen and even tried to get me to drink some cheap wine cooler in celebration. More than that, she *promised,* over and over, to drive me to New York. She babbled on for days about how we'd make a trip out of it, a girls-on-the-town kind of thing. And now she's making that trip happen. We're really going. Mother and daughter, making our dreams come true. Our wishes.

So, *I still have my keyboard?* Really?

"My keyboard fits on my lap," I say. "It has no dynamics, no pedal. It doesn't even have eighty-eight keys. It's not a *piano*. I can't practice fucking Rachmaninoff on that thing!"

Jay whispers a "damn," and Pete clears his throat before tossing back a swig of beer. Luca stares at his lap, chewing his lip. Mom glances at all of them, gauging their reaction for how to respond.

Finally, she says, "I'll thank you to watch your language."

I gape at her.

"Besides, baby, that thing was always out of tune. It's hardly a loss."

As usual, her assessment is a hair shy of accurate. Tuning wasn't my piano's problem. It's the A key, nearest to middle C. It buzzed and sometimes it stuck. But it was a real piano, something I never thought I'd have, so I made it work. When I was ten, a local church was getting rid of its old piano to make room for a beautiful black-lacquered baby grand. Mom haggled with the pastor, really amping up her charm, and we got the scarred upright for next to nothing. Its keys were yellowed, some of them chipped, but I took care of it and kept it in tune and it was mine. My canvas, my escape.

"I'm sorry, baby," Mom says, setting her hand on the back of Pete's thick neck. "But sometimes sacrifices are necessary when you're going to be part of a family."

I flinch like I've been slapped. Pete and Jay have the decency to look away, but Luca watches me calmly, his palms braced on the table like he's prepared to get up and bolt, a gentle hand leading me away from the mayhem. He's done it before, distracting me from drama at home or from sexts pasted all over the Internet with pizza-fry-eating wars and daydreaming about rearranging Mrs. Latham's beach gnomes into R-rated positions.

Mom watches me too, her expression all reprimanding mother. Family? Sacrifices?

"Grace," Mom says, taking a sip of her beer, "don't make a big deal out of this. It's *just*—"

"Right. It's just music. I know."

Mom lifts her chin, defiant, but her eyes have gone soft. Pleading. "I don't mean it like that, baby. We'll figure it out."

"Right," I say, always the acquiescent daughter.

Usually. Usually I say okay with my mouth and bitch about everything in my head. Usually I move into the next apartment, deal with the next mess, figure out how to pay the next bill.

But today, I'm sort of done with *usually*.

Without another word, I turn my back on her—on the family dinner—and disappear into my room, slamming the door behind me like any normal red-blooded American teenager would.

# chapter seven

I REPAINT MY FINGERNAILS. MOM STARTED PAINTING MY nails when I was three. She taught me how to do my own when I was five.

Always glossy dark purple.

Same as her.

"Like sisters," she had said, pressing a kiss to my thumb and closing her eyes. I knew she was making a wish. "We wish on our fingertips, baby, not the stars."

"Why?" I had asked, wide-eyed and still a little in love with my wild, beautiful mother. She held her hand over mine, showing me how to paint from the center of the nail out.

"Because," she said slowly, her tongue pressed to her top lip the way it does when she's concentrating. "If you really want something, baby, the stars won't help you. You have to reach out and take it."

It's been several years since we huddled on the couch and did our nails together. It used to be fun, giggling and gossiping and carving a space out of reality where we were just sisters and the mother and daughter were the illusion. But I got tired of that script around the time I turned twelve and Mom decided I was old enough to hear about her occasional one-night stands in between boyfriends, which wasn't really something a girl who hadn't even had her first period needed to know. Plus, aside from my immaculate nails, the rest of me — my hair, my attempts at makeup, clothes — was a total freaking mess for all of middle school until Emmy finally taught me how to put on mascara and match a top to a skirt.

Still, I haven't been able to shake the nail habit, though unlike Mom's loyalty to aubergine, I dabble in all the purples. I tried red one time. Blue another. But other colors just looked weird on me, a stranger's hands. Varying the shades is the closest I've been able to get to nail polish rebellion.

Tonight I paint with Lavender Sunrise, every nail except my middle fingers. Those I coat in an almost bloody-looking blackberry color.

"Is that supposed to be a subtle *fuck you*?" Luca asks, getting up from my bed where he's been weaving together some old guitar strings into something that vaguely resembles a napkin holder. My roommate in Boston played guitar to blow off steam from piano performances and the workshop, which was pretty tense most of the time. She threw away a bunch of used strings, but I grabbed them out of the trash can, knowing Luca would love them. He's always creating stuff out of totally random materials. Anything he can bend or melt or break into something weird and functional.

After he graduates, he and Macon have big plans to start up some sort of industrial design business here on the cape. His mom pushes college, but he just waves her off.

"Too obvious?" I ask, grinning up at him where he's hovering over my shoulder.

He paws at the clip I've been using to hold my hair in a messy pile on top of my head, and soon my face is covered.

"Hey!" I swat at him, grabbing for the clip.

He laughs, patting my head. "You need to come by the diner tomorrow. I want you to meet Eva."

"Oh, lord, here we go." Luca is perpetually in love or trying to fall in love or thinking about how he might fall out of love so he can fall in love again.

"It's not like that," he says.

I smirk at him.

"Okay, maybe it's a little like that, but only because she's really pretty. But life just crapped all over her. Half the time I don't know what to say or do. She needs friends."

"Friends."

"Yes, friends. You know. Conversation. Time spent in each other's company. Inside jokes. That sort of thing."

I growl at him. Literally.

"Easy, tiger."

I growl louder.

"You don't have to be her bosom best friend—"

"Did you just say *bosom*?"

He inhales deeply through his nose, a sure sign I'm annoying the hell out of him. It's so damn fun. Plus, I'd rather not go down this path. It's not that I'm opposed to new friends. Okay, maybe I am a little opposed, at least historically. And then there's the fact that I haven't told Luca I've already met her. I'm not sure why. Our whole interaction on the beach just felt sort of . . . I don't know. Sacred. I got the impression that Luca and Emmy didn't know she was weeping on a usually secluded beach, so I keep my mouth shut for now. Besides, it was just a few moments. Not a friendship.

"I've got to go," he says when I don't say anything else. Setting the guitar-string creation on my desk, he picks up my bottles of nail polish, base and top coats, and ragged nail file, and places them all in the little taco-shaped contraption.

I smile at him.

"You going to be okay?" he asks.

I look away. "I'm always okay."

He frowns.

"Luca, I'm fine." I stand up and stretch. "Just tired."

"See you tomorrow?"

"Yup."

After he leaves, I wait a good five minutes, listening for human sounds in the house.

Nothing.

I crack open my door and peer out. The hallway is clear and glowing slightly blue from the moon shining through the big living room windows. Jay's door is shut and no light peeks out from the crack near the floor.

I run to the bathroom on my tiptoes, clicking the door closed behind me as softly as possible. I flip on the light and rest my palms on the counter, breathing in deeply through my nose. A laugh bubbles up as I envision myself skulking through my own house just to take a piss.

I wash my face with cold water. After I brush my teeth, I snap off the light and fling open the door, moving fast through the hall toward my room.

Except I run into a wall that reeks of Calvin Klein.

"Ugh, dammit, Jay." His hands reach out to steady me, but I back up before he can touch me.

"Sorry."

"Sure you are."

"Grace, don't make this weird."

I peer up at him in the half-light. He peers back down at me, his dark eyes intense.

"I'm not making anything weird. I'm not making it anything. Because it's nothing. You're nothing and I'm nothing. In fact, this" —I wave my hand between us—"isn't even real. Let's just mind our own business, okay?"

I go to move around him, but he stops me.

"Don't tell me you're still pissed about that whole Tumblr thing."

"Jay. Don't. Just don't."

"It was a joke."

"Ha-ha."

"No one cares about those dumb texts."

"I care."

"You do, huh?"

Lightning fast, he reaches out and hooks a finger through my belt loop, pulling me closer.

"Let go of me," I say, trying to untangle his finger. "If you rip my pants, I swear to god—"

"Come on, Grace. We had some good times. Don't ruin my memories."

"You're the one who ruined it, you asshole." I finally get my thumb under his finger and twist it free. He releases me, his mouth bending into a sort of sad-looking smile that makes me feel completely off balance. I cover it up with a string of obscene insults.

The sad smile vanishes. "You've got such a dirty mouth." Then he's back in his room, a door and air and dozens of feet between us that feel like they'll never be enough.

My entire body hums from where his fingers brushed my hip. And not the good kind of humming. God knows, Jay's fully capable of the good kind, but this is all wrong. That sad smile felt like some sort of slap in the face. Coupled with the almost-aggressive finger-in-the-belt-loop grab, I feel dizzy. But Jay's always been a little confusing. One of those guys who knows he's hot and can hook a girl with one lazy grin. But when we had sex for the first time, I was the one who initiated it. He asked if I was sure so many times, I snapped at him to shut up and kiss me.

When I get back to my room, I flop onto my bed and inspect my fingernails. As I expected, my forefinger is smudged from prying Jay's claw off my shorts. I'm about to get up to fix it when I hear a *tap*.

I sit up, holding my breath and listening until I hear it again.

*Tap, tap, tap.*

I turn my head toward the window and nearly scream when I see a face peering back at me on the other side of the glass.

A girl's familiar face.

# chapter eight

E VA GESTURES TO THE LOCK ON THE WINDOW. INSTINC-
tively, I flip it free, out of curiosity more than anything.
She pushes the window open and then blinks into the sudden brightness spilling into the yard.

"What the hell are you doing?" I ask as she folds her body
through the opening.

"Emmy sent me over for a dozen eggs," she replies. She tumbles
onto my bed and looks around, legs crossed underneath her like I
invited her over for a freaking slumber party.

"I'm assuming that's a joke."

She grins. "Yes, Grace, that's a joke."

"Ever heard of the front door?"

My tone comes out a little harsher than I intended, because
her face falls and she looks down, picking a tiny hole just starting
to form in the knee of her black jeans. She's wearing black-framed
glasses, a fitted black T-shirt, and black Chuck Taylors. It's like she's
on some sort of hipster spy mission.

"Sorry, I'm just really tired," I say, sinking onto the bed next to her.

"You *did* unlock the window."

"Momentary lapse of judgment."

"I'll use the front door when I leave."

I can't help but laugh at that. "What are you doing here, anyway?"

"I wanted to ask you if I could see the lighthouse."

"You saw it."

She smiles. "I mean from the top."

I lean against my headboard and rub at my sleep-desperate eyes. "Oh my god, who the hell *are* you?"

"Didn't we already establish that?" She points to her chest. "Eva." She points to me. "Grace."

"I meant the question in more of an existential sense."

"Oh, well, when you figure that one out, let me know. I haven't got a damn clue. But my full name is Evangeline, if that helps. It was my mom's middle name." Her voice, teasing and even flirty at first, softens at the end, nearly tapering off into a whisper.

When I don't say anything, she blinks at me, then looks away, folding her arms over her chest. "Sorry. I don't know why I told you that."

We sit there, drowning in a damn river of awkward for what feels like years. Do I say I'm sorry about her mom? Ask how she likes the cape? I'm about to offer something, anything, but she's got this look on her face that makes me stop. It's the same look Mom wears every November tenth—my father's birthday—and every March twenty-first—their wedding anniversary. It's the *Please don't talk about it* look.

"Listen," I say, rubbing at my forehead with both hands. "I'm exhausted. The lighthouse is cool and all, but it's my first night here, so—"

"Will I get you in trouble?"

"I don't know, will you?"

She smiles and slips off the bed, starting a slow amble around my room, gliding her hands over my few possessions. "Emmy's a hard sleeper, and lately I can't sleep. Plus, the ocean—"

"Let me guess. It *called* to you." Carpe diem, baby.

She tilts her head at me. "Yes, it's been whispering sweet nothings in my ear since this afternoon. I had to see it."

I shake my head at her, but laughter bubbles in my chest.

"Irresistible wooing notwithstanding, it *does* look beautiful under the moon." Eva stops her tour and faces me, resting her butt against the dresser. "Come with me."

"I've seen the ocean under the moon before."

"Not with me. Not from the top of the lighthouse."

She has me there, but still. I grasp for some fresh excuse, but something makes me keep my mouth shut.

She smiles a slow smile—she knows she's got me.

*This is ridiculous,* I say to myself. But I need a little ridiculous right now. A leap off a balcony, of sorts.

I get off the bed, and her posture snaps straight, ready for action.

"Hold your wad," I say, holding up both hands. "I'm not even sure how to get up there."

"There's a door on the outside," Eva says. "Locked. But surely the current lighthouse keeper has a key."

"I'm not about to go digging through my mother's boyfriend's trousers."

She frowns but moves toward my door. "Let's just look around."

I hold up a finger and listen for a few seconds, straining my ears for music or low murmurs or creaking floorboards. Nothing.

"Fine. But when I open this door, stay quiet."

She mimes zipping her lips.

"You're not one of those elephant walkers, are you? These are old floors."

"I assure you," she says after a beat of silence, her voice suddenly dreamlike, "I'm like a fairy on my feet."

I run my eyes down her long legs. She even stands gracefully. "Just be quiet."

Eva hovers close to my back as I ease the door open. It squeaks and I stop, then try to open it an inch at a time.

"It'll make less noise if you do it quick," she whispers, and her breath tickles my neck.

"Lot of practice at this?"

"You could say that," she says. "At least lately."

I don't even want to know what that means, but I'm starting to suspect that traipsing around the cape at night might be a regular occurrence for this girl since she got here. *Stays in her room mostly* my ass, Luca. Emmy would flip if she knew.

But I don't say any of this. Instead, I yank the door wider. It doesn't make a sound. We sneak down the hall, and I barely take a breath until we're past Jay's room and safely into the living space. Moonlight streams in through the wide windows, silver streaks through the blue-dark.

"It's so amazing that you get to live here," Eva says, stopping to stare out the window.

"Yeah, it's a freaking miracle." I tiptoe toward the kitchen. Mom and Pete's room is around the corner, but I still don't hear anything, so I assume they're asleep. A light over the stove glows just brightly enough that I can look around.

"Did you find any keys?" Eva asks, coming up behind me so quietly I nearly yelp.

"Does it look like I found any keys?" I hold up my empty hands.

"Um, prickly."

"Um, intruder." But I'm smiling. She moves along, her fingertips on a delicate search through the moonlight.

"Here," she says, pointing to the wall near the side door, and I walk over. Three sets of keys dangle from grungy brass hooks. One is my mom's, adorned with a tiny red plastic flip-flop and packed with at least six different keys that have absolutely no current purpose, keys to old apartments and condos that she never gave back to the landlord. The other two I don't recognize, but one has a clunky Ford truck key, so I assume those are Pete's. The last set has only two keys and they look old. Not skeleton-key old. Just aged and well-worn.

I grab them off the hook and flip the deadbolt open on the door.

"Let's go."

Outside, Eva takes the lead. It's cold as ass. I stuff my hands under my armpits and follow her around the side of the house. The salty wind bites through my tank top, and I'm a few muttered curse words away from going back inside when we reach the old wooden door on the north end of the lighthouse. To my right, high tide is at full throttle, and the ocean churns against the rocks that act as a barrier between the water and the lighthouse's tiny yard.

"Keys," Eva says, holding out her hand. I drop them into her palm, and she wiggles one and then the other into the lock. After a few jabs and twists, the door swings open. Cool, stale air curls out through the entryway. In the dark, I can just barely make out a spiraling staircase, cobwebs lacing in between the rails.

"This is a scene from a horror movie," I say. "You realize that, right?"

Eva laughs and tugs on my arm, pulling me into the dark chasm.

Aside from a toolbox and a folded-up ladder in one corner, the space is pretty much empty except for the staircase, so we start climbing. We spiral up and up and up. The air grows even staler, mixing with salt and something softer. A musky, flowery scent I can't pin down.

It's dark and the stairwell narrows more and more the higher we climb. Relief filters through me when we reach the top, but there's another locked door and my breath comes in short spurts again. Eva messes around with the other key. Despite the chill in the air, her body heat is all I can feel, and it's making me sweat in that sort of way that precedes passing out.

Finally, the door bursts open, and we spill out onto the circular balcony. The space between the wall and the edge is about three feet all the way around, lined with flat cement. Above us, light sweeps over the earth and ocean, igniting the silvery dark with pale yellow every few seconds. It's windy as hell, and, I swear to god, the lighthouse sways like a drunk idiot.

My lungs feel like they're shrinking, and I press my back against the cool white wall. Eva props the door open with a brick before basically skipping to the edge, her hands curling around the railing as she looks out at the world. Her hair dances in the wind, dark swirls ignited every time the light grazes over the tips.

"This is amazing!" she yells, turning to look back at me. Her smile dissolves as she takes in my fingers clawing at the wall. "Are you scared of heights?"

I shake my head. I have no problem with heights in general. I do have a problem with heights that make me feel like I'm an apple balancing on the top of a toothpick.

She comes over and that subtle floral scent washes over me again. Like jasmine under a spring sun. She reaches behind me and grabs my hand. I let her guide me to the railing. My fingers close around the cool metal, and she settles in next to me, her arm brushing mine as she peers out over the side of the world.

I try to relax and focus on the water, the rocks below, and the sky above. Try to empty my mind of Jay and Mom and pianos. Strangely, after a few minutes of just looking, Eva warm at my side, I do. My shoulders descend and my eyelids feel pleasantly heavy, the salty wind and a formidable ocean whispering a gentle *hush-hush*.

"I can't believe I've never come up here before," I say.

Eva laughs. "I can't either."

"There's a boring-as-hell museum on the main floor, but the top hasn't been open to the public since—" A humid gust bites off my words, and my fingers tighten on the railing.

"Since what?" Eva asks.

"Since some girl jumped off the edge, like, a hundred years ago."

Her eyes widen. "Are you serious?"

I nod.

"Why?"

"Everyone has a different story. Her lover was a sailor and he died at sea. Her father was a brute and was going to make her marry his brutish pal. She got caught with her girlfriend, and her parents were going to send her off to an insane asylum."

Eva sucks in a breath. "Is that true?"

I let out a light laugh. "I don't know. Hence all the conflicting stories."

"God, that's awful."

"Which one?"

"All of it. And that no one really knows the truth, no one really knows *her*." She gazes out at the ocean, her eyes wide and thoughtful. "I mean, her whole story is swallowed up by how she died. By that one thing. Nothing else really matters."

"No, I guess not." I've heard all of these stories a million times. The lighthouse museum has little key chains with the brassy image of a girl in a long, old-fashioned skirt, her metal arm held out in front of her like she's trying to hold on to something. The cape can't even agree on her name. Harriet. Helen. Hattie. But Eva's right. It is sad.

We stand there in silence for a while. Next to me, Eva inhales deeply and lets it out slowly, her breath matching the rolling waves below us. I try to think of something else to say, but, weirdly, it feels needless, like the words would be intrusive. It's a peaceful kind of silence. Easy. And dammit if it isn't nice to let something be easy.

"It makes me feel safe," she says, leaning her forearms on the rail.

"What does?"

"This. Being this high, above everything, the world huge around us. Makes it seem like my life is small, you know? Like it's not the only thing. There's a lot more, more to be, more to experience. More to feel."

I breathe in the briny air, and the world around us does feel big. It does make me feel small. Hemmed in by the vastness. It's strangely comforting.

"Why are you doing that?" Eva asks, interrupting my calm. She taps the back of my hand and I look down, stilling my fingers that had been silently moving over the railing, a silent song pouring out of the tips.

"Oh. 'Riverside.'"

She turns so she's facing me. "Is that supposed to make sense?"

I laugh. "Not really. It's a song by one of my favorite singers. She's a pianist too, and this song gets stuck in my head all the time." I don't mention how effing gloomy the song is. It's depressing as hell, but I love it, love playing it. I've even been known to sing it a little when no one's around. Not that I'll have too many opportunities to do that now that my piano is gone.

I stretch my fingers out, joints cracking. "I didn't even realize I was doing it."

"So you were playing this song? On the railing?"

I shrug. "Not note for note. It's mostly in my head. Fingers just move a little here and there. It's more nervous habit than anything."

"It still looked pretty involved. Are you any good?"

Again, I shrug.

"Oh." She gives me a slow smile. "You're good."

"You can't possibly know that from me tapping on a railing."

"Sure I can." She takes my hand and lays it on her own palm. "Long fingers, elegant movements. All the makings of an excellent piano player."

"Again, fingers have very little to do with it. Just ask my mother. Her fingers are longer than mine, and she's completely tone-deaf."

Eva just smiles, my hand still in hers, running her thumb over my darkly painted middle fingernail. "Is that what you want to do? Play piano?"

I swallow hard, that word *want* tripping me up. It's hard to want things when your life is like mine. Dangerous, even. So I settle for the facts. "I have an audition at Manhattan School of Music at the end of July."

Her eyebrows lift. "Wow. That's serious."

I smile. "Yeah, I guess it is."

"I'd like to hear you play sometime."

"Only if you do it with me."

She frowns. "I don't play piano."

"But you dance, right? Ballet? You could dance while I —"

"No, I couldn't." She turns her face toward the ocean, her expression completely closed-off and blank. The silence that settles between us is so thick, I can almost chew on it.

"Sorry," I say, even though I don't know what for.

She shakes her head, her curls springing around her face. "It's fine. Just . . . don't ask me again, okay? I get enough of that from Emmy."

"What do you mean?"

"She thinks I should get *involved,* start dancing again. I guess there's a good-size studio in Sugar Lake or something."

"And you don't want to?"

She doesn't look at me, but her eyes go hazy over the water. "It's not about want."

There's that dangerous word again — *want.* Next to me, Eva is stiff, her shoulders curled inward toward her chest as though trying to shield herself.

"I'd still like to hear you play," she says, finally glancing at me.

"Why?"

"Why not?"

"No. I mean, *why?* What the hell are you doing up here with me in the middle of the night?" I laugh as I ask it, but I'm dead serious. This girl is beyond strange, and I feel strange around her. Grounded and light, tense and nervous, all at once. I haven't felt like this around anybody for a long time.

Not since Natalie.

She stares at me for a few long seconds. Too long. In fact, she takes her damn time, letting her gaze slip over my features like she's memorizing them. She opens her mouth, and I expect some bullshit answer, a joke maybe, because she doesn't seem to want to linger on anything too deep, but what I expect is not what I get.

"Because I'm miserable," she says quietly, her eyes still locked on mine. "And today, on the beach with you, I felt a little less miserable."

"Oh."

"Yeah."

"Well. Okay. But I don't have any more sand on me, in case you get hungry."

She laughs and I smile back and I feel myself sort of giving in. What I'm giving in to—a new friendship or just another moment in time with this girl, I'm not sure.

But for now, that's okay.

Wordlessly we turn side to side, our shoulders pressed together, the wind lacing around us, both of us staring into the light-swept black, feeling small and big all at once.

# chapter nine

I'M JOLTED AWAKE. SOMETHING THAT FEELS THE SIZE OF A house lands next to me on my bed and jerks me out of a dream where a girl in a long white dress kept swan-diving off the lighthouse. Over and over. She'd catapult over the edge, land in the water, then climb back up the tower while I watched from the beach.

And right before she hit the waves, every time, her face morphed into my mother's.

"Ugh," I groan, rubbing my temples with both hands.

"Wake up, lazybones," Mom says, sprawled out next to me. She's definitely not the size of a house, but she reeks of cigarettes and hot glue. I don't know what time it is, but it's too damn early for whatever she wants.

But then she glides soft fingers down my cheek and, with the dream clinging like a hangover, I find myself curling into her side. She scoots closer, tucking my head under her chin, running her hand over my back. Mom's taller than me, but my body is all hills and valleys where hers is straight highways and plateaus. In the rare moments when we tangle together like this, when the only thing between us is blood instead of men and cigarettes and unpacked boxes, I feel like a little girl. Her little girl. She hums a tuneless melody, and I let her feathery voice strip away the remnants of that dream.

"I need you to come with me to LuMac's," she says, breaking the spell. It never lasts long.

"Why?"

She sits up, straightening her spaghetti-strapped tank. "Because I'm craving the Philly cheesesteak omelet, and I want to meet Ella."

"Eva."

"Yes, Eva."

"So go eat an omelet and meet Eva."

Mom groans. "I can't go alone, you know how Emmy is. She'll want to *talk* and ugh. I can't deal with her this morning."

"She'll probably just say hello, Mom. She's polite."

"I'm polite! I just always feel like she's judging me. Like I can't do anything right, and I don't know what to say to her. You and I are doing fine. We're always fine, aren't we?"

I make an ambiguous noise. I'm not touching that one. I've spent what feels like ten lifetimes trying to get Mom to see how her behavior affects me, affects other people, how it's not exactly healthy to chase toast with a Bud Light for breakfast, but she's totally blind in this area. She's a freaking paragon of motherhood and mental health. Just ask her.

"But, oh, this poor Eva girl" — Mom releases a wistful sigh — "I have to meet her, baby. Plus, you need to set up your job schedule, don't you?"

"Yeah, yeah. Fine." I pull on a pair of shorts and a black T-shirt before twisting my hair into a messy topknot. "I need to find a piano somewhere to practice on anyway." I shoot her a look, but she only nods and tells me what a "great idea!" that is.

Out in the kitchen, Jay sits at the table, slurping up cereal.

In nothing but his boxers.

I grit my teeth as I pour a glass of water, but I can feel his eyes trailing me. Mom chats him up, giggling and patting his shoulder like he's not seventeen and half naked.

I gulp down the water so I don't puke and head out the door. Mom can follow me if she wants, but there's no way I'm going to stay in here and watch whatever the hell that is.

Mom joins me halfway down the driveway.

"You didn't even say good morning to Julian," she says, lighting up a cigarette.

"I don't say good morning to slobbering cretins."

"Oh, he's not that bad. He's been very polite to me."

*Yeah, well he nearly ripped my belt loop last night. That's real polite.*

The words almost slip out. Seems like a no-brainer: tell your mother about the ass-wipe who makes you feel nervous in your own house, but nope. Because I know what she'll say.

*You're just being dramatic now, Grace. I know he wasn't nice to you when you broke up, but try to be civil, will you?*

I press my mouth closed and keep it that way the four blocks to LuMac's.

The first thing I notice right away when we walk into LuMac's is the decor. Two weeks ago, it was an all-retro-fifties diner. Now it's a retro-fifties diner with an industrial flair. Luca's creations are everywhere. Copper and nickel napkin holders, a soldered iron cake stand, twisted metal frames around the art on the walls. He's always had few pieces here and there, but now it's like a junkyard got artistic and then threw up all over a sock hop.

Mom gasps and mutters, "Well, this is an interesting choice," but I think it looks pretty freaking cool.

Buttery, fried-food smells fill the space as Mom and I settle into one of the only booths still available. With summer starting up, tourists are spilling onto the cape, and they flock to LuMac's at all hours of the day.

My butt has barely hit the sparkly red pleather cushion when Emmy descends upon us.

"My two favorite ladies!" she exclaims, sliding in next to me. Her long, rust-colored hair is pulled into her usual sleek ponytail, and her soft arms wrap around my shoulders. I lean into her a little. She smells like sugar and warm toast and looks exhausted.

"Hey, Em," I say, my eyes scanning the dining room for Eva. "How are you?"

"I'm all right. We're getting there." She pops a kiss to my cheek. "Are you ready to work for me?"

"Yep. Just say when."

"How about tomorrow morning? Luca should be done training Eva by then. Of course, Macon could train you just as well, but he's been busy building up our Internet delivery service."

"Yeah, that sounds fine." I smile at her, searching for signs that she knows Eva spent a good two hours at the top of the lighthouse last night, like that's information she'd just wear on her face or something. I roll my eyes at myself.

"How's the new place, Maggie?" Emmy asks.

Mom nods. "Wonderful. You know Pete, right?"

"Yep. His family moved here when he was around fourteen, so I've known him since high school. He's a character, that one."

"He swept me off my feet, I'll say that." Mom grins, like her fortieth romance of the year is the cutest damn thing either of us has ever seen.

"Well, good," Emmy says. "Let me know if you girls need anything as you settle in, yes?"

Mom's gaze narrows a bit, and she rolls her shoulders back. "Thanks, but I'm sure you have your hands full. I think all we really need right now is some breakfast."

I don't look at Emmy, but Mom's *Piss off and get me some food* tone makes my cheeks fill with heat.

"Of course," Emmy says through a tight smile. "Let me get Eva. She needs some practice, and I know she's safe with you girls." She squeezes my arm before disappearing into the kitchen.

Mom releases a huge breath, which I don't address. A few seconds later, Eva emerges from the back, Luca at her heels. Her hair is tied back into a ponytail, curls escaping around her face, and she's in all black again. Or still. Who knows with this girl.

They approach our table, Luca talking a mile a minute and pointing here and there, Eva nodding and *uh-huh*ing. When she sees me, she breaks into a grin.

I offer back a close-mouthed smile that says I'm cool as a damn cucumber, but my stomach does a weird little flip that I ignore by burying my head in LuMac's massive menu.

"Since when do you need to peruse our fine establishment's even finer choices?" Luca asks when he gets close enough.

I glare at him over the top of the tome. "Since today, I guess."

"So you *don't* want cinnamon pancakes and scrambled eggs and that nasty wheat-berry toast only you and Macon will eat?"

I shrug casually and continue my investigation of the menu I've had memorized for about two years.

"Hey, by the way," Luca says, "this is Eva."

I look up, meeting Eva's softly narrowed eyes and tiny smile. A smile that's tossing the ball into my court. It'd be so easy to tell Luca we've already met. Twice. I mean, why the hell not? I tell Luca everything and what I don't tell him, he figures out in a ridiculously short amount of time.

When we were fourteen, Luca listened while I talked on and on about Natalie Fitzgerald, the new lifeguard at our community pool. And when he caught me staring at her, transfixed by the way the sun glinted off her smooth thighs, he simply asked me what was going on in my head. He didn't smirk or frown or freak out or crack a threesome joke. And then, this past winter, Luca enlarged a copy of Jay's yearbook picture, and we hurled darts at it for hours in the shed behind LuMac's. He knew I needed to blow off steam, and darts were an infinitely smarter choice than setting fire to Jay's football gear. Slightly less satisfying, but smarter. Luca knows all, sees all, is perpetually levelheaded about all.

Still. I like that big world Eva and I created at the lighthouse last night. So big there was only enough room for the two of us, hemming us in from all the bullshit. Plus, Emmy's a force when she's angry, and Eva and I on top of the off-limits lighthouse is definitely angry-making material.

"Nice to meet you," I finally say, and she grins wider.

"You too."

"Oh, honey," Mom says, nearly talking over us. She reaches out her hand to grab Eva's. "We're so glad you're here. You and I are going to chat sometime soon, okay?"

I expect Eva to frown, sort of pull back or squirm under Mom's sad puppy-dog eyes and emotional intrusion, but she doesn't. Instead she locks gazes with my mother for what feels like hours. That little mischievous smile vanishes, replaced with something so raw and naked, I almost feel like *I'm* the one intruding.

"Okay. Thank you," Eva finally says softly. Then she squeezes Mom's hand. *Squeezes* it.

Mom nods and sort of wiggles Eva's fingers before releasing her. She orders coffee and the omelet she'll eat a fourth of, claiming she wants to save some for Pete, no doubt. I don't know what the hell that moony look Eva and my mom just shared was all about, but I'd rather not think on it too long.

"How do you like living on the cape so far, Eva?" I ask while Luca watches her scribble down Mom's order.

"Oh, it's fabulous," she says drily. "Everyone is super friendly and helpful, showing me the *sights* and all that."

"Have you tried any of our local ocean-side delicacies?" I ask, and Luca looks at me like I've grown a second nose.

"Yes, I have," Eva says. "Lovely textures, if a little gritty. Bit salty for my taste, though."

"Are you talking about the lobster?" Luca asks. Eva and I crack up. I feel sort of bad, deceiving Luca like this, but it's not like I won't eventually tell him.

"Gray," he says, his gaze narrowed on mine.

"What?"

"Order. Food. Breakfast."

"Fine, fine." I close the menu and fix my eyes on Eva, who's waiting with a pen poised dramatically, her glasses slipping down her nose a little. I fold my hands demurely. "I'll have cinnamon pancakes and scrambled eggs with two slices of that nasty wheat-berry toast only Macon and I will eat."

Eva laughs, and Mom kicks me under the table but smiles at me nonetheless. She can't resist a smartass, that's for sure. Luca just smirks and snatches my menu from the table before smacking me on top of the head with it.

"You realize I don't even feel that, right?" I pat my chaotic bun.

"You're going to feel this." He reaches across the table and digs a finger into the hollow of my collarbone. Predictably, I yelp and let out a swear or two. Eva watches our exchange, that tiny smile on her face.

"Luca, stop harassing the customers!" Emmy calls from the kitchen.

"She's not a customer—she's Gray-Gray."

"Get back here," she says.

He snaps his body into perfect posture and salutes his mother. She laughs and disappears into the back.

"Remember, Gray," Luca says. "Bonfire, tonight."

"Aw, shit."

"Grace, enough with the foul mouth," Mom warns, looking around like she's scared Pastor Alan is hiding in the next booth to bust me. I ignore her.

"You promised," Luca says. "Plus, it's Eva's first bonfire. I told her we'd show her the way it's done."

"It's a pile of logs aflame on the beach surrounded by our drunken peers—I'm sure she can figure it out."

"I don't know," Eva says. "That sounds pretty complicated."

A laugh slips out of my mouth.

"Come on, Grace, it's tradition," Luca says.

"Fine, I'll meet you there."

He shoots me a thumbs-up and heads off toward the kitchen, but Eva lingers.

"I'm going to go check and see if there's anything in the back I can use to spice up your eggs," she says as she tucks her notepad into her apron.

"Hold the seaweed, please."

"Your wish is my command." She grins and I watch her walk back toward the kitchen.

"Why don't you want to go to the bonfire?" Mom asks, interrupting my observations.

"I don't *not* want to go."

"Sure sounded like it."

"I just got back. I'm tired." It sounds like a sorry excuse before I even finish the sentence. Truth is, I love the bonfire the baseball team from our high school puts on every summer. Those guys are statistics-obsessed, smelly-sock-wearing weirdos, in my opinion, but they know how to throw a damn party. Problem is, our entire school is always in attendance, and I'd really rather avoid the brouhaha that will ensue when everyone finds out I'm freaking living with Jay.

But whatever.

I'm sure no one will care all that much. I'm sure Jay will be too busy with his friends to pay me any attention. I'm sure Mom will be fine handling the unpacking while I'm gone.

*I'm sure, I'm sure, I'm sure.* Maybe if I say it enough, it'll all just happen, like Dorothy clicking her heels together and—*whoosh!*—home again, home again, jiggety-jog.

"I think you should go, baby," Mom says, fiddling with something on her phone. "You deserve some fun. Plus, Pete and I are driving over to Portland."

"What?" Portland is about an hour away, and she already used a ton of gas picking me up from the bus station yesterday. "Why?"

"There's this fancy-schmancy art supply store there that I've been meaning to check out for a long time. Now I finally have a reason."

"What reason is that?" I know for a fact she doesn't have any orders on her Etsy shop. I have the password, and I check it every day to make sure she doesn't miss anything.

"Eva," she says.

I blink at her. "Eva."

She nods, still tapping away at her phone. "I'm so heartbroken for her, and I can tell she's feeling . . . well, a little lost. I have some ideas of a few things I can make for her, just little things to make her feel more at home. Supported."

"Emmy supports her plenty. Emmy's a grief counselor, Mom."

She waves a hand and sips her coffee. "That shrink mumbo jumbo doesn't help, trust me." She sighs, her gaze going soft. "She's so lovely, isn't she? An only child, missing father, too young to deal with losing the most important person in her life."

Her voice has this dreamlike quality to it, and I stare at her as she grabs a napkin from the funky copper holder, her eyes blurry from actual tears over a girl who might as well be a total stranger. Something in my chest closes up, squeezes, and breaks open again. I'm an only child. I have a missing father. I'm too young to deal with half the crap I handle every day. At least I think I am. And I'm . . . well, *lovely* has never been a description attributed to me, but I'm not a damn ogre or anything.

Not that I really expect my mother to notice any of these things.

Last year she got me two dozen purple roses for my birthday. They're my favorite flower. They're my favorite flower because they've always been her favorite flower, and I used to love that we shared that. The morning of August second, she crept into my room before the sun came up. While I slept, she took a few individual flowers and crushed up the petals, spreading them around my floor, covering the dingy carpet with beautiful color. Then she divided the bouquet into several smaller ones, tucking them into vintage bottles and vases and putting them all around my room. On my nightstand. On my desk. On my dresser. On my windowsill. She set a plateful of my favorite pumpkin-apple muffins next to my bed.

When I woke, it should've been perfect. It *would've* been perfect if my birthday was actually August second.

It's not.

It's August twenty-second.

I told myself it wasn't a big deal. *It's the thought that counts* and all that. I knew the roses were expensive, and she had to special-order them. I knew she probably baked those muffins—the only food in the world she's actually good at making—after I had gone to bed the night before. We went about the day, her jabbering on about my birth and even talking about my father a little bit, how he cried when he first held me and how he sneaked a cheeseburger for her past the hospital nurses.

It took until almost dinnertime—and a few curt words to a bewildered Luca about *him* forgetting my birthday—for her to realize she'd totally messed up the date.

And now, here she is, ready to spend money we don't have and sing "Kumbaya" for a girl she's only just laid eyes on in real life.

Suddenly, that big world shrinks to the size of pinprick and I'm too small inside of it.

Too small for my mother.

Too small for my town.

Too small for this summer, for the next year weighing on me like a fur coat in the heat of July.

Too small even for Luca and his concerned shoulder squeeze when I don't lift my eyes to meet his as he sets my food down in front of me.

Nothing fits and no amount of inside jokes or new friends or lighthouse trips will change that.

"See you tonight?" Luca asks.

I nod without looking up, picking at my eggs. Mom slurps her coffee. She slurps all her drinks. Loud, wet, annoying gulps that are the equivalent of nails on a chalkboard to my ears.

As Luca walks away, I glance up, half hoping Mom is leveling me a worried look. She's not. She's buried in her phone, slurp-slurping away.

# chapter ten

B Y THE TIME I GET TO THE BONFIRE, THE SUN IS LONG gone and half the partygoers are already sloshed. I find the beer keg a few feet from the fire, a bunch of dudes hovering around it. Some guy whose name I'm pretty sure is Chad with arms the size of my thighs starts to show me how to work the keg, but I grab my own red cup and fill it before he can get an oh-so-masculine word out. I turn away, but one of them—Victor Dinnon? Vince Dannon? Something with a V and a D—snags my wrist.

"Hey, where you going, Glasser?" he asks. "I've got my phone with me, so we can, you know"—he pumps his hips and makes these guttural noises I hope some poor girl never, ever has to hear in real life—"*text*." His buddies break into laughter. I yank my arm from his, spilling half my beer in the process.

"Tempting, but I'm not really into bestiality."

Venereal Disease frowns, and his posse laughs harder. I move away from them quickly but still feel their eyes on me as I go, and it makes my face flame up. None of the texts Jay posted featured pictures, thank god, but they were detailed enough to leave little to the imagination. Since then, I've never felt fully clothed around anyone from my school, so that's lots of fun.

Music from some unidentifiable source blares through the crowd. Everyone's in shorts and hoodies, although some girls are clinging to their bikini tops, trying to force summer into existence. I weave in between swaying bodies and rocks topped with couples making out, my eyes peeling through the moon and flame-licked darkness for Luca. I tip my cup into my mouth, swallowing a few gulps of the mostly flat brew.

"Tastes like piss this year," Luca says from behind me, startling me into snorting some beer up my nose. I cough and spew while he slaps my back.

"Dammit, Luca." I wipe my mouth. "And also, yeah. But all beer tastes like piss."

"Not good beer."

"What the hell do you know about good beer?"

"Macon's all into microbrewing now. He's been cooking shit in his kitchen for the past few weeks."

"Cooking shit? Is he brewing beer or running a meth lab?"

"You know Macon. Always enterprising."

I laugh. I do know Macon. He's five years older than us and is sort of a jack-of-all-trades. He made straight A's in school, can figure out anything if you give him about an hour of silence, and has never lost a game of Trivial Pursuit because he's a wealth of useless information. He also never went to college, even though Emmy begged him to. Instead, he married his high school sweetheart, Janelle, and stayed in Cape Katie, helping his mom run LuMac's and raise his equally enterprising little brother. He and Luca have already started selling a few of Luca's weird creations around town, but after Luca graduates, LuMac Designs will launch full force.

Every time I think about it, a little pang of loneliness shoots through me. I've never been without Luca. Not for longer than a couple of weeks, at least. The thought of leaving him — and leaving him *here,* both of us knowing I'm counting on him to make sure Maggie doesn't fall off the edge of the planet — has always filled me with a lot of relief and a lot more guilt and a hell of a lot more fear. Every time I'd start freaking out about it, doubting that I could leave, that I *should* leave, he'd make this really annoying game-show buzzer sound.

"*Mraaaa!* Wrong answer! Try again!" he'd yell.

"Jesus, Luca," I'd say, covering my ears.

"Gray, you and I both know you need to get out of this town. Me? I'm good here. I'm happy. I'm not a college boy. But you? You need that concert hall, and you need your own damn life, so *Mraaaa!* Shut up about it."

And so I would shut up for about a week, and Mom would even cook a meal or two and buy me a new top or something. I'd get comfortable and start snuggling into a little normal and then — *BAM!* — Mom would do something wildly alarming, like drive to the duplex we lived in *two duplexes ago* and bang on the door because her key didn't work until the current resident called the cops on her ass.

"Did you find a piano?" Luca asks now.

"Yeah. Luckily. Though it's a bigger piece of junk than mine was."

"Where?"

"The Book Nook. Patrick Eisley has an old upright in the storage room that used to be his dad's or uncle's or someone's. Who cares? It's got eighty-eight keys. I got in a couple hours of practice this afternoon."

He puffs out his cheeks with held-in air before letting it out with a little *pfft* sound. A sure sign he's holding back *opinions*.

"I know," I say. "You don't have to tell me."

"I didn't say anything."

"You wanted to."

"Gray, I always want to when it comes to Maggie. You know I love her, but—"

"This is a party, Luca."

"So what you're saying is, shut up and party?"

"Basically."

"I can do that." He nudges my shoulder playfully before he mumbles, "For now."

We both drink and watch our peers drink, most of them getting more and more sloshed by the mouthful and spilling half the contents of their cups into the sand.

"Oh, finally," he says.

"What?"

"Kimber's here." He tosses back the rest of his beer and drags a hand through his hair about five times, a sure sign he's gearing up for some grade-A flirting.

"Kimber Morello?"

"Yeah."

"Since when do you like Kimber Morello?"

"Since she came into the diner earlier in this little short skirt and a halter top."

I pull a face. For all his chivalry, Luca is still such a guy. But he could do worse than Kimber. She's an honest-to-god nice person and one of the few who didn't smirk at me whenever I passed her in the halls after the whole sexting debacle. Plus, she's cute as a damn button, with this stick-straight black hair I'd kill for, and she's a hell of a photographer. This past year when I was Martha Ireland's assistant, Kimber was her intern. Her black-and-white candids were off-the-charts amazing.

"I thought you liked *Eva*," I say, drawing out the vowels in her name. Kimber spots Luca from across the bonfire and tilts her head at him, a clear invitation to join her.

"I said she was pretty—there's a difference."

"Please. You were practically drooling when you told me about her."

He snorts. "Whatever. Besides, I've got no shot, trust me."

"Why not?"

He waves me off and takes a step toward Kimber, but I grab his arm. "Why don't you have a shot?"

He raises his brows at me, and I let go of his arm, swallowing some beer to cover up my interest.

"I just don't," he says. "If you're so curious about it, you should ask her yourself. She's around here somewhere."

"What happened to 'showing her the way it's done'?" I ask, hooking finger quotes around my words.

"Oh, she's got it under control. But check on her for me, will you? Mom'll have my ass if Eva gets trashed." Luca snags one of my hands, pulling it toward his mouth like he's trying to bite me.

I jab my forefinger into his bottom lip.

"Hey! Damn, Gray! I might need that later." He rubs at his lip and pouts.

"Then don't put my finger in your mouth next time."

He laughs and shakes his head, before his expression softens. "I'm glad you're back."

Quick as heat lightning over the ocean, my throat thickens. "Yeah. Yeah, me too."

He huffs a little through his nose but nods. We both know *glad* isn't exactly the word for it.

Kimber calls Luca's name, and he waves at her. "I got to go. And you need to have some fun. Go get drunk. Practice safe sex."

"Thanks, Dad."

He shoves my shoulder a little but plants a kiss on the top of my head.

And then he's gone, his arm slung over Kimber's shoulders, a laugh already on his lips as they stroll off down the beach.

After I finish my beer, I toss my cup into a pile with the others and search the crowd for a familiar face. But this is Cape Katie —a lot of faces are familiar, but I don't really know anyone. A few names. Hobbies. Who so-and-so dated for how long and why they broke up. Nothing that really matters.

I move here and there to keep busy and look interested, giving myself a good half-hour before I can get the hell out of here. With Luca otherwise occupied, he won't notice and I'll stay long enough that tomorrow I'll be able to tell him, "Oh my god, yeah I *did* see Melody Caruthers hurl all over Layla Simms!" Melody's sick stench floats around on the sea wind, and I'm just about to hightail it home when I hear laughter erupt near the bonfire. It's all male and greedy-sounding. I step around a sobbing and soaked Layla, walking toward the fire as music laces through the sand-dusted air.

I see her before anything else about the scene really registers. She's on top of an old picnic table, dancing with a few other girls. She's got on a filmy black tank top and white shorts, smooth skin everywhere. The firelight reflects off her hair and her eyes are closed, though she's not smiling. Her movements are nothing like ballet —the pounding bass and electronic rhythms aren't exactly graceful —but every roll of her shoulders and hips is mesmerizing.

"Yeah! Exotic new girl has some damn moves!"

The familiar voice jolts me out of my staring. Jay claps his hands above his head, his gaze tilted up as his eyes roam all over Eva. His douche-hat friends elbow each other and laugh, but they don't look at one another. They only look at her. Point their phones at her. Yell at her. Whistle. Jay reaches out a hand and skims it up Eva's calf. She pulls back a little, her dance faltering just enough that I know his touch unnerved her.

Not one to be ignored, Jay hops up on the table and starts moving. Jesus, he has absolutely no class, but the guy can undulate a hip. He presses close, his stomach against Eva's back. Her eyes flip open, her mouth parting in surprise. He grips her waist and tries to sway with her. At first, she plays along, but her smile tightens, all of her previous carefree motions gone.

Then suddenly, I can't see her. Boy after boy gets up on the table, spilling onto its surface like an army of ants. They surround her, arms waving in the air, hips circling, laughs echoing into the wind. Eva's completely disappeared.

*Grace!*

Mom's plea bounces around inside my head, and I'm lost in the memory, my feet crunching on the peanut-shell-dusted wood floors, the stench of sweat and beer stinging my nostrils, the bodies pressing too close.

*Gracie!*

Right off the cape, in a little town called Sugar Lake, there's this dive bar Mom loves to frequent. Ruby's, it's called, like it's this dainty little jewel in the rough. It's not. It used to be a semi-classy dance club back in the eighties, but now it's a total dump. Mom gets lonely or breaks up with her latest boyfriend or we get kicked out of an apartment because we didn't have the rent, and Mom usually ends up there, plastered and making out with some creep in a dark corner. One time this past winter, I went with her. She was particularly unnerved by her breakup with some guy whose name I can't even remember. I sat at the bar, sipping ginger ale, while she danced and drank. At least this way, I'd make sure she got home. But it got later and later, she got drunker and drunker, dudes got handsier and handsier. Close to two a.m., I went to the bathroom. Five minutes later, I couldn't find her. She was covered in a wall of men, the music moving their bodies closer.

At first I wasn't even sure she was in there, but then I heard my name, a tiny high-pitched plea rising out of that huge mass of stupid. I elbowed my way in, enduring a few ass grabs along the way, and pulled her out.

She was laughing and then she was crying, and I've never been so terrified. She hasn't been back in few months—at least, not that I know of.

After that, I decided not to go to college. No way in hell. Mom would never bodily *survive* without me, and there's a community college in Sugar Lake. Good enough.

Luca strongly disagreed.

A shout from the crowd pulls me back to the bonfire.

Teeth gritted, I push through the crowd, elbows flying, curse words trailing behind me. When I reach the table, I hop up and shove even more until I find Eva in the middle. She's trying to play the whole thing off, shuffling her feet and gently pushing guys' hands away. Luckily Jay has both of his paws to himself or I'd castrate him right here, right now. Still, Eva looks totally freaked out. I grab her arm, yanking until she nearly tumbles off the table. She lands on her feet, and I push her in front of me.

"Hey, Grace!" Jay calls from behind me, totally oblivious. "Come back and dance!"

I ignore him, keeping my hand on Eva's back as I steer her through the gaping crowd. Some laugh. Some leer. Some don't even notice us, but I keep moving until we break through the edge of the group.

When we pass a cooler, I grab two water bottles, but then I keep walking toward the ocean. Adrenaline buzzes in my ears, in my chest, and my fingertips fizz like I've been sucking in too much oxygen.

"God, that was wild," Eva says, still breathing hard.

I uncap one of the waters and gulp some down, the cold a shock to my sand-scratched throat. I don't stop walking.

"Hey. Grace, wait."

A hand on my arm whirls me around. Her eyes are bleary, mascara smudged, hair disheveled. It's too familiar. Too easy for me to try to fix. Too hard for me to walk away from.

I turn my back on her again.

"Grace, come on."

But there's nothing to really say, because if she's into that kind of partying, the kind that's basically a show for jerks and a balm to soothe some unseen wound, more power to her, but I'm out. Because that's the bitch about having a mom like mine. Lines get blurred. Half the time, my attempts to help Maggie with anything relating to one of her boyfriends result in a tongue-lashing followed by tears, capped off with another round of *It's none of your business, Gracie!*

So yeah, this is all just too damn familiar.

"I've got to go," I say.

"Grace, wait. Please."

Right now the only thing I want is to go home—whatever home that is at the moment—and curl up in my mother's bed. Maybe talk to her more about Pete and Jay and get her to understand, because I always, always hope that one day she'll understand.

But she's not there.

She's in Portland, buying a bunch of shit for . . . well, a girl who's not me. The thought causes me to stop and turn around to look at her, this girl who's not me.

"What?" I ask.

"Are you mad at me or something?"

Am I?

It's not her fault a bunch of assholes decided to try to dance with her. It's not her fault she lost her mother. It's not her fault I can sense my own mother latching on to her, pulling her in as her new pet tragedy.

"No," I say quietly, still trying to convince myself. "No, I'm not mad. You were just dancing."

She visibly relaxes and runs her hands over her hair. The motion smooths down her locks until she lets go, and then all her curls pop up again. "I wouldn't call that dancing."

"What would you call it?"

She shrugs. "Faking it." She exhales as she sinks down into the sand. Ahead of us, the sea slams against the shore, high tide on its way. She looks so small, all the jokes and fearlessness that led me to the top of the lighthouse stripped away.

Except the lonely. The lonely is still all over her.

I sit down next to her and open her water, nudging her arm until she takes it and sips.

"Thanks for helping me," she says. "Really."

"No problem." I say that, but I know I'm lying. I can feel a ball of anger—*a problem*—coil together in my chest. Not at Eva, but at my mother, who's slowly turning me into something inhuman. Unfeeling and cold.

"Hey." She touches my arm, and I lift my eyes to hers, which are a little bleary-looking. "I'm serious. I haven't been to many parties, and you were a total badass back there."

*I've had a lot of practice,* I want to say. But I don't. I can't. That'll lead to questions. And questions will lead to me explaining my mother, my life, and that's something I've vowed not to do with anyone except for Luca, and even sharing it with him sometimes is hard enough. Talking about Mom feels like a betrayal. It all sounds so tragic, almost cliché, like something out of a Lifetime movie. And my mom . . . well, she's my mother. And things aren't that bad. *They're not that bad.*

"Okay," I say instead. Profound, I know.

"You know that one guy? Jay?"

I snort. "Yeah. You could say that."

"He smelled like roast chicken."

I laugh. "Oh my god, that's right. He always smells like that when he drinks and gets wild. It's like he sweats out all the meat he eats. It's totally bizarre."

"And totally disgusting."

"And that."

"He called me exotic. I really hate that."

I tilt my head at her. "Why?"

She shakes her head. "You'd think having a white dad and a black mom means I have three legs and feathers. I'm biracial, not some rarely spotted species from some barely populated island."

"Well, Jay's an idiot. So he might literally believe you're a rarely spotted species from some barely populated island."

Eva snort-laughs, choking a little on her water. "Or he's an entitled white asshat in America and he's horny."

"Oh, that's a given."

We laugh a little more, drink a little more, watch the ocean roll over itself a little more. I'm not sure how much time passes before I fill the silence with a whole bunch of stupid.

"So, you've really never met your father?"

She sucks in a breath.

"Sorry," I say. "I shouldn't have asked that."

"No. No, it's fine. Just surprised me is all. I didn't know you knew that."

"Luca told me."

"Right." She lifts the water bottle to her mouth, gulping until it's empty. "And no, I haven't."

"You don't even know who he is?"

"I know his name, a white dude my mom toured with when she was performing with a ballet company in Philadelphia."

"Oh. Mine too," I say. "I mean, my dad was some white dude, not that he was a dancer. And he wasn't just some dude. I mean, my mom was married to him. God, sorry. I shouldn't have brought this up."

She laughs a little at my babbling. "It's fine. And yeah, I figured your dad was a white dude." She gestures to my pale-as-hell arms. "Anyway, my parents weren't married and he didn't want to be involved, I guess, so my mom didn't put his name on the birth certificate. She only told me his name last year."

"That must've been so hard on her, doing it all alone."

"We did okay, but back then it was, I think. And then her company was all pissed that she got pregnant and fired her."

"Really? Can they do that?"

She shrugs. "They did it anyway. I mean, from the start she wasn't a favorite. Had to pretty much claw her way into the company, even though she was one of the best dancers."

"Why?"

She gives me an *Oh, come on* look and presses her fingertips onto my wrist, her skin even darker against all my pale.

"Oh," I say softly.

She waves a hand and then wraps her arms around her knees. "She had me and opened up a studio with a couple of friends of hers from college. It's just been me and her ever since. I think meeting my dad now would just confuse me."

"How do you mean?"

"I don't know. I mean, he's white. He's a man. He may be a stellar human being, but how would I know? I'm curious, sure. I think about him a lot and maybe someday I'll look him up, but I think he'd just . . . complicate how I see myself. It's already hard enough."

"What's hard? I mean, about how you see yourself?"

She smiles, but there's no mirth in it. "Other people's voices can get really loud. When I was a kid, hardly anyone looked like me and I'd spit back stuff I heard people say at school and at dance. My mom would get so mad. She was really good about building me up, pointing out all the great things about being who I am, about being myself. And it worked. I like myself, I do. But I'm still—" She presses her lips flat and looks away. "It's just hard sometimes, that's all. I get really anxious, like there're too many things in my head, too much to feel. I've always been like that, even before Mom . . . anyway. You wouldn't really understand."

I frown because I *want* to understand. No, I'm not a black girl and my mom's not dead and I have no idea what that's like, but I feel this weird tug in my chest, a hook pulling me toward her. Like some foundational part of me, while different from Eva's experience, *does* understand. Needs to.

"That's why I like to color," she says. "Chills me out, slows down my thoughts, and makes everything make sense. Colors, lines, patterns. No matter how intricate, it's still ordered, you know?"

"Piano does that for me."

She nods. "Ballet used to. I loved the method to it, you know? Choreography, positions, technique, the beats of the music. But how I still had all this freedom to—"

"Make it your own."

She smiles at me. "Exactly."

"And ballet doesn't do that anymore?"

She shrugs and looks away. "There's a lot of freedom in coloring, too."

Her answer reeks of bullshit, but I don't push her. "Sounds like I need to try it out."

"You do. Preferably on a windy day at the beach."

"With some peanut butter."

"Always with peanut butter." She smiles and rests her cheek on her knee, watching me. "So what about you? Where's your dad?"

"Oh. He died in Afghanistan."

Her eyes widen. "I'm sorry."

"It's okay. I was two. I don't really remember him."

She nods and we fall silent. I'm sure she's thinking about her mom. I want to ask more, ask if she's okay, ask what I can do, but it all sounds so formulaic. Besides, I've been trying to help my mom through her grief for years. *You don't get it, Grace. You don't understand,* she'd always say when she was really struggling. And maybe I don't. Maybe I can't. There's a huge chasm of difference between losing someone you never really knew and losing someone who encompassed your entire world.

"Why doesn't Luca have a chance with you?" I finally ask. Apparently, when silence gets too oppressive, I like to vomit up some awkward-as-ass questions.

Her eyes widen in surprise, but one corner of her mouth ticks up in a little smile. "He told you that?"

"Yep."

"Damn. Boy is ruining my mystique."

She laughs and I laugh, but she won't look at me. Instead, she trains her gaze on the water. A yellow-orange ray from the lighthouse's beam a few miles away swings over the waves and she follows it.

*Up, over, away.*

*Up, over, away.*

I hear her take a few breaths, the inhale before speaking, but the words never come.

Until they do.

"I like girls, Grace."

Her words seem to flutter on the wind, tossed this way and that until they land between us.

# chapter eleven

I LIKE GIRLS, GRACE.

*Well, sure, who doesn't?* I think at first. Because that's exactly what my mother said to me once, her oh-so-maternal retort to a very similar confession.

*I like girls, Grace.*

I look at Eva, the way she chews at her bottom lip and focuses on the swirls she's drawing in the sand, nervousness cascading off her in waves. Still, her mouth bends into the tiniest of smiles.

My mind slows and retreats to three years ago and Natalie Fitzgerald, the sixteen-year-old lifeguard at the cape's community pool. All the boys fawned over her, brought her sodas, and offered to slather her back with SPF 40. Girls got to the pool early so they could see her arrive and catch a glimpse of what en vogue outfit she had on over her red one-piece.

Me? I was somewhere in between. Always had been with girls. For a long time, when I was a little younger, I thought that was how every girl saw other girls—this mix between beauty and awe and curiosity, a thin layer of lust just underneath. Took until I was fourteen to realize that no, the way I thought about other girls was a little different.

Natalie's long dark hair tumbled down her back. She always wore it loose, even when she was on duty, and her tanned body was smooth and lean from years of swim team. I couldn't help but watch her every time she got out of her chair to check the pool's chemical levels, every time she dove into the water during adult swim. If she was moving, I was watching, something stirring low in my stomach. The same kind of feeling I knew was flaring in Luca's gut as well. His mouth practically hung wide open for that entire summer.

I didn't tell him the thoughts swirling around my head about Natalie, not even when the three of us struck up a pool-only friendship, but he asked anyway. That's how Luca was and is and always will be.

"So, you like Natalie, right?" he had asked one hot day. I'd just flopped back on the towel after Natalie had called me over to her chair to make me listen to some new singer she liked on her phone.

"What do you mean?" I'd asked back.

He tilted his head at me. "Natalie. You *like* her."

"Um . . ." I thought about denying it, only because I wasn't sure *what* I felt exactly. But then his question Ping-Ponged around in my head as I caught a glimpse of Natalie pulling up her perpetually slipping bathing-suit strap. My mouth went dry and my heart felt too heavy in my chest.

"Yeah. I think I do," I'd said quietly.

Luca nodded and smiled, like it was the most natural thing in the world. And for me, I guess it was.

Later that fall, he was pretty baffled when I started dating and messing around with guys, but I liked them, too. It took several conversations with Luca, both of us sitting cross-legged on his *Star Wars* bedspread, for him to get it. For *me* to get it.

"Is Grace only kissing guys because she thinks she should?" he'd asked a Magic 8 Ball, shaking it so vigorously, the whole bed vibrated. We were fifteen and I'd just made out with Nate Landau at a party the previous weekend. Luca made a face at the ball's answer, then presented it to me.

*My sources say no.*

I'd laughed and grabbed the 8 Ball out of his hands. "Does Luca still suck his thumb in his sleep?"

*Without a doubt.*

Luca fake-gasped and knocked the 8 Ball out of my hands. He grinned, but it melted quickly. "Seriously, Grace. Help me understand this."

I huffed loudly, lying back on the bed and staring at the ceiling so I didn't have to look at Luca's earnest gaze. "I *like* kissing guys, all right?" And I did. I still do.

"So you're not gay?" Luca asked.

I remember blinking about a million times, the ridges in the ceiling's plaster flashing in and out of my vision. I rolled the word and all that it entailed around in my head a few times. It didn't fit. It wasn't me and I said as much.

"Okay," Luca said. "But would you have kissed Natalie? I mean, if she'd wanted to?"

God, the thought alone made my arms break out in goose bumps. All that softness. Sameness. "Yeah. Yeah, I definitely would have."

His eyes narrowed on me. It wasn't a judgmental look, only curious and just . . . Luca. He watched me for a few seconds before he broke into a grin, tapping his finger on his chin. "You know, I think there's a word for this."

I looked away from him and my cheeks flamed up — not from embarrassment, but from *knowing*. From realization, because I was pretty sure there was a word for it too.

"You're a little baby bisexual." And even though my stomach flipped over, a little rhythmical *yes* humming through my veins, I laughed at the way Luca was trying to make sure I felt okay about it all, slipping something lighthearted into the middle of a large truth. He reached out and patted my shoulder, but I arced out of his reach and snapped my teeth at him.

"Bad bisexual," he said.

The conversation devolved into laughter and noogies, but then that was that. Luca never made me feel weird about it. Never questioned when I dated guys. Never cocked a suspicious brow when I looked a little too long at some pretty girl. He let me be. And I knew the word fit me. It felt right. Not as a label, really, but more as a way to simply understand myself.

Still, I'd never dated a girl. I'd never even *kissed* a girl. Before and after Natalie, there had been a few on the cape and at school who made me feel the same way she did, at least physically, inspiring daydreams during school and those quiet moments alone in bed, my body pulled taut with thoughts that felt so easy and natural to give myself over to.

With the few girls I've been attracted to, there was always this guessing game attached to it. And I'd never gotten more than a friendship vibe from any of them. Hell, I barely got that. As Eva said yesterday, I can be a little prickly. I *am* my mother's daughter, after all. Either way, there sure as shit hasn't been any love, with anyone. Jay used to turn me into a puddle just by smiling at me from across the cafeteria, but I wasn't in love with him. I'm not even sure I *can* fall in love. All I do know is that there has never been a *person* who intrigued me enough to find out. Not since Natalie.

Until now.

I mean . . . maybe?

God, I'm dizzy, because like I said, it can be a guessing game with girls. A constant push and pull of hope and crushing that hope so you're not disappointed. Maybe it's just me.

I press my fingertips to my forehead to try to get my brain back in place and think of some brilliant, affirming response to Eva's confession.

Instead, "Oh" is the eloquent retort that comes out of my mouth.

Eva tenses next to me. "Does that . . . bother you?"

"No!" We both startle at how loud my damn voice is. "I mean, no. Of course not. I . . . it's fine."

A silence settles over us—a hovering sort of quiet that's waiting for me to fill it with more words, more truths. But I can't get it out. It's not that I'm ashamed. It's just so damn new, this flesh-and-blood *possibility* sitting right next to me, the heady jasmine scent coming off her skin and mingling with the salty air and sand.

Eva offers a little laugh, leaning back on her hands and stretching out her legs. "Well, I'm glad it's fine."

"I didn't mean that you needed my approval."

"No, I know. But you never know how someone will react. Took my mom a couple weeks to get her thoughts around it all when I told her."

"But she was cool with it?"

"Yeah." She looks down, picking at a loose thread on her shirt. "She loves me no matter what. *Loved* me. God, I don't think I'll ever get used to this past-tense way of thinking." Sighing loudly, she rubs at her forehead.

"Eva—"

"So what about you?" she asks.

I watch her, feeling again like I should say something comforting. Feeling again like she doesn't want me to. "Um. What about me?"

"You and Luca? Have you and he ever—"

"Oh my god, no."

"Why not?"

"He's like my brother. No, he *is* my brother." I cringe for effect and Eva laughs.

"But you and Jay?"

I breathe out a long breath. "Yeah, me and Jay. Unfortunately. But that's over. Way over. So over."

"So you're over?"

I splash some sand onto her feet, and she kicks it onto my legs.

"Are you dating at all right now?" she asks.

My gaze drifts to hers, a slow crawl. "Nope."

She nods and looks away. "I've never even kissed anyone."

"Are you serious?"

She winces a little, and I feel like a total jerk.

"Sorry," I say, then put on a fake British accent. It's really awful. "What I meant was, *How very demure of you.*"

It does the trick. She laughs. "Trust me it has nothing to do with being demure. I only just came out about a year ago. I mean, I've had crushes on a few girls, but they were all straight. Let me tell you how fun that was."

Natalie's pitying smile at the end of that summer flashes into my mind. Her soft hand on my shoulder as she turns me around and points out her college boyfriend waiting for her by his black Beamer.

*Oh, I think I have a pretty good idea.*

"And, I mean, I lived in New York, so I definitely knew girls who were gay. Just no one I liked. At least, not when I was brave enough to act on it. And I was dancing, like, all the time. There wasn't time for much else. Like I said, this is my first real party."

"Wow."

"Yeah. Depressing, isn't it?"

"Kissing isn't all it's cracked up to be."

Her eyes widen. "For real? Because it looks freaking awesome."

I laugh. "Okay, you caught me. It's pretty great."

"Just as I suspected."

Laughter explodes behind us. Turning, I see Jay, bare-chested, twirling his shirt around his head to a Beyoncé song like he's a stripper or something. Girls flock around him, waving dollar bills and honest-to-god squealing.

"Good lord, he's totally smashed," I mutter, getting to my feet and brushing the sand off my butt.

Eva reaches out a hand to me, and I help her up. Her fingers grip mine a little longer than they need to. But maybe that's all in my head. Maybe every look and smile and flirty smirk is forever and always in my head, just like it was with Natalie.

Ugh. Ugh infinity.

"Time to go?" Eva asks, ticking her head toward the bonfire.

Jay's belt buckle now hangs undone, football-printed boxers on display.

"I'd say so. You going to head back to Emmy's?"

She nods and lets out a sigh. "Home sweet home." But she doesn't move. She just watches the water roll over itself, her eyes hazy in thought.

There's no doubt in my mind that Emmy and Luca, even Macon and Janelle, are really trying to give Eva a good home. Make her feel loved. Watching Eva, there's no doubt in my mind that it's not working. Maybe nothing *can* work right now.

"You want to meet me at the lighthouse later?" I ask before I can think better of it.

She turns to me, her eyes brightening. "Yes."

No hesitation. No doubt.

*Yes.*

# chapter twelve

THE NEXT MORNING, I'M BRUSHING MY TEETH, HALF
awake, when I hear my mother unleash a string of curses
loud enough to rattle the windows.

It's the ass-crack of dawn — I'm up early for my first shift at
LuMac's — so I'm pretty surprised she's even out of bed. She and
Pete weren't home when I got back from the bonfire last night, but I
waded through a trail of fresh beer cans when I sneaked out to meet
Eva after midnight.

As always, my heart rate gallops and my feet itch to hurtle me
toward my mother before my brain can catch up, slow me down,
prepare me for whatever tiny nothing or huge something I'm about
to face. I spit out a mouthful of foamy toothpaste and follow the
eff-bombs.

Mom's in the kitchen, a soldering iron in her shaking hands.
My stomach sinks to my feet when I see an open can of Bud Light
close to her elbow. I'm already inching closer, wondering if I can
slip the can into the trash without her noticing, when I spot three

pieces of thin, triangular sea glass, all hued in various shades of aqua. Next to them lie skinny strands of copper, ready to be mixed with the solder. I feel an annoying flare of childlike joy.

Approaching the table, I pick up a familiar and ragged notebook open to a drawing of a necklace. In the picture, the pieces of sea glass fan out on a delicate, nearly translucent chain. The copper, a rusty red color, encases each piece. I've seen this necklace in its final form so many times, and the effect is magical.

I love this necklace. Mom designed it a few years ago, and it's her most popular item in her Etsy shop. For a long time, she's been promising to make me one, but most of the time, it takes every bit of initiative in her bones to get her to fulfill an order, so making a necklace for zero profit—even for her own daughter—isn't likely. It even became a sort of running joke. Every time she'd get an order, she'd smile at me and say, "Another call for the Precious."

"Gollum is so demanding," I'd say.

"But we needs it, Precious," she'd say in a freakishly accurate impersonation of Gollum, and we'd laugh and I'd help her get out all her materials, and the world was small and okay and ours.

"Goddammit to hell," Mom says now, pulling my eyes from the sketch. She's attempting to edge a sliver of gorgeous blue-green in the soldered copper but keeps smearing it onto the surface of the glass. That stuff is hot, too. Her fingers are red from little burns and flecks of copper.

"Can I help?" I ask, pushing the beer out of her reach.

She startles in her chair. "Oh, baby. I didn't hear you come in."

"Alas, I am here." I look around for an order form to get some idea of how much time we have until it needs to ship, but there's nothing but the notebook and materials. "Who ordered the Precious this time?"

Not even the hint of a smile. She doesn't look up, just cleans the glass with some Goo Gone and starts edging again.

"Mom?"

"What?"

"The order? How long do you have to make it?"

"Um . . . there's no time limit." She finally gets the edging right and moves on to the next piece.

"Oh." I fight a smile, finally understanding why she's acting so weird. I start to back away from the table. "I'll just pretend I didn't see all this, then."

She finally glances up at me. "Why would you do that?"

"Because. The necklace." I sweep my hand over the table.

Mom frowns at me. "Yes. The necklace. I'm making it for Eva."

My stomach plunges to my feet. "What?"

"Eva. I told you I thought of some things that might make her feel more at home."

"And that thing is . . . a necklace."

She shrugs, her eyes never leaving her task. "You'd be surprised what makes you feel loved when you lose the person you love the most."

I blink. Over and over again, hoping the scene will change, but it never does. When I don't move or say anything else, she looks up.

"Ugh. Baby, don't look at me like that." She returns her gaze to her noble task. "Can you help me, please?"

I keep staring at her, her too-big tank top hanging off her shoulders, her long fingers growing more and more steady as she works. She always gets better, more confident, the longer she sticks with something, her chronic creative paralysis fading with each motion. I know this about her.

It makes me wonder—what does she know about me? What would she say if someone asked her my favorite food or what scares me or about a sure way to get me to laugh? Would she have an answer at all?

"Gracie?" she says when I don't answer. "A little help?"

Closing my eyes, I inhale through my nose and let it out slowly, something Emmy taught me to do a few years ago when I'd get stressed about piano recitals. When I feel a little less violent, I open my eyes and find Jay standing in the doorway to the kitchen. He flicks his eyes from me to my mom to the necklace and back to me. He looks concerned, and I wonder how long he's been standing there and how much he overheard.

The violence floods back in, but it's a childlike kind of violence. The kind that wants to stomp my feet and bury my face in my mother's skirt and ask her—beg her—to *see* me.

But I can't ask her to do that.

Because if I do, she'll tilt her head at me and smile, maybe even cup my face in her hands and kiss my forehead.

*I do see you, baby.*

And that answer is almost worse than nothing at all.

"I have to go to work," I say flatly.

Mom doesn't say goodbye as I walk out the door.

Jay stops me when I'm halfway down the driveway. I don't hear his feet eating at the gravel until he's right next to me, hooking a hand on my arm and swinging me around. I jerk away from him, nearly losing my grip on my bike, and keep walking, pushing it along next to me.

"Grace."

"I have to go to work, Jay. Shouldn't you be asleep or playing Mario Kart or jerking off or something?"

"Nice. And I have work too, you know."

"No, I don't. And I don't care."

"Jesus, I'm just trying to check on you. Your mom —"

"What, run out of flirty material to try out on her?"

"You're impossible."

I stop, turning to glare at him, my fingers white on my bike handles. His hair is all mussed and his eyes have turned soft. I remember how he used to whisper my name, over and over, while he kissed my eyes, my nose, my ears, my mouth.

*Grace.* Kiss. *Gracie.* Kiss.

What a load of shit.

"I'll be impossible if I want to," I say. "And you don't know what the hell you're talking about."

His gaze turns hard. "And whose fault is that, huh? But I *do* know your mom's a bitch who needs to grow up."

I shove him. Hard, in the chest with both hands. His eyes pop in surprise, and he stumbles back a few steps. Early-morning sunlight spills over his hair, turning it into gold. I shove him again.

"Shut. Up. You don't know a damn thing about my mother. Your oaf of a father might be in her life for now, but that doesn't give you the right to make judgments, to *comfort* me like we're some sort of sick family. You don't have a right to anything, Jay. So butt out."

He straightens his shirt, his expression an angry cloud. "What the hell, Grace? Look, I'm sorry about the other night, okay? You think I'm happy about this whole act our parents are putting on? I was supposed to be in Chicago with—"

His expression darkens even more and closes up. He takes a deep breath, hooking his hand on the back of his neck as he stares at the gravel.

"Look," he goes on, "I knew you moving in here would piss you off, so I went with it, okay? But now I'm just trying to help. Jesus, I'm trying to say you deserve better."

My next string of words gets stuck in my throat. I hate Jay Lanier. He betrayed me out of spite. Took my right to move on from him and turned it against me. He mocked this situation we're in, like it was all a big joke. Even when we were together, in those quiet name-whispering moments, he never knew me. Never. And yeah, that was my fault, my choice, but it still stings that he never even realized it. Never knew I was holding back.

"Don't pretend like you give a shit, Jay. Just don't."

And then I toss my leg over my bike's seat, the knot in my throat thick enough that it pushes hot tears out of my eyes. I pedal away from him and convince myself it's just the salty wind making them water.

# chapter thirteen

I T'S NOT HER *FAULT.*
It's not *her* fault.
It's *not* her fault.

As Luca babbles on and on about the right way to roll silver-ware, this phrase echoes in my mind over and over again. I watch Eva weave through LuMac's tourist-packed dining room pouring coffee through a smile, tucking her tips into her aqua-blue apron.

*Well, that will pair just beautifully with the necklace . . .*

Ugh. Stop. It's not her fault.

And it's not. I know this. It's not like Eva threw herself into my mother's arms and begged her to love her and share with her all the secrets of life. She's not even *aware* of how fucked up my relationship with Maggie actually is. On top of that, I know Mom gets like this — she hooks herself on to a sad story and rides it until the bitter end.

But this is the first time that story has been a person I know, someone I have to see and interact with and work with. Usually it's cats at the animal shelter and orphans in some war-torn country or flood victims along the Mississippi. Usually I can ignore Mom's fluttering and heart-clutching, and she's over it in a couple weeks. Usually it's not quite so . . . *real*.

Okay, that one time Mom brought home a worm-filled dog from the pound was pretty real, because I was twelve and *I* had to take care of him, get all attached to him, and name him Noodles because of his curly, sand-colored fur, only to realize there was no way we could afford him and then I had to find a good home for him and say good-bye. That was pretty real. But still. Noodles was a dog.

Eva is a whole live girl.

"Hey," Luca says, bumping my elbow. "Earth to Gray."

"What? Sorry."

He follows my gaze over the counter to where Eva's delivering an armful of plates to table . . . eleven? No, twelve.

"Uh-huh," he says after few more glances between us.

"What?"

"Did you hang out with Eva last night?"

"Yeah," I say, dragging out the word. I'm just going to assume he means the bonfire and not the lighthouse at two a.m.

"What did you talk about?"

"Stuff."

"Stuff."

"Yes, Luca, *stuff*."

120

"Like, serious stuff or fun stuff?"

"Oh my god, pry much?"

He shrugs and presents his palms. "Just wondering. You're not exactly Cape Katie's Miss Congeniality, but you and Eva . . ."

"Me and Eva *what?*"

"Seem to get along. Damn. Sensitive much?"

I take a deep breath, rolling up some more silverware. "Sorry. And yeah, we do get along. She's cool."

He nods, smiling an infuriating little smile.

"What?" I ask.

"Did you *share* things?"

"Luca, I swear to god, I'm about to stab you with this knife."

"It's a butter knife—it'll barely break the skin."

"Try me."

"I'm just asking if you talked about yourself at all. Your mom or whatever. Jay didn't even know your middle name."

I ignore the *whatever* and focus on the most innocuous part of his inquiry. "First of all, Jay didn't care about my middle name. Second of all, what does my relationship with Jay have to do with Eva?"

He starts to say something, but I power on.

"And third, *why* would I tell her about Maggie?"

He frowns. "You're not going to?"

"Again, why? Poor girl's been through enough."

His frown deepens, but he nods. Luckily, Eva chooses that

moment to come over, a few credit cards and guest checks overflowing in her hands.

"Oh my god, does anyone tip with cash anymore?" she asks, brushing her hair out of her face with her arm.

"Nope," Luca says. "Or anything over fifteen percent, at least in Cape Katie."

"Lovely."

"But you can expect some nice plum preserves around Christmastime."

She blinks at him, and he shoots her a double thumbs-up, coupled with a goofy grin. They banter back and forth for a few seconds, but I don't hear it. My eyes seem to have a mind of their own, traveling from Eva's tired eyes and laughing mouth, down her long neck to the hollow of her throat where the necklace would rest next to her heart.

"How's your first day going?" she asks, turning toward me.

"Fine, I think. I've mastered the very challenging silverware roll." I hold up an admittedly sloppy creation.

"Lucky. Better than dealing with *people*."

"How dare they want coffee refills."

"Right? So entitled."

We laugh and Luca bats his eyelashes at me over Eva's shoulder. I stick my tongue out at him while Eva runs the credit cards.

"I'm exhausted," she whispers, leaning toward me so only I can hear her.

"I wonder why."

She smiles and nudges my shoulder a little. Last night we climbed to the top of the lighthouse again and talked about nothing. Stupid stuff. How Eva's never been on a horse. My uncharacteristic love for *Anne of Green Gables*. Eva's addiction to eating peanut butter right out of the jar. My irrational fear of water beasts.

"Water beasts?" she'd asked, barely holding back a laugh.

"Sharks. Giant alligators in tiny ponds. Piranhas traveling in packs. Dolphins."

"Dolphins. Who's scared of dolphins?"

"They have teeth. They're freakishly smart. They wig me out, okay?"

She tossed her head back and laughed, and it was a little embarrassing how much I loved the sound.

We talked about all this nothing for a good two hours, steering clear of anything to do with mothers or future plans or girls or first kisses. Yes, we stayed far, far away from that. But it was so easy. Up there, I didn't belong to a messed-up mother. She wasn't the grieving daughter. We were just Grace and Eva.

"Secrets don't make friends, ladies," Luca says while he puts a fresh filter into the coffeemaker.

"Good thing I don't care too much about making more friends," I say.

"You're so charming, Gray."

I flip my hair dramatically. "You love me."

His eyes soften on me. They flick to Eva once, who watches us with an even softer smile, before settling on me again. "I do."

His sudden seriousness makes my throat tighten. There aren't many things I'm sure of in life, but Luca's undying loyalty is one of them. Honestly, I don't think I'd be alive or half as functional as I am without him. I should tell him this more often. Should tell him I love him more than once every five years.

Instead I sock him in the stomach.

I mean, I do it gently, but I still punch him.

He releases a laughed *Oof* and pulls me into a headlock. Emmy blasts out the kitchen door just as he's starting up his legendary noogie.

"Luca!"

He releases me, frantically trying to pick up some rolled silverware that clattered to the floor in our scuffle. Emmy just glares at him.

"I never know if you two are madly in love or hate each other's guts," she says.

I feel Eva's eyes on me while Luca pretends to consider this. "I'm thinking somewhere in between."

Emmy shakes her head at us. "Well, please keep that *in between* out of the dining room and show Grace how to work the POS."

I frown. "Piece of shit?"

Eva chokes a laugh.

"Point of sale," Emmy says, gesturing to the register, but she's biting back her own smile.

"I'll show her," Eva says as she swipes another card. "I'm here anyway."

"Thank you," Emmy says before resting her hand on Eva's shoulder. "Everything okay today?"

Eva immediately stiffens. It's subtle, but I definitely notice her rolling that shoulder back a little, dislodging Emmy's hand. "Yeah, fine."

"Good." Emmy's hand drops, her mouth smashing into a straight line. She watches Eva stack up her receipts for a few seconds before shifting her gaze to me. "Grace, before you learn the POS, can you come to the kitchen and get this tray of muffins for me?"

"Yeah, sure." I throw Luca a glance as he rounds the counter to attend to a new three-top. He just tousles my hair as he passes me.

I follow Emmy into the kitchen, where a couple of gleaming silver trays full of fresh raspberry muffins sit on the prep counter, waiting to be piled into the pastry case near the register. Malcolm and Kaye, Emmy's cooks, are busy at the stoves grilling sausages and prepping fries for lunch.

"These smell amazing," I say as I take a tray from Emmy.

"Thank you. You're welcome to one on your break."

I nod and head for the dining room, the tray heavy on my forearms.

"How does Eva seem to you?" Emmy asks before I reach the swinging doors. I freeze, then turn around slowly, meeting her worried gaze. Heaving a deep breath, I walk back over to her and set down the tray. Before I respond, I try to gather my thoughts, wondering if Emmy's hunting for evidence of Eva's midnight escapades.

I finally settle for "She seems okay. I mean, I know she's sad, but she's . . . I don't know. Coping, I guess? I just met her, but yeah. She seems okay."

Emmy's shoulders descend a little. "Good. That's good. Luca told me you two spent some time together at the bonfire. She barely speaks to me. At least, nothing more than a curt sentence or two, so I'm glad to hear she's talking to you. I arranged for her to join a dance company in Sugar Lake, take a few lessons. It's not New York, but it's something. But she refuses to go."

"Well, from what she told me . . ."

Emmy tilts her head when I hesitate. "What did she say?"

"She just doesn't seem like she wants to do ballet right now."

Emmy presses her mouth flat. "I know she doesn't, honey, but ballet was her life. Like you and piano. Can you imagine giving it up? And at a time like this, when she needs as much *normal* as possible?"

I'm not sure what to say because, no, I can't imagine ever giving up piano. It keeps my feet on the ground, my heart in my chest. But I *can* imagine giving up a dream, settling for some other form of piano because there's no other choice. Like Eva said, sometimes it's not a matter of want.

"I just want to take care of her," Emmy says, looking down, her hands worrying at her apron strings.

I reach out and squeeze her arm. Emmy's the sweetest woman on the planet. Hands down. She's saved my ass multiple times, slipping a twenty into my jacket pocket every now and then when I've been hanging out at their house. I never find it until I get home —she knows I'd never accept it if she just handed it to me—but she always seems to know exactly when I need it.

"And how are you, sweetheart?" she asks before I can say anything else about Eva. "The lighthouse working out okay?"

That question has way too many possible answers so I stick to my usual. "Everything's fine."

Emmy narrows her eyes at me. She's nearly impossible to bullshit, but she lets me off the hook and offers a tiny smile. "Well. Strawberry-rhubarb pie won't bake itself. Let's get back to work, shall we?"

I nod and watch her pull cartons of strawberries and long stalks of rhubarb from the refrigerator. I grab the muffins and join Eva at the register. While I unload them into the pastry case, she starts her spiel about the POS and I half listen, wondering about Emmy's eager concern and the obvious tension between the two of them. Wondering about that aqua sea-glass necklace forming under my mother's hands at home.

But underneath all of that, there's something else. This pull to Eva. Loneliness to loneliness. Like to like. Missing mother to missing mother. Wish to wish.

For the rest of our shift, she keeps catching my eye. I keep catching hers. And every time she smiles that little smile—a little hint of the girl on top of that lighthouse—it makes me smile back.

# chapter fourteen

AFTER A FEW GRUELING HOURS WITH FRÉDÉRIC Chopin at the Book Nook's piano, I walk into the house to the sound of voices.

Soft female voices.

And something that smells like puke. At first, I wonder if it's me because I went straight from LuMac's to the bookstore. But no, I smell like onion rings, which is decidedly different from puke.

I follow the voices through the kitchen, half expecting to find a pool of vomit somewhere that I'm going to have to clean up. But then there's Mom, bright-eyed and bushy-tailed, seated at the dining table, a dish of something drenched in cheese and slightly green-colored steaming in front of her. Hence the puke smell.

And Eva is sitting right next to her.

Hence the female voices.

". . . You don't have to do anything you don't want to do," Mom is saying, her voice a little teary-sounding. "Everything is different now."

"It's not that I don't want to do ballet," Eva says, flicking the tab on a can of Diet Dr. Pepper. "I miss it a lot. I just . . . feel like I physically can't do it."

Mom nods. "Emmy's never lost anyone the way we have, baby. If giving up ballet gets you through the day, then give up ballet."

Her words fit all wrong on my ears. I'm about to take a step back into the kitchen when Mom glances up.

"Hi, baby." She says it happily, but she wipes under eyes like she's also been crying at some point. Eva smiles, her eyes a little watery-looking too. "Where've you been?"

"Piano."

"Oh good, you found one!"

"I did. What's going on?"

"We're just waiting for Pete and Julian to get home. I ran into Eva at the Trading Post when I was picking up some groceries and invited her for dinner. We've just been having a little girl time." Mom winks at Eva. "Haven't we, hon?"

Eva nods. She wraps her hand around her soda can and crinkles the aluminum. "Much needed. Join us, Grace."

I can't answer her because my eyes are glued to her nails, which are painted a fresh eggplant purple. They're glittery and super shiny, glossed in my mother's favorite hue, the bottle she only takes out for special occasions, like first dates or that one time she actually made it to one of my piano recitals before it was halfway over.

"Girl time," I deadpan. Approaching the table, my fingers dig into the strap of my bag, and I let my gaze pass right over what I see now is *my* brand-new bottle of top coat, to stare at Eva. She looks peaceful and relaxed, if a little tired, nothing like she did when she shook off Emmy's touch earlier.

Eva tilts her head at me, her smile faltering. I try to cover up whatever expression is on my face right now, but I can't muster up the barest hint of a smile. Instead, I look away from her and peer down at the green concoction in a casserole dish.

"You cooked?" I ask Mom. "What is that?"

She beams. "It's lasagna verde."

"I don't think that's a thing."

Eva laughs. "Oh, come on, you're going to love it. It smells great, Mags."

*Mags?*

"It smells like vomit," I say.

Mom flinches and her smile flips upside down, but I don't say anything. I can't. Because if I open my mouth right now, I'll scream like a banshee and scare our nearest neighbor a half mile down the beach. Without a word, I turn around and walk out the door.

When I was a kid, my mom and I used to take these midnight walks. She had nightmares a lot, so she'd wake me up—school the next day be damned—and take my hand, and we'd walk on the beach or the bike path, circling the cape until I could barely keep my eyes open and she'd have to carry me home. She'd smoke cigarettes, and I'd always wait for her to start talking about my dad. His favorite color. How they met. What kind of music he liked.

Anything.

But she'd never say a word.

We'd just walk, hand in hand.

Now I walk too. I'm not sure for how long. A couple hours at least because the sun starts to set when I'm on the beach and the day gets swallowed up by an inky black when I'm on the bike path. It takes me that long to suss out why I'm so mad, who I'm mad at, if I'm mad at all or just tired.

My feet pound the pavement as I spill off the path and onto the sidewalk of a residential neighborhood about a mile from Lu-Mac's. I'm stomping and my skin feels buzzy, a familiar sensation that catapulted me off of Colin McCormick's balcony. I stop, my hands on my hips as I try to figure out what I want to do. What I need to do. Not a year from now, not at my Manhattan audition, not next week. Now. Because right now, I can feel myself coming out of my skin, sloughing off Grace the girl to make more room for Grace the caretaker, the worrier, the fixer. The hopeless nitwit who thinks some new girl showing up in her life means *possibility*, when really all it means is more damn worrying.

A flash to my left draws my attention. I turn my head just in time to catch the flicker of the outside light blinking off on Mrs. Latham's porch. Her tiny gray house is impeccably maintained, her prized beach gnomes spread across her pristine yard in various states of leisure and, if you ask me, ridiculousness. They're each about the size of a cat, and Mrs. Latham loves those damn things. Mrs. Latham has also despised Luca and me ever since we were twelve and used to share a paper route. Luca hurled a rolled-up *Cape Katherine Chronicle* onto her porch with a little more vigor than necessary, and it tipped over a potted begonia or azalea or who-the-hell-cares-what, which knocked over one of her gnomes and busted his bulbous nose. She got so mad and yelled so loudly, Luca actually cried. Since then every time she ventures into public, she glares daggers at us, and we vow afresh to one day rearrange those gnomes into compromising positions.

But we've never done it, because it's completely immature and stupid.

I laugh softly, taking out my phone and tapping on Luca's name. He answers almost immediately, and my lungs open up, that pent-up, antsy feeling slowing down into a steady heartbeat.

I could use a little immature and stupid right now.

# chapter fifteen

THE NIGHT AIR IS COOL AND CRISP, THE USUAL HINT OF sea salt in every curl of wind. I wait under LuMac's aqua-blue-and-white awning for Luca, my adrenaline kicking up a notch with every second that passes, but this is the good kind of anticipation, one full of excitement rather than dread.

"Gray."

I turn toward Luca's voice, the grin on my face fading when I see he's not alone. Kimber smiles at me, her long hair tied into a low ponytail.

And Eva is right behind them.

"Hi, Grace," Kimber says, her yoga pants clinging perfectly to her thighs.

"Uh, hi."

Luca bumps my shoulder. "I can't believe we're actually doing this."

I grunt acknowledgment, but my attention is on Eva. She's staring right back at me, a million questions in her eyes.

"What exactly are we doing again?" Kimber asks as Luca slips his hand into hers. She leans against him. Definitely a familiar, we've-made-out kind of lean, which means Luca must really like this girl. He talks a big game, but he's a total sap when it comes to girls and he's never hooked up with someone for only a night. Aside from a round or two of spin the bottle, Luca's only ever kissed girls he's actually dating. Now, he may only date her for a week, but, dammit, he makes sure she knows his noble intentions before he plants one on her.

"We're going to make it look like beach gnomes are doing the nasty," Luca says casually, like we're talking about watching a movie or something.

"Why?" Kimber tilts her head at me, her gaze curious.

"Why not?" I say.

"That's not really a reason."

"Do you need a reason for everything?"

"Usually, yeah. Especially if it involves handling someone else's property without their permission."

I feel my eyes narrow into slits. "You don't have to do it, Kimber. I called *Luca*. Not—"

"All righty, then," Luca says, slinging an arm around Kimber's shoulders. "It's just something Grace and I have joked about doing for the past few years." He proceeds to tell her about our paper route and Mrs. Latham's subsequent eye daggers. I watch Kimber as Luca talks. She watches me back. We've always gotten along in the past, working together last summer and sharing some classes.

Back in ninth grade, she even lent me a pair of sneakers for gym for about a month when my own got so ratty that the soles nearly disintegrated during a rousing game of four square. I wouldn't call us friends. I wouldn't call us *not* friends, either. But now she's looking at me like she's not quite sure who the hell I am or why her brand-new boyfriend is friends with me.

"Sounds like Mrs. Latham has one too many well-behaved beach gnomes," Eva says. "I say let's do this." She meets my gaze for a split second before I flick mine away.

"Fine," Kimber says. "But if we get arrested, I'm claiming hypnosis."

"Because that's believable," I mutter. Luca elbows me in the ribs, and not very gently, either.

We make our way down the sidewalk toward Mrs. Latham's neighborhood. Luca and Kimber walk in front, hands linked and whispering.

"Why did you leave like that?" Eva asks. We walk side by side, but I keep my eyes on Kimber's ass. That is, until I realize I'm accidentally staring at Kimber's ass, then I shift my gaze to Luca's curly head.

"Leave like what?"

"You pretty much bit your mom's head off for making lasagna, and then you stormed out."

I keep walking, keep staring at Luca's hair, which now has Kimber's hand twined into it. I have no idea how to answer Eva. To

136

answer her is to *explain*. And to explain is to become a kind of sad story you see on Lifetime movies.

"What were you doing there?" I ask instead.

"I ran into your mom at the store, like she said. And then . . ." Her voice fades and I dare a glance. She blinks into the night air and stuffs her hands into her pocket. "I was having a shitty day, okay? And we started talking, and your mom . . . I don't know. She seemed like—"

"Like she'd do anything to make you feel better?"

Eva swings her eyes to mine. "Yeah."

I nod. I get that. I *live* that every single day. New York City itineraries to soothe the sting of a new move and an asshole ex-boyfriend, promises of beautiful necklaces, early-morning cuddles that make me forget she ever disappeared on me for those few days back when I was thirteen.

"And I was sort of hoping to see you," Eva says, her voice as quiet and full as the night around us.

All thoughts of Eva and Mom fizzle from my thoughts. Now there's only Eva. Maybe even Eva and Grace.

"Okay, what's our plan of attack?" Luca asks, yanking my attention toward him. Mrs. Latham's house comes up on our right, all the windows dark and shuttered. I breathe deeply and look around, gauging the rest of the neighborhood, but all is quiet and sleepy.

"I say we partner off," Eva says, her voice now steady and sure.

"And then, you know, just position them and go. I mean, right? No other way to do it, really."

"Sounds good," Luca says, taking Kimber's hand and crossing the street, his shoulders all hunched over like he's in some spy movie.

"Guess that leaves you and me," Eva says.

"I guess it does." I hear the flirting lilt to my voice and, honestly, I sort of love it.

"Meet back at LuMac's?" Luca asks when I join him and Kimber behind a juniper bush at the edge of the sidewalk.

I nod as Eva comes up behind me. "Wow," she whispers, peeking around the bush at Mrs. Latham's yard. "Looks like a bunch of *Lord of the Rings* characters got together for a luau."

Luca snorts a laugh. Then he squares his shoulders, his eyes meeting mine for a splinter of a second before they dart away. "This luau's about to get kinky. Ready?"

Kimber starts giggling, and he presses their joined hands to her mouth playfully, which only makes her giggle harder.

"Set?" he goes on, biting back his own laugh.

Eva slips her hand into mine. I don't hold hands a lot, not even with people I'm dating. I hated that twining, enclosed feel, like Jay or whoever was trying to wrangle me into submission. So when Eva's fingers glide in between mine, I mean to pull back. Really, I do, but there's this little *zing* that slides up my arm and then down into my stomach. It'd be rude to just wrench my hand away. Not only rude, but also directly in contrast to what I actually want.

Kimber's eyes flick down to our joined hands, her brow furrowed, before she links her arm with Luca's and looks back toward the lawn. I feel myself flush hot. Instinct kicks in and this time I do try to pull away, but Eva's hand tightens on mine. I heave a deep breath, almost glad she's making me stay put.

"Go!" Luca whisper-yells before I can think any more about the fingers linked with mine or what Kimber thinks about it or what it means.

The four of us bolt into the yard. I run straight for three gnomes under a ceramic palm tree that seem like easy targets. Eva's hand is still in mine, her long legs slowing to keep pace with my five-foot-four frame. When we hit the gnomes' pine straw bed, we separate, and she aims for some limboing gnomes nearby. The house is still dark, the only light a faint, orangey glow from the streetlights. My heart pounds as I take one gnome who is for real bending over with a pink shovel in his hands like he's digging in the sand, and position him in front of another gnome who appears to be snuggling with a pineapple. I snort a half-terrified, half-hysterical laugh under my breath.

Suddenly, a loud, splintering sound echoes through the silence, as though two gnomes collided and the outcome was gory. Luca curses and the house lights up like a million suns. Floodlights pour gold through every part of the yard. I'm so surprised — not to mention temporarily blinded — that I lurch backwards, tripping over my own feet and sprawling on the dewy grass.

"Luca Michaelson!" a voice yells from the front door. "I know that's you! You better get your scrawny butt off my property before I call nine-one-one!"

"I am not scrawny," Luca mutters from behind a bush somewhere to my left, his tone ridiculously calm and even.

"Abort!" I call, rolling myself onto my stomach. I stand up and look for Eva. She's near an oak tree, frozen in place with a gnome in a pink bikini clutched in her hands. When we lock eyes, she sticks the gnome on the back of another one already seemingly sucking face with a red-bearded gnome and runs toward me, our hands joining again like it's a habit.

A door slams and a growling noise starts up and increases in volume behind us.

"Oh, god!" Kimber says, tripping to my side, a twig tangled in her long ponytail. "I knew this was a bad idea. I can't believe she let Sugar out!"

"I can't believe she named him Sugar," Luca says as we all run. "That thing is like Cujo — goes straight for the nads."

"Maybe you should sacrifice yourself," I say, "since you're the only one with actual nads."

"Unlikely."

"Unlikely that you have nads?" I ask. Luca reaches across Kimber and tries to noogie me, which is damn near impossible, considering we're running.

"Just *move*, idiots," Eva says, shoving Luca's arm away.

We hit the pavement and bolt down the dark street. Glancing behind me, I see the outline of a huge dog barreling toward us, its paws scraping the asphalt as it snarls its way closer and closer.

"Uh, guys . . ." Kimber says, nearly whimpering.

I imagine my mother identifying my torn-to-shreds body in the morgue tomorrow morning. Maybe she'd make me a necklace then, lacing it around my cold, dead throat for burial.

A deafening bark pulls me from my morbid thoughts. "Split up!" I yell, pulling Eva with me off the main road and onto a sandy path leading into the woods. A quick glance behind me shows Luca and Kimber, hand in hand, running toward LuMac's. That quick glance also shows that Sugar has chosen Eva and me as his conquests. Foamy drool drips from his snout.

"I'm pretty sure *this* is a scene right out of a horror movie," Eva says.

"Just run!"

A little chuckle bubbles up and escapes Eva's mouth as I zigzag us through trees.

"I can't believe you're laughing," I say, gasping for air. "We're about to get eaten."

"Hey, this was your idea. Besides," she says, barely winded, "I grew up in New York City, I can handle a damn Doberman."

We carve a path across the sandy floor as Sugar's bark reverberates through the blue-dark. It's not long before I feel him nip at my heels. Literally.

The pull on my pants makes me lose my footing and trip over a root. Sprawling on the ground for the second time tonight, I mutter a thanks to the gods of teenage stupidity that Sugar seems startled by my fall and stops in his tracks instead of taking a chunk out of my leg.

Before I know it, Eva is pulling me to my feet and shoving me toward a huge and gnarly oak tree. Then she's pushing me up, pushing my waist, my ass, my thighs. Good god, her hands are everywhere, but we're moving up and away, one branch at a time until only barks trail behind us. Sugar has two paws on the tree trunk, blinking up at us like he's sort of sad the game is over.

"Holy shit," I say, my lungs gulping air. We're both perched on a thick branch at least ten feet off the ground. Sugar whines for a few seconds, but then starts sniffing around the trunk.

"I can't believe you wanted to do that for fun," Eva says.

"Oh, come on, that was totally awesome," I say, laughing. My tone is sarcastic, but this is exactly what I wanted. Not to get chased by a rabid dog exactly, but *this*. Heart pounding, fingertips tingling with adrenaline, an energy lighting up my veins that has absolutely nothing to do with paying rent or freaking out when my mother won't pick up her phone.

Or lasagna verde cooked for a girl who's not me, nails that aren't mine coated in aubergine.

I push the thought away and take another deep breath. Beside me, Eva only sips at the air, barely out of breath and clearly in amazing shape from years of ballet. Like I couldn't tell from her sleek calves and plank-like stomach.

Not that I've noticed.

Okay, I've definitely noticed.

Below us, Sugar lies down under the tree. He yawns and then rests his massive head on his paws. He looks pretty damn comfy for a bloodthirsty beast.

"Great. Now we're stuck up here until he goes home," I say. The tree, however, is not pretty damn comfy. The branches are gnarled and barely thick enough to hold my butt without lopping me over the edge.

"Sorry about earlier," Eva says. She shifts around, scooting until her back is pressed against the trunk. At first, I think she's talking about my mother, the dinner and the nails and the storming out, but then she goes on. "All the"—she circles her hand in my direction—"groping."

"Oh." I release a single laugh. "I think I can forgive a little ass grab. At least I still *have* an ass."

"Good point."

A silence settles over us. The air has turned even cooler, stars blinking in between the tree's leaves. It's quiet, the normal summer night noises hushed, giving me an unwelcome chance to think too many thoughts. Tonight has been one giant cluster.

Eva exhales and it sounds so content, I feel it relaxing me too. "Actually, that *was* really fun," she says, smiling. "Just what I needed, really."

"What do you mean?"

"You know, just . . ." She waves a hand. "Distraction. Forgetting."

"Is that what that was earlier?" I ask before I think better of it. "With my mother? Forgetting?"

She turns to look at me, her expression turning almost unbearably sad. "No. That was remembering."

"Oh."

"Does that bother you? Me hanging out with your mom?"

I don't know what to say. What *can* I say? This girl next to me is sad and lonely. How can I begrudge her comfort, even if it's found in my own mother?

And if I said, *Yes, back the hell off,* what then? Because, god help me, I don't want to be a mess with Eva. I just want to be me.

"No," I say, forcing my eyes on hers, forcing the tremors out of my voice, forcing myself to mean it.

Her shoulders visibly descend, relief clear in her exhaled breath.

"Good. That's good," she says softly, rubbing a hand across her forehead. She doesn't look at me, but I watch her as a few tears bloom and slip down her cheeks. I'm aching to hold her hand, press my fingers against her back, anything to help. Surely my mother's not the only one who can. Surely, Eva's and my big world is still out there, waiting for us to slip back into it where we belong.

"Are you okay?" I ask instead, lacing my fingers together in my lap.

She nods and looks down, picking at a hangnail.

"Tell me something about her," I say. "Something good. Anything you want."

She lifts her head, staring into the tree branches cocooning around us. After a few moments and a few deep breaths, she starts talking. "There was this café on Sixtieth Street. It's pretty famous and sort of a tourist trap, but it's near the dance studio and my mom and I would go there after class every Tuesday and get frozen hot chocolates."

Her eyes mist over with the memory. "I miss those stupid over-priced drinks. There was usually a huge line outside the café, but it never mattered to Mom, even though she was always tired after teaching. We'd stand there for an hour, talking about everything and nothing. Even when it was freezing outside, we'd wait. I miss that. Just . . . standing there with her, you know?"

I nod, even though I'm not sure I do know.

"I miss ballet," she goes on. "I miss the movement, the line my arms would make with the rest of my body. The smell of resin and varnish that coated the hardwoods in the studio. I miss New York."

"Do you really hate it here?"

She shakes her head. "I don't know. It's where I need to be. I miss home but I can't *be* there, you know? It's not New York without her. It's not anything."

"Eva—"

"I want to go back. I just don't know if I can. New York, ballet, any of it. I used to want to teach ballet like my mother did. She loved it so much."

"Do *you* love it?"

A line creases between her eyes. "Mom made me try out different things when I was little, but I always came back to dancing. It's

145

in my blood. I loved that I could forget everything and anything. Or remember it. Whatever I wanted. I was in total control when I danced, but I also wasn't, like something bigger than me, bigger than everything that made me anxious inhabited my body, moving my arms and legs. I wanted to help other girls feel like that. Especially girls like me."

"Wow."

She laughs. "You mean, *Wow, that sounds ridiculous.*"

"No. Not at all. I get that."

Her mouth tilts up in a smile, and she tilts her head at me. "Pianists are very important to dancers, you know. To shows and studios."

"Are you still a dancer?"

Immediately, I regret my question. That tiny smile fades like a chalk drawing in the rain, and Eva's mouth parts as though my question is a literal shock.

"I'm sorry," I say. "I only meant that when you talk about dance, you always talk about it in the past tense."

She nods but doesn't take her eyes off of mine. "Are you a pianist?"

"Always." I blink at her, surprising myself with my lack of hesitation. But it's true—there's no way I'll ever not be a pianist, even if I spend the rest of my days in the Book Nook with Patrick as my only audience.

We sit in silence for a few seconds, Eva's breaths steady and thoughtful next to me. It's easy, this quiet between us, and I can't help but think that piano isn't the only thing that makes all the bullshit fade into the background for me. At least not right now.

"So, riddle me this," she finally says. Her voice is light, her posture straightens against the tree trunk, and I know we're done talking about ballet. "*Jay* walked into your house after you left earlier. Your mom called him Julian."

I groan dramatically and bury my face in my hands. "Well, he would. He lives there."

"I mean, I got that, but *why?*"

I rub at my forehead. "Yes, that is the question, isn't it?"

"Your mom is actually dating his dad?"

"And—here's the real kicker—she had no clue who he was until I pretty much grabbed her by the shoulders and spelled out his name really slowly."

She frowns. "Seriously?"

"True story."

"Holy crap."

"'*Shit,*' Eva. The phrase you're looking for is 'holy shit.'"

She laughs, bracing her hand on the branch. Her pinkie touches mine, and neither of us moves our fingers away. "That's so wild. Maggie doesn't seem—"

Her words cut off abruptly, and she bites on her lower lip.

"Maggie doesn't seem what?" I ask.

"She doesn't strike me as that clueless."

I swallow down a bitter laugh. Because, no, at first Maggie seems charmingly charismatic to most people. Beautiful and free. I know better than anyone how alluring those things are. And Mom *is* all those things, times a hundred.

"She's many things, Eva," I say quietly, looking down at my hands. Next to me, I feel Eva's eyes on me, waiting for me to go on, and I want to. Maybe I even *should,* so she'll get what's going on in my head right now, so she'll understand what those purple nails mean to me, but it's so hard to *say* it. To confess that my own mother, the woman who gave me life and is supposed to love and cherish me above all else, forgets my age half the time. Letting all this crap about Jay and Pete spill is enough.

"Tell me something else about you," Eva says, and I'm grateful for the subject change.

"Like what?"

"I don't know. I know you're a pianist. I know you hate dolphins."

I crack a smile.

"I know you're beautiful and you're fond of swearing and that Luca would commit legit murder for you and you'd do the same for him."

I force my thoughts away from the *beautiful* comment and the fact that when she said the word, her pinkie moved closer and covered mine. "That's about all you need to know."

"No way. Tell me . . ." She narrows her eyes, thinking. "Tell me about your first crush. The first time you really liked someone."

"Why?"

She shrugs. "First crushes are unforgettable and scary as hell.

It's something real and I'm naturally nosy, okay? Mine was a girl named Clara, and she had red hair and brown eyes. We'd been dancing together since we were six, and one day during a costume change, I overheard her refer to me as a 'desperate dyke' in front of her friends."

"Oh, god."

"Yeah, it was lots of fun."

"Sorry."

She shrugs, keeping her eyes on me, clearly waiting for my own story, probably expecting me to moon over some guy with floppy hair and a lopsided smile. This whole conversation is starting to make me squirm. But it's not an uncomfortable kind of feeling. It's an opening up, a hovering on the edge of a cliff after a long climb, the view and height stealing your breath and thoughts.

So I push my hand over a little, twining my pinkie around her ring finger.

And I tell her about my first crush.

"There was this girl," I begin. Eva's eyes widen, but I keep going. "Her name was Natalie." I tell Eva about meeting Natalie at the pool, my fourteen-year-old self instantly enamored with this older girl. How I watched her. How I couldn't breathe around her. How she'd smile at me and bring me different shades of purple nail polish, and we'd paint our fingers and toes during her breaks. How she *listened* to me, let me tell her all about my mother and piano and how I wanted *more* from life. How guilty I felt, even then, for wanting more. How she told me it was okay to want more, to want the world, even. I tell Eva about the way Natalie smelled—like coconut sun lotion and oranges. I tell her how Natalie's skin hypnotized me, how one day when we were getting Diet Cokes from the vending machine in the clubhouse's tiny breezeway, I slid my hand softly down her forearm before linking our fingers. How good it felt to finally touch her.

"What happened?" Eva whispers when I pause, my throat thick from the memory, which is just freaking annoying. It's been three damn years.

"Nothing. She looked down at our hands and smiled. Pulled away and said I was cute. Later that day, she made sure I saw her boyfriend pick her up and then promptly stick his tongue down her throat."

"Ugh."

I shrug, the tree bark rough against my shoulders. "Not her fault."

"It's not yours, either."

"I guess not. I just felt stupid."

"Yeah, I can imagine. Thanks for telling me all that."

"Sure."

"Can I ask you something?"

"Yeah."

"You and Jay . . . he was your boyfriend, right?"

"Yes."

"And you liked him?"

"I liked him okay. I didn't love him. But I liked being with him while it lasted. We had fun until we didn't."

She frowns. "Oh."

"Just ask me, Eva. Just say it."

Her fingers twitch on mine. "So . . . Natalie . . . did you . . . *like* her like her?"

"Yeah. She was the first person I really, really liked. You asked me to tell you about my first real crush, remember?"

"I did, didn't I?" she says, her mouth curved into a half smile.

"Before Natalie, it was just little infatuations and spin the bottle."

"Okay," she says, but the question is still there, hovering.

"I guess I'm bisexual," I say, inhaling a deep breath with my words.

She lifts a brow. "You guess?"

"I mean—"

"No. Crap, I'm messing this up. Wherever you are with this, that's totally cool. I *guessed* I was queer for a long time before I really let myself just . . . *be* queer. I just want to make sure that I understand what you're saying."

I nod. I've only ever said all of this to Luca. I tried telling Mom, and that was so wildly unsuccessful I never really tried again. But I haven't shied away from talking about it because I'm confused.

I glance at Eva's face—her open, curious expression. Her amber-flecked eyes. Her gorgeous mouth, slightly parted and patiently waiting for me to go on. The little dip at her throat created by her sleek collarbones.

Nope. Definitely not confused. But with my confession, Eva and I are edging away from impossible, edging closer to possible. We're shifting from a gay girl and a straight girl to two queer girls.

"It's just a word, you know?" I say, meeting her gaze. "And sometimes words help; sometimes they don't. But . . . well, I like who I like. I like the person."

A little smile lifts her mouth.

"That makes a lot of sense. Cool."

I wait for more—another question, a scoff, even an untangling of our fingers—but nothing comes. She stays still, stays quiet, presses her fingers into mine a little more.

Then her whole hand slides across my whole hand, and our fingers are all mixed up, pale and dark, lavender on dark purple, wrapped over and around. The tree creaks ominously, but I don't care. I forget about everything that came before this—every pissed-off and jealous emotion I had from earlier tonight, gone.

Sugar snores loudly right below us, but I don't care about him, either.

I lean closer, needing her closer, needing me closer, and soon she's right there, her mouth inches from mine. I stop, remembering she's never kissed anyone before. She searches my face, and *wonder* is the only word for her expression. I close the tiny distance between us, just a bit, and let my lower lip brush hers. She sucks in a breath, so I stay there, letting her make the last move.

And she does. Her eyes flick down to my mouth once, then she presses her lips to mine. Soft and warm. I cup the back of her neck to pull her closer. Our tongues touch, gently at first, but then her thumb sweeps over my cheek, and I feel wild, like I need to devour her right here. She tastes like summer, like running and laughter, and the combination is so heady that I have to force myself to slow down and savor this moment. It's a first for me, too.

She pulls away and I almost groan in protest, but I hold it in when she rests her forehead against mine.

"Did we just kiss in a tree?" she asks, a giggle edging her words. "K-I-S-S-I-N-G."

She cracks up at that and her lips find mine again, both of us laughing between the soft press of mouths.

"Ready to go?" she asks when we break apart.

"Absolutely not."

"Me neither, but I think I'm one scoot away from getting a splinter in my ass."

"Well, we wouldn't want that."

She guides me down the tree, her feet as light as the cool breeze over my skin. When we hit the ground, Sugar stirs but doesn't wake, grunting in a way that sounds exactly like a pig. We stifle giggles as we tiptoe around him. Then we run toward town, holding hands the entire way.

# chapter sixteen

THE NEXT MORNING, I WAKE UP TO SHOUTING. I'M OUT of bed so fast, I don't even think about the fact that I'm in nothing but a thin camisole and a pair of fraying sleep shorts. My door cracks against the plaster wall as I fling it open and run down the hall into the living room.

"—can't just take my money without asking, Maggie," Pete is saying. He's dusting something out of his hair and off his shoulders that looks like Fruity Pebbles. "That's not how this works."

"I thought we were in this together!" Mom yells.

They're standing in the kitchen, a red box of cereal torn and empty on the counter, more colorful flakes scattered all over the floor. Mom's dressed in nothing but one of Pete's button-up shirts, dangling to her mid-thigh. At least, I think it's Pete's.

"Together doesn't mean stealing," he says.

*Oh, shit.*

"I did not steal," Mom says. "I borrowed. For a good cause."

"Always a cause with you. You need things for your jewelry

business, fine. Ask me. I told you I'd help out, but don't dig through my wallet when I'm sleeping. I won't have that."

Mom pops her hands on her hips. "You won't *have* that? What is this? Nineteen fifty-five?"

"What happened?" I ask when they both take a breath.

Mom inhales sharply and whirls around to face me. Her affronted expression dips a bit, but she presses her lips flat and barrels on. "Nothing, baby. Pete's having a hard time adjusting to a woman in the house, that's all."

"You've got to be kidding me, Maggie," he says. He gestures toward the mess of cereal. "Is this what it means to have a woman in the house? Cereal dumped on my head for asking you about my own damn money?"

Dread fills my stomach. "Mom, did you—"

"I borrowed it, Gracie. I needed more copper for Eva's necklace I messed up the first one, and she needs—"

"Then. Ask. Me!" Pete booms, his face and thick neck red as a beet. I immediately move toward Mom, wrapping my hand around her arm and pulling her closer to me.

"What the hell?" Jay comes around the corner, rubbing his bed-head hair and blinking heavily. "It's seven a.m."

"It's eight thirty, genius," I say. My entire body feels caught in a vise.

"Whatever. Too early. What's wrong?"

"We're fine," Mom says, but her voice shakes. "Just a simple misunderstanding."

I keep my hand on her arm, both of us as tense as spooked cats. Pete shifts his gaze between the two of us for a few seconds before he closes his eyes, releasing a huge sigh. When he speaks, his voice is calm and even. "Grace, can you and Julian excuse us for a minute?"

"No, I cannot," I say.

"It's okay, baby," Mom says. "Pete and I need to talk."

"So talk. I'll stay right here." Pete is huge and was all crimson-faced and pissed-off two seconds ago. And yeah, okay, it sounds like Mom stole his money and he has every right to be mad about that, but there's no way in hell I'm leaving her alone with him.

"Come on, Grace," Jay says, taking my hand and pulling.

I jerk back. "Get your hands off me."

"Gracie, go," Mom says.

"No way in hell."

"Margaret Grace." She turns toward me, prying my fingers off her arm. "You watch your mouth and get your little butt back in your room. This is between Pete and myself, and I do *not* need you here. I can handle this."

I blink at her, speechless. She's never said that to me before — that she didn't need me. I'm so shocked, I don't even fight Jay guiding me away and down the hall.

In my room, I sink down onto the bed, but my senses are still on high alert. I listen for more yelling or shattering of thrown objects, but there's only a low murmur. Jay hovers in the doorway.

"He won't hit her," he says.

I glance up. "What?"

"He can get pretty loud when he's mad, but he won't hit her. He's never hit anyone in his life. Not even a dude."

My body relaxes and I let out a bitter laugh. Because this is ridiculous, right? That *this* is what I'm worried about. Because I never know exactly what we're getting into; with every new guy, every fight, every scream, there's always a chance it'll turn ugly.

On my rumpled bed, the fingers of my right hand move subtly, tapping out the bass clef of Schumann's *Fantasie.* Jay stays put, watching me. I can't look at him. Yeah, he's an ass, but I'm acutely aware right now that I'm the girl whose mom just stole from his hard-working dad—the man whose house we're living in, whose food we're eating, who could kick us out at any minute. I can't remember the last time Mom sold a piece of jewelry or worked a shift at Reinhardt's Deli. If she's slipping twenties from Pete's wallet or wherever, then things are bad and could get worse any minute. I feel an overwhelming urge to apologize, and I swear to god, I'm about to, when I think of my own stash of tips from LuMac's.

It's not much. I've only worked one shift, but when I got home yesterday, I put the thirty bucks in my *Wizard of Oz* music box that I've had since I was five, a birthday present from Emmy. Jay's eyes follow me as I get up and cross the room to my dresser, flipping open the box's lid. "Over the Rainbow" twinkles through the room, slightly off-key after so many years of play. Dorothy spins slowly in her ruby slippers.

The box is empty.

I knew it would be. Just like I know I won't ask her about it. Just like I know if she had asked me for the money, I would've given it to her.

I stare at the dingy, emerald-green velvet interior, a little yellow brick road curling through the faux forest floor. Gently, I close the box and lift my eyes to the mirror. My hair is stringy from being outside last night, the wind and running tangling it up, and there's a mess of smudged eyeliner I was too exhausted to wash off when I got home.

I look like her.

"Where's your mom, Jay?" I ask, eyes still fixed on my reflection.

"Huh?"

"Your mom. I assume you have one."

He clears his throat, and I turn to look at him. He's staring at me, his lower lip tucked under his teeth. "She's in Chicago. Has been for about four years."

"Why?"

"They got divorced, obviously. She moved there for work. She's a lawyer. A career-obsessed bitch, honestly, with a whole new family. I usually see her at Thanksgiving."

"Oh."

"Yeah."

"You were supposed to stay with her this summer, weren't you?"

"Her new husband surprised her with a trip to Key West," Jay says, shrugging and picking at a loose fleck of paint on the door frame.

"How did I not know all this about her? I mean, when we were together?"

He tilts his head at me. "You never asked."

After a couple of awkward seconds, he turns around and leaves. The house is quiet now, my senses filled with the image of a girl in a mirror—the girl I am, daughter of a sad woman who takes what isn't hers and never, ever asks.

# chapter seventeen

THE KEYS FEEL ROUGH UNDER MY FINGERS. THEY'RE yellowed and a few of them are cracked. Hell, the lowest A key isn't even *there,* but it's a piano with pedals and it's only a tick out of tune, and I can create music on it, practice for my audition, distract myself, and focus on a future I'm not even sure I can have.

Except I can't concentrate. I bang on the piano, the dissonant clang causing the Book Nook's owner, Patrick, to *tsk* from the front of the store. I ball my hands into fists and stretch them out before starting the piece again. I drift into autopilot, my hands obeying me for a few seconds, but my mind wanders. It creeps over to Mom picking Fruity Pebbles off the kitchen floor as I left this morning, but I can't think about her right now. Don't want to. Don't even know *what* to think about her stealing and necklaces for Eva and not needing me and whatever else the hell.

So I let myself think about Eva. Last night we ran all the way to the lighthouse driveway, and only when our feet slowed did our hands falls away. Eva kissed me once and then kept heading farther into town, a little smile on her lips as she waved goodbye.

And my hand. My mouth. They tingled. I couldn't get them to stop. They're tingling right now just thinking about it all, and my fingers slip and hit an E-minor chord when it's supposed to be E major.

I shove my hands into my hair and groan. The early-morning sun filters in through the window in the storage room, blinding me for a split second.

"Scholarships don't win themselves!" Patrick calls from behind the register. He's in his midthirties, completely bald—by choice, he swears—and is a classic Cape Katie busybody, one of those who feasts on Bethany Butler's radio show just so he feels like he knows everything about everybody in town.

Still. He has a piano, and he lets me sit in here for hours a day, free of charge.

"Thanks for clearing that up, Patrick," I call back, but he's got a point. If I don't get a scholarship, I don't go, plain and simple, and a lot of other pianists vying for a spot at a school like Manhattan come from performing arts high schools and money. I'm miles behind just by simply existing.

Patrick grunts acknowledgment, and I get back to work. This time forcing every thought other than college, scholarships, dorm rooms, and ice cream socials in the quad out of my mind.

Schumann's *Fantasie* unfurls from my fingers. It's soft and haunting and I love it. I pour myself into it—every wish, every shitty duplex, a girl named Eva, a mother who steals from her daughter—it all rises and falls with the piece's dynamics. The first movement unfolds in a sort of stream of consciousness, various states of the mind and heart mimicked under my hands.

Fear. Fury. Hope. Love.

I let it all fall out of me and onto the neglected keys. It's a rush, a complete letting go, and I can *think*. Everything is clear when I'm at the piano. I know who I am. I know what to do.

I know how to leave.

Blasting through the rest of the first movement, my fingers ache and tingle, but it's a very different sensation from last night. This one is pure drive, surety, confidence. The last notes reverberate through the store, my hands suspended in midair. The mad dance I always fall into with the piano whenever I play tosses my hair into my face. I push it back just as a tiny exhalation of air reaches my ears.

I whirl around on the creaking bench to find Eva gaping at me. She's in a slouchy tunic and a short denim skirt, legs for literal days.

"Wow," she says. "You *are* good."

I smile. "Don't sound so surprised."

"Humble, too."

"Hey, I don't have a whole lot else going for me."

She sits down on the bench, pushing my hips over with hers. "Humble *and* self-deprecating. How attractive."

"I try."

"Are we flirting?" She leans against my shoulder a little and lowers her voice, her hair brushing my cheek. "I think we're flirting."

I can't keep the grin from my face. "I don't know. Do you want to be flirting?"

"I might. Do *you* want to be flirting?"

"I think talking about flirting sort of nullifies any actual flirting."

She laughs, pulling one of her curls straight before releasing it. It springs up to her cheekbone. "Maybe we should stop talking about it, then."

"Maybe."

We lean into each other, and I feel this huge wash of relief. We're about to kiss again. It wasn't a one-time thing. It was real.

Then, out of the corner of my eye, I see Mom in the doorway. I pull back from Eva—way back—and stare at my mother. She's hugging a large cream-colored paperback book with intricate flowers printed all over the cover to her chest. She looks at ease, her makeup fresh, her posture casual, like this morning never happened.

"Hi, baby. I didn't know you were here."

For once, she's right. I didn't tell her where I was going when I left this morning, and she didn't ask. She was too busy cleaning up cereal.

"What . . ." I flit my gaze between the two of them. "What are you doing here?"

Mom holds up the book. "I was listening to Bethany's radio show the other day, and Nina Alvarez was talking about how she struggles with anxiety. She mentioned these fancy-schmancy coloring books for grownups. They're supposed to be great for relaxation and even mediation. Then Eva told me she uses them all the time, so we're going to head over to the picnic tables at the park and try it out."

"You should come with us," Eva says, sliding her hand over mine. I yank it back. Hurt blossoms in her eyes. I want to apologize, to explain that it's not about us or even the fact that my mom is standing right there while I sit extremely close to another girl. Mom doesn't really know about me, but not because I haven't tried telling her. She just doesn't listen. Regardless, I'm not embarrassed.

I'm furious.

Because, my god, I kissed this girl last night, and today she's buddying up to my mother. I know Eva's having a hard time, and if coloring with Maggie helps, then so effing what? I can't pretend that Mom doesn't understand grief or whatever a hell of a lot better than I do, no matter how screwed up her coping methods. Still, I can't help but feel cheated by both of them.

Standing, I collect my music books and stuff them into my bag. "I have to work."

And that's all I say before I head toward the door, Patrick eyeing me as I speed-walk past the history section. I can't help but think Luca would be proud as hell right now—I'm already getting better at this leaving thing.

# chapter eighteen

THE MAGIC OF ALL THAT ADRENALINE AND HAND-holding and kissing from last night is gone. Poof, bye-bye. So when Eva starts her shift at LuMac's about halfway through mine, I pretend like I don't even see her side-eyeing me in the break room while she clocks in and I exchange my ketchup-soaked apron for a clean one.

"What happened there?" she asks, nodding toward the bloody-looking apron.

"Harrison Jensen didn't like his fries."

"Ah."

Harrison is a notoriously temperamental three-year-old Luca warned both Eva and me about during our training. He takes to throwing food when he's displeased, and his server rarely escapes unscathed whenever his parents drag him to LuMac's. So of course, when he and his harried-looking mother walk in for a midmorning snack, they sit in my section.

I finish tying my apron, sticking my order pad and pencil into the front pockets before turning to leave.

"Grace, wait."

"What?" I stop and turn around.

"What happened at the bookstore? Did I do something wrong?"

"No, of course not." I don't even try to enliven the flat tone of my voice.

"Are you sure? Because you seem . . ."

"I seem what?"

She tilts her head at me. "Angry."

"I'm not." I can't look at her. If I look at her, I won't be able to lie, and if I can't lie, the truth of how much I hate seeing her around Maggie will come tumbling out right here in the break room, and I'm not ready for that. Still, I can't seem to keep the snap out of my voice. "I'm just tired and smell like ketchup, and my fingers hurt from practicing, okay?"

She visibly flinches at my tone. "I don't believe you."

"Well, that's your choice, but that's all I've got."

Her eyes narrow and her jaw tightens. "Fine."

"Fine."

She gives me one more baffled look before shaking her head, whipping an apron off a hook, and all but running out of the break room.

"Whoa," I hear Luca exclaim in the hallway leading to the

167

kitchen. "Slow down, Eves, or you'll be wearing maple syrup in about two-point-four seconds."

He sticks his head in the break room door, his eyebrows cinched in concern. "Who spit in her coffee this morning?" he asks, jutting a thumb in Eva's direction.

"Me, apparently," I say, digging my fingers into my eyes.

"You?" He frowns, setting his backpack on the small metal table.

"I thought you were supposed to start an hour ago," I say, ignoring his question. I drag a hand down my face as though I can wipe away this whole cluster of a day.

"Oh. Well, yeah, about that. Mom pushed back my shift."

"Why?"

"Let's just say she was not amused when she found out what we did last night."

"What? How'd she find out?"

"Mrs. Latham came in for breakfast at the crack of dawn, apparently."

"Oh. Oops." *Hi*

"Yeah, oops. So I had to go back and put the gnomes in their rightful and pure positions."

"Spoilsport."

"Right? Though I swear to god, Mom was trying really hard not to laugh while she chewed my ass out."

I smile and take a deep breath to steel myself for three more hours of dodging Eva in a very tiny restaurant.

"Hey," Luca says when I'm on my second deep inhale. "Don't forget, July Fourth party on the boat."

Every year, for as long as I can remember, Luca and Macon take out their boat—their *dad's* boat, which he left as a sort of pathetic consolation prize and is huge and beautiful and fun as hell—and anchor it a few miles off the coast. They invite whoever they happen to be dating—until Macon roped himself to Janelle for life, that is —a few of their less annoying guy friends, and me. We drink beer and eat hot dogs and Cheetos and watch fireworks kaleidoscope over the sprawling sky, their reflection a sparkle of color on the water.

"The Fourth is two weeks away," I say.

"Yeah, but last year you and Maggie had just moved and you couldn't find your swimsuit or any of your summer clothes. You came in sweatpants. Remember how bitchy you were the entire time because you were so hot?"

I scowl at him. A big dramatic glare that I hope covers up the tightness in my jaw and the ache behind my eyes from the fact that my life is a total effing mess and has been for years. Sweatpants because I couldn't *find my clothes?* Christ on a cracker, it sounds so ludicrous coming out of his mouth.

He shrugs like it's no big deal. "I'm just reminding you so you can start looking for your swimsuit now."

"Not like I'm going to swim in deep water anyway. Hello, water beasts."

He rolls his eyes several times to let me know how ridiculous I am. "Just find it."

"Fine. Who all's coming?"

"You, Kimber and me, Macon and Janelle, and Eva. Going simple this year."

"Oh. Eva's coming?"

Luca pulls a face. "Um, yeah. Considering she lives with us and all, I figured it'd be pretty rude to not invite her."

"Right. Right, okay."

"What the hell's up, Gray?"

"Nothing." I pull my order pad out of my pocket and fiddle with the pages. "It's just—"

"Grace!" I hear Emmy call through the swinging door into the dining room. "You have a four-top!"

"Okay, thanks!" I stuff the pad back into my apron. "I've got to go."

"Hang on." Luca hooks his finger through the waistband of my apron. "What's going on?"

"It's nothing. Eva and my mom are just hanging out some, and it's weirding me out." I say it really fast, like speed can make it less weird.

"Oh," Luca says, wincing a little. "Yeah. Mom and Eva have had some *words* about that."

"What do you mean?"

He rubs the back of his neck. "You know . . . Mom's just concerned. I mean, she hasn't told Eva too much about Maggie's . . . history. She wouldn't do that, but Eva's having a hard time settling in with us, and Mom's trying to figure out the best way to help her. Maggie told her to quit dance, for crying out loud."

"She didn't tell her to quit. She told her she didn't have to do it."

"Is there a difference?"

"I think so."

Luca frowns. "Well. Mom's still worried. And you know how Maggie is."

I fold my arms. "Yeah. I do."

He presses his mouth flat and gives me this *Come on, Grace* sort of look. "Then you know she's probably not the healthiest influence on Eva right now."

"Are you serious?"

"Yeah. I mean, don't you think?"

"No, I don't think."

He stares at me before shaking his head and walking over to the time clock on the wall. "Kimber was right; this always happens," he mutters.

My stomach clenches. "Kimber? What always happens?"

"You and your mom. You can't be pissed off about her bullshit, Grace, and then get pissed at me when I call her on said bullshit. You can't have it both ways."

"I'm not trying to have it both ways." But even as I say it, I know that's exactly what I'm doing. In the back of my mind, I know Emmy has every reason to be wary. She and Mom have a precarious relationship for a reason. Healthy moms don't take off on their kids for a few days, only to turn up like nothing happened. But the minute anyone actually says this, my hackles go up.

"Have *you* told Eva anything about Maggie?" he asks.

"No. You think it's easy to talk about?"

"Of course not, Gray. But I don't want Eva to get hurt," he says, jabbing at the numbers on the screen. "And if you're really friends, if you're . . . if you like her, how could you not tell her?"

I ignore that last part, because I don't know. *I don't know.* "She won't get hurt."

He turns to me, his eye narrowed in unbelief. "You can't know that. *You* get hurt every single day. And usually I don't say anything because I know that's not what you want, but that doesn't mean I'm not thinking it."

"Eva can take care of herself."

"Like you, huh?"

My mouth falls open, but I quickly snap it shut. Still, Luca sees it and rakes a hand through his hair.

"Grace!" Emmy calls again.

"Just go," Luca says. "I'm doing inventory today, so I'll see you tomorrow."

God, I hate fighting with Luca. *Hate* it. "You want to do something tonight?" I ask, needing to smooth this out.

He shakes his head. "Kimber and I are hanging out at her place."

I press my lips together to keep them from trembling. I don't know what else to say or do, so I leave, unsure how things with Luca went south so fast.

# chapter nineteen

THAT NIGHT I CAN'T SLEEP. WHEN I GOT HOME AFTER logging a few more hours on the piano at the Book Nook, Mom and Pete were arguing about how much of his beer she's been drinking lately, and then they disappeared into their bedroom, dinner be damned. They haven't emerged since, and, honestly, I really don't want to know why. I feasted on a bowl of maple-and-brown-sugar instant oatmeal. Jay had some of his miscreant friends over until long past midnight. And while he did offer a pretty human-sounding invitation to join them, I declined and locked myself in my room. By the time the house quiets, it's nearly two a.m. and I still haven't slept.

Nights like these, when Mom is totally unavailable—either physically or emotionally, which, let's be honest, is a lot of the time —I actually miss my father. I don't know what I miss, exactly, because I literally have zero memories of him. It's just *him*. The other half, a presence to help me with Mom, to take me out for ice cream, to have some sort of healthy litmus test when dealing with guys and my suddenly temperamental best friend. Then again, if Dad were here, my mother would be a very different person. *I* would be a very different person. Maybe we wouldn't even live here; I wouldn't know Luca; I'd never have met Eva; I'd be cute and sweet and easy to trust and love.

Sometimes I wonder if Mom glosses right over me because of the way I look. I have her coloring—the same blond hair and pale eyes and freckles spilling over my cheeks, but that's it. My mouth and nose and ears, the shape of my face, even the arc in my eyebrows, are all James Glasser. When Mom looks at me—*really* looks at me—I always get the feeling she's looking at a ghost. And maybe, if Dad were still here, I'd be flesh and blood to her instead of a memory. I'd just be her daughter.

I let out a shaky breath and turn over on my side, facing the dark expanse filling the window. Thoughts finally begin to still, and my eyes are just starting to grow heavy when I hear a *plink* against the window. I prop myself up on one elbow, barely registering what I'm seeing when the window begins to lift, a brown hand curling under the sill and pushing it up. Cool, briny air blows in as Eva squeezes herself through the opening and lands on my bed with a soft *Oof.*

"Of all the bad habits to choose from," I say, "sneaking in through people's windows is a poor choice."

"I don't know," she says, closing the window before tucking her legs underneath her. Moonlight paints my room silver, and I can see her smile. "Keeps you guessing."

"Trust me, I'm always guessing. I've got enough of that."

Her smile fades. "What do you mean?"

I swallow hard. "Nothing. Just . . . you know. Life."

She nods, then turns her head away to look around my room. When she doesn't say anything, I lie back down, suddenly exhausted. Eva's hair is wild around her face, her chin a sharp line as she looks everywhere but at me.

"Why are you here?" I ask.

She turns to face me, but I can't make out her expression in the dark.

"Eva."

Still silent, she kicks off her shoes, and they slide off the side of the bed. She removes her glasses and places them on the windowsill before she pulls back my sheet and slips in next to me. I'm in a pair of boxers and a thin tank top. She's in all black, but black *shorts,* and her legs are smooth and long against mine. She nudges toward me a little, and I scoot over so she can share my pillow. All the air leaves my lungs as she tucks her hands against her chest, her forehead nearly touching mine.

Nearly, but not quite.

"I was waiting for you," she says. "At the lighthouse wall."

"Why?"

She shrugs. "It's what we do, right?"

"We've done it twice."

"More than enough times to form a habit. You said so yourself about my breaking and entering."

"I don't want to go up to the lighthouse, Eva." Although my heart feels like a herd of gazelles right now, I keep my voice calm and even, and it's enough to flatten out that little smile pulling up one corner of her mouth.

"Okay. We don't have to," she says.

"I thought you were pissed at me."

"I thought you were pissed at *me*."

*I was,* I think. *Wasn't I?*

"I'm sorry," she says when I don't say anything.

"For what?"

"I don't know. But I can tell you're upset, and I just . . . I want to be friends. I feel like I did something wrong. Maybe I moved too fast or—"

"You didn't."

"But something's wrong," she says. "You're sure this isn't about last night in the tree?"

"It's not about anything."

She nods, but her brows are creased with unbelief. "Is it about your mom?"

I stare at her for a few minutes, wondering how much I let leak to the surface today in the bookshop and in the break room at work. She looks so concerned, so I give her something true. Something safe, something that gives us both what we need right now.

"My mom and I . . . we have a . . . weird relationship sometimes."

"She doesn't know, does she? That you're bisexual?"

"Honestly? I don't know."

"What do you mean? Did you tell her or not?"

See, these seem like simple questions, but they aren't. Did I tell her? Yes. Did she get it? No.

"I'm not embarrassed for her to know. It's just . . . like I said. Weird relationship."

Eva nods and I can tell she wants to understand. She searches my eyes, seeking unspoken truths. "It seemed tense today, in the bookstore."

"Did she say anything? After I left?"

"No."

Of course she didn't. Mom is an expert at telling herself everything is all glitter and rainbows between us.

"Mom and I have just been through some crap, Eva, and we . . . I don't know what else to say. It's not always easy."

"I know."

I suck in a breath. "You do?"

"She's still dealing with so much after losing your dad."

A cavern opens up in my stomach. "Oh. Right. My dad."

"I mean, that's sort of why she helps me. I just feel so helpless all the time, and she gets that. She's still there, you know?"

"And you don't find that kind of weird?" I ask before I can stop myself. "My dad died fifteen years ago."

Eva frowns, like the idea never dawned on her. Hell, it probably hasn't. "Grief doesn't follow a pattern. It's not linear."

"Did *Maggie* tell you that?"

"No, Emmy did."

"Well, doesn't Emmy help you too? She used to be a grief counselor. She knows you better; she knew your mom."

Eva nods. "I know, but, like, that's why. It's easier talking to your mom because she *doesn't* know me or my mom or about ballet, but she knows this." She taps the side of her head with her forefinger. "She's not pushing me to dance so I can get back to *normal,* whatever the hell that is. I don't want someone to spout some 'time heals all wounds' bullshit to me. I just want someone to say how much this sucks. Let me do what I need to do. Maggie does. And she's not always trying to fix me. She just lets me hang out with her and talk if I want to, shut up if I want to. Does that make sense?"

It does make a weird sort of sense. I nod and lean toward her, inhaling. God, I want to kiss her again. Want to so badly, it almost feels like a need. Even if she wanted to as well, it doesn't feel right to close these last few inches between us when just hours ago I couldn't think about her without dropping the eff-bomb. I want her to make the first move. I *need* her to, if nothing else to prove that me freaking out over her and my mom in the bookstore didn't scare her off.

She doesn't kiss me, though. Doesn't move even a centimeter closer. Just searches my face like I'm an abstract painting she can't quite figure out.

"You really do play beautifully," she finally says.

"Really?"

She nods, her hair tickling my face. "So gorgeous. Today when I heard you, watched you play, I was . . . God, Grace, you belong on a stage."

Her words feel like the first spring day after weeks of snow. I want that—me on a stage, an audience rising up in front of me and waiting for me to spin them a story with my fingertips. It's an old, deep ache. No matter how much I tell myself I'll never make it, never measure up to other pianists my age who haven't had to work two part-time jobs for years just to pay for lessons, I can't stop wanting. And every time I look at Eva, I see all that want reflected back at me.

"I don't think you should quit dance," I say.

She blinks and puts a few inches of space between us, her little smile now a slack frown.

"I don't mean go back to it right away. Maybe you're not ready and I get that, but I can tell you love it, Eva. I think you're still a dancer."

Her expression softens, and she brushes my forehead with hers again. "I don't know. Maybe I . . . I just don't know. It almost feels like . . ."

"Like what?"

Her throat bobs with a hard swallow. "Like I'm betraying her. Because I can dance and she can't."

"Eva . . ." I don't know what else to say, so I don't even try. But I do reach out and touch her hair, gliding my hand over her curls.

She looks down and all I see are tear-dolloped lashes and cheeks, a kind of sad beauty that makes my chest hurt.

We lie there for a while, breathing quietly in the dark. I love this almost as much as talking—just being.

"You smell like peanut butter," I finally say.

She laughs softly and wipes at her eyes. "Probably because I feasted on some Peter Pan on the way over here."

"That sounds kind of dirty."

"I meant it to."

I smile at that, then push back the covers. Lying here with her is pure bliss, but the longer we lie here, the more likely we are to talk about things we've both had enough of for now.

"Let's go," I say, handing over her glasses and pushing the window up.

"Where?"

"The lighthouse."

Eva smiles and slips on her glasses.

"I'll meet you by the wall," I say. "I've got to grab the key."

"You promise?" Eva asks, one leg out the window. "You're not just trying to get rid of me, are you?"

She's smiling, so I start to crack a joke, but there's a sliver of uncertainty in her tone.

"I promise. Bring the peanut butter."

She grins before disappearing out the window.

It doesn't really matter who we are during the day. These nights —they're ours. We're not Grace Glasser or Eva Brighton. Just

Grace and Eva. Two girls who need to feel young and free, need to feel like girls. Need to scream from the top of a lighthouse and eat peanut butter out of a jar and swear and accidentally brush up against each other and giggle about it.

So that's what we do.

# chapter twenty

FOR THE NEXT TWO WEEKS, EVA AND I FALL INTO A PATtern. The days pass in a blur of serving onion rings and Emmy's famous Better Than Sex pie—yeah, that's what it's called on the menu, although all the little old ladies of Cape Katie call it BTS—practicing for hours and hours at the Book Nook in the afternoons, and trying not to think about anything beyond the next sunset. My audition still feels so unreal, but as we move into the beginning of July, my stomach coils into knots every time I sit down to the piano.

Eva and I don't talk much during the day. We work together, circling each other like acquaintances, communicating the status of ketchup bottles and fresh coffee. Twice, Mom came in for lunch. She fawned over me for about three damn seconds before smacking a kiss to my forehead and disappearing with Eva into a corner booth on Eva's meal break. Once, they even left for the halfhour, meandering down the beach with their shoes hooked on their fingers.

I try not to think about what they're talking about, what Eva is getting from all this. I try not to think about what Luca said about Eva getting hurt, about *me* getting hurt all the time.

Meanwhile, Luca and Emmy watch Mom and Eva's interactions with narrowed eyes and tight smiles, panic brimming just under the surface. Actual *panic,* like Maggie's going to swipe Eva right out from under their noses and go into hiding. It pisses me the hell off. And it worries the hell out of me. I can't decide which emotion is stronger.

Still, I say nothing. Share nothing. Act like it's no big deal.

But then at night, everything changes. We start at the lighthouse, eating peanut butter and laughing into the black air. Then we usually go on a bike ride or a walk on the beach. There's a secretive quality to doing all of these things under the moonlight and stars that makes it exciting, makes it special. We talk about everything and everyone except our mothers.

Sometimes we dance around them, hinting at these two women—one dead, one alive, both lost—but we never quite land on them. Under the dark sky, we're two motherless girls.

We're whoever we want to be.

And apparently, who we want to be is friends who snuggle in bed until dawn, when Eva sneaks back to the Michaelsons' before Emmy wakes up. Because every night, after our moonlighting, we've ended up back in my bedroom.

In my bed.

Under the sheets.

Legs entwined, backs pressed against chests, arms slung over waists, but never, ever more than that, and Eva's always gone by the time I wake up.

So, as usual, on the morning of July fourth, I open my eyes to an empty bed and a tightly closed window. Also, as usual, I go through the previous night in my head—more specifically, the minutes right before we fell asleep, when I couldn't tell where my body stopped and hers started—and wonder if the whole thing was a dream, some hallucination brought on by acute stress or acute exhaustion or acute what-the-fuckery that has been a staple in my life for the last fifteen years.

But there's a little concave dent on the right side of my queen-size pillow. An Eva-shaped impression. And I know without a doubt that I fell asleep with her chin resting on top of my head, my back pressed against her stomach.

In the pale morning light, I stare at the ceiling. The dopey smile on my face slowly fades as my thoughts burgeon, because in all honesty, this whole thing Eva and I are doing is more than a little confusing. Every night our bodies wrap each other up, secrets are whispered, breath is shared—it's like the world's longest make-out session without ever actually kissing.

I've been here before—that weird zone after a hookup where you're feeling each other out to see if it was just a one-time thing or has relationship potential. Except it's always been the guy feeling things out, with me on the other end pretty much avoiding him. Eva's certainly not avoiding me, but she's not doing anything to confirm that what happened in the tree was more than a casual kiss to her. Maybe she just wanted to check her first kiss off her never-have-I-ever list.

So many times, I've wanted to just grab her and press my mouth against hers, dispel all these damn doubts. A few nights I got so bold as to brush my lips across the back of her neck, but she didn't acknowledge it. Didn't turn in my arms to kiss me. Once, she released a contented sigh, but that's it, and the doubts continue to drive me nuts.

So, yes, Eva and I must be only friends. But this morning, the affectionate little friend zone we've got going doesn't keep me from remembering the smell of her skin, the silky slide of her thighs against mine, or that kiss in the tree. It certainly doesn't keep me from closing my eyes and letting my hand drift down my belly and under the waistband of my underwear. It doesn't stop me from imagining Eva's warm breath on my neck, her voice whispering my name as my hand dips lower. My fingers are her fingers, circling and seeking, gentle then rough. I give myself over to the whole illusion, whispering her name under my breath until the slowly building tension breaks and I bite down on my lower lip to keep from making any noise.

My body relaxes back into the mattress as my vision clears and my breath returns to normal. I lie there for a long time, listening to the house come awake, wondering what I'll meet with when I walk outside my bedroom door. Mom drops a few eff-bombs as something that sounds like a coffee mug or a bowl crashes in the kitchen. I roll over and pull the covers up over my head. All of my nerves are still tingling, and I hug my pillow like it's a lean, smooth-skinned body.

Yup. Totally just friends.

Cape Katie really pulls out all the stops for the Fourth of July. As I leave the bookstore and walk through town toward Luca's, it looks like someone vomited red, white, and blue everywhere. Crepe paper snakes up lampposts, sparkly-colored streamers drip from store awnings, and the air smells like a mixture of hot dogs and sugar, which is not a totally unpleasant combination.

Luca lives in a yellow ranch-style house near the marina. Before Paul Michaelson moved to California, he was always on the water, fishing, and had even started getting into lobster fishing. He had a beautiful boat ironically named after his wife, *Emmaline,* that Luca and Macon have impeccably maintained since he left. If Luca's house is my one true home—and let's be honest, Mom and I don't stay anywhere long enough to make it a home—the Michaelsons' boat is my second. We practically live on that thing during July and August. I love the feel of the cool sea air blowing across my skin. It's freedom and comfort, and my feet itch to feel that weightlessness underneath me today.

And, okay, maybe I'm itching to see a certain someone, but only because she's my first real friend other than Luca.

Right?

Right.

I can't help but laugh at myself a little as I turn the knob on Luca's front door. It feels damn good—being silly and giddy over someone I actually like.

My smile vanishes when tense voices spill out of the kitchen and into the foyer.

"—trying to give you your space," Emmy says. "I understand that. What I don't understand is this disrespect. We've done nothing to deserve this. If Luca knew, it would break his—"

"I told you I'd think about starting ballet again, but I need some time. I don't see why it bothers you so much."

"I'm not talking about ballet, and you know it."

They're quiet for a few seconds. Then Eva says, "I'm not trying to be ungrateful. I'm really not. I know this has been hard for everyone. I just want to make my own choices."

"You don't always have that option. Not when you're part of a family."

"This is *not* my family."

There's another beat of silence, and I hover in the hallway, out of sight, breath held painfully in my chest. Someone inhales deeply, then, quietly, Emmy says, "Well. We're the closest thing you've got. And legally, this is where you belong. So the answer is no."

"Fine. Whatever." I hear some shuffling and then Eva appears, her eyes flaring bright, her hair wild, probably from twisting curls around her fingers the way she does when she's stressed. She stops in her tracks when she sees me.

"Grace."

"Hi." I take a step closer, but she shuffles back a little. I'm not sure if it's intentional, but it makes me plant my feet. "I came a little early to see if Luca needed help getting stuff down to the boat."

"Right. I think he's still asleep or in the shower or . . ." Her voice trails off as she moves toward the bedrooms. "I need to get ready. Meet you there?"

I nod and before I can get another word in, she's gone, her bedroom door clicking shut and echoing down the hall. In the kitchen, Emmy is stirring up a bowl of some chocolate-flavored batter, which could be anything from a cake to brownies to pie filling. Her hair is pulled into a smooth ponytail, her mouth a thin line.

I clear my throat and she looks up.

"Hi, sweetie," she says brightly. Too brightly, with a tightness around her eyes.

"Everything okay?" I ask, then wave my hand toward the bedrooms. "With Eva?"

Her expression falls a bit. "Oh. I think so." She wipes her hands on her apron, which has a picture of a hamburger, the phrase *Hands off my buns* replacing the meat between the bread. Every Christmas, Luca and Macon buy their mom a new apron, each one more ridiculous than the last. This past year, the apron featured the curvy body of Wonder Woman from the neck down. Pretty sure that one got packed up before the tree ornaments did.

Emmy comes over to me and cups my cheek. "You're a good

girl, Gracie. Don't worry about a thing." Her eyes are a little misty, her voice a little thick. I'm about to press her, because while Emmy is usually pretty affectionate, she's sort of freaking me out. Still, I can't help but inwardly cling to her assessment of me, no matter how wayward it might be.

She opens the fridge and takes out a stick of butter. Unwrapping it, she plops it into a bowl and puts it in the microwave. "Now, tell me about you. How's your mom?"

"She's . . . she's okay."

Standard answer. I know Emmy would do anything for me—at least, I've always thought she would—which is probably why I don't make a habit of going into too much detail around her about Maggie since their huge argument when I was thirteen. I'm sure Luca tells her stuff, but he'd never tell her *everything*. The whole town already sees too much for comfort. It's embarrassing as hell, and I can't stand the pitying glances.

"She and Eva seem to be getting along pretty well," Emmy says, eyes on the wooden spoon swirling the batter into chaotic circles.

"Yeah."

I don't know what else to say, so I say nothing and the silence gets thicker and thicker. Finally, Emmy cracks. "So. Tell me all about this upcoming piano audition."

"Oh." Nerves flare in my stomach just thinking about it. "Well. It's in about a month. Though I haven't decided if I'm going or not."

She stops mid-stir, one eyebrow lifted. "To the audition?"

"No. I'm going to that." There's no way I can't go to that, no matter how conflicted I feel about it. Last winter, after I pulled Mom out of the fray of men at Ruby's and decided to bail on college, Luca pretty much kidnapped me and drove me to Portland.

"For Manhattan," he'd said as he all but shoved me into a video-recording studio that belonged to some friend of Macon's. The guy looked like a black-haired Chris Evans, so I didn't complain at the time. Plus, Luca literally beamed while I recorded.

He also paid for the whole thing.

Then Manhattan invited me to audition, and things started happening so fast. It's all blurred in my mind and heart and gut, a swirl of nerves and confidence and insecurities.

There's also this trip Mom planned . . . I try not to think about the fact that she hasn't mentioned it since the day I got home from Boston.

"I just mean, if I get in and get a scholarship," I tell Emmy. "If I moved to New York, I'd be like five hours away, and I'm not sure if Mo—"

"One step at a time."

"I'm trying, but you know it's not that simple, Emmy."

She nods as the microwave dings. That delicious melted-butter scent fills the room as she pours it into the batter. "Nothing ever is. The question is what do *you* want, Gracie?"

I stare at her. "What do *I* want?"

She smiles, but it's a sad smile, full of years of Maggie drama and pity over the fact that I'm clearly shocked by the question.

Because what the hell *do* I want?

Life with Mom has never been a matter of want. It can't be. It's a tangle of needs and necessity, paycheck to paycheck, the future like a distant city on a map in the middle of some foreign land. All those wishes pressed into my fingertips were just that—*wishes*. And no one really expects a wish to come true.

Do they?

# chapter twenty-one

J ANELLE MICHAELSON LOOKS LIKE A BALL HAS BEEN surgically attached to her stomach. A huge perfect-for-dodgeball kind of ball. She waddles onto the boat, a few packs of hot dog buns in her arms.

"Hi, Grace," she says, her face red, like the simple greeting totally drained her.

"Hey. Here, let me." I take the buns from her and toss them into the laundry basket full of bags of chips and ketchup and mustard bottles. "Haven't seen you in a while."

"Yeah." She collapses onto the cushioned bench seats near the stern and rubs her belly. "I've been setting up the nursery for Emily, and considering I move about a foot an hour, it takes me all day."

"Emily? Is that what you're naming her?"

Janelle nods. "After Emmy, but still different enough to be her own, you know? Macon was *very* insistent, and I love the name, so I didn't fight him."

"That's sweet." And it is, but for some reason, a knot rolls up my throat and I have to look away. I distract myself with unwrapping packages of hot dogs so Macon can grill them on the little stove down in the boat's cabin.

"Did Luca tell you he designed her crib?" Janelle asks, pulling her gold-brown hair off her neck and fanning.

"No. That's awesome."

"It's shaped like a boat. I mean, sort of. As much as a crib can be shaped like a boat. Macon's building it and taking his sweet time."

I laugh. "He does like to do things right." When we were kids, Macon always made Luca's and my Halloween costumes and was beyond meticulous. He enjoyed doing it, but I think Emmy mostly put him up to the whole thing. She knew Mom could never afford to buy me one. The time I went as a rain cloud—sparkly silver rain included—and Luca was the Stay Puft Marshmallow Man from *Ghostbusters* and kept falling down porch steps because he couldn't bend his legs remains one of the best nights of my life, which is laughingly depressing when you think about it.

"Don't worry, Nelly, I've got this," Macon calls, stepping aboard with a flowery canvas bag overflowing with food hanging from one arm, a pile of blankets in the other.

"Oh, I'm not worried," Janelle says, winking at me. She and Macon have one of those relationships where they're constantly heckling one another, all of their jokes eventually leading to massive and very public make-out sessions.

Kimber and Luca come up from below deck, her cheeks flushed and a grin on his face. Speaking of massive make-out sessions. The three of us walked here together, Eva still in the shower when we left, and I don't think there was a single second when Luca wasn't touching Kimber's shoulders, waist, neck, hair, hand, whatever. Now they've both stripped down to bathing suits only, and it seems like Kimber's hot-pink bikini is about to make Luca combust. He keeps glancing at her ass and then her boobs and then ripping his gaze away like he thinks he shouldn't be glancing at her ass and her boobs because he's a *gentleman*. Kimber's doing her share of ogling Luca's slim and toned chest, his tanned skin golden under the sun, so I think it's okay. The two of them would be pretty damn cute if I wasn't slightly annoyed with both of them.

"Did you remember your suit?" Luca asks, elbowing me.

I pull my tank top over my head, revealing my faded black halter-style tankini top that's bordering on too small. He shoots me a thumbs-up, but that's it. No threat about tossing me to the dolphins, a joke he cracks nearly every time we board *Emmaline*.

We haven't really talked about our argument two weeks ago, nor have we argued again. We've just . . . *existed*. We've been polite, laughed a little about picky or crabby customers, helped each other cover tables when a rush hit LuMac's. Once he asked if I'd told Eva any more about Maggie. I offered an ambiguous shoulder shrug that Luca clearly took as a *no,* because he shook his head and silently refilled sugar dispensers, a muscle jumping in his jaw.

This new awkwardness sucks, honestly. I'm not used to this sort of surface-level crap with Luca, both of us completely wrapped up in other people, barely talking to each other about it all.

Fifteen minutes later, we're waiting for Eva before we can set sail, and I've got a beer in my hands. I tuck myself into the seats near the bow and sip on something Macon microbrewed or whatever you call it. The amber liquid is cold and slightly less pissy-tasting than any beer I've ever had before. In fact, it goes down just fine.

"Grey Goose!" Macon calls, a ridiculous name he's called me ever since Luca and I were ten and got violently ill off a bottle of Grey Goose that Emmy had neglected for too long in the freezer. Everyone's got their precious little nicknames for Grace.

He comes up from below deck, where *Emmaline* sports a cozy cabin, complete with nautical-themed bedding and a mini-kitchen. "Leave some for the fishies, huh?" he says, flopping down next to me.

"Oh, the fishies'll get plenty when she pukes it all overboard later," Luca says. Like he's even seen me drunk more than once or twice. Like I've even *been* drunk more than once or twice. I may like jumping off balconies here and there and rearranging beach gnomes, but, dammit, I do it all with a clear head.

Luca doesn't look at me, focusing very intently on a bottle of SPF 55. He moves down the boat toward the stern, where he hands the sunscreen to Kimber. They smile at each other as she squirts a white glob into her hands and spreads it over his bare shoulders.

"He's touchy lately," Macon whispers. He's a stockier, darker-headed version of Luca. Same curly mop, same easy grin, same fierce loyalty. "You'd think he'd be a little more relaxed since he's finally getting some."

Janelle joins us, a water bottle the size of my thigh in her hands. Her blue-and-white polka-dotted one-piece looks adorable over her round stomach. She smacks him on the shoulder.

"Ow, what?"

"Don't talk about Kimber like that."

"Hey, I love Kimber," he says, reaching out and pulling Janelle close to his side. "I adore Kimber. Worship her, in fact."

"High praise," I say, taking a swig of beer.

"She makes him happy. We've all been a little tense since Eva joined us. Everyone's adjusting."

I frown but say nothing. *Tense* is mild for whatever vibe Eva and Emmy were putting off earlier.

"Plus, Kimber tells it like it is," Macon says, shrugging. "I admire that."

Janelle stares at her fingernails, and Macon opens a bag of pretzels, crunching loudly. I get the overwhelming feeling that *telling it like it is* means talking about how messed up I am when it comes to Maggie. Maybe I'm being paranoid, but there's definitely a *tone* to the air after Macon's comment, and it makes me squirm. I swallow a huge mouthful of beer.

Then another.

I'm on my third giant gulp when I spot Eva, walking gracefully down the pier in a pair of tiny denim shorts. The string of a kelly-green bikini is knotted behind her neck and peeks out from underneath her light-gray tank top like a little secret.

"Like I said, go easy on that beer, Grey Goose," Macon says, digging a ginger ale out of the cooler near my feet and handing it to Janelle. "Higher alcohol content than that Bud Light nonsense." He chucks me under the chin and calls to Luca to help him untie the boat from the dock, but I keep staring at Eva.

And she keeps staring at me, her smile free of all that awkwardness in the Michaelsons' hallway earlier. I want to know what's going on, why she and Emmy are fighting and what Emmy won't let her do, but right now, with the warming sun on my back and Eva walking closer and closer, I just want to have fun and laugh and, to be honest, get a little tipsy on some non-pissy beer.

The finally hot July sun soaks into my skin, imbuing me with a sort of giddy-hysterical feeling I'm sort of enjoying.

Or maybe that's Macon's beer.

Either way, once Macon and Luca untie *Emmaline* from the pier and we're moving over the sun-sparkled Atlantic, the atmosphere on the boat is a little less tense and a little more Fourth of July. After we drop anchor about a mile offshore, Luca and I even manage to eke out a few jokes. As usual, I rag him about putting mayonnaise on his hot dog, and he finally gives me crap about my fear of Flipper.

"Dolphins are super friendly," Kimber points out. She is real as shit sipping her beer through a bendy straw.

Macon laughs. "Just wait until she goes for a swim and a teeny-tiny fish brushes her ankle." He mimes silent screaming and pulls on his hair. Janelle smacks him on the shoulder. It's like their love language.

"Well, you'll never know," I say through a bite of hot dog. "Because there's no way I'm getting in that water. It's still cold as hell."

"It's always cold as hell," Luca says.

"You're only making my point."

He smirks at me. Then he swallows the mouthful of barbecue chips he's chewing and steps up on the edge of the boat.

"Luca," Janelle says, but that's all she gets out before he launches himself off the boat and into the ocean, releasing a high-pitched yell when he hits the water.

In minutes, he's climbing up the ladder and dripping the salty sea all over the boat's floor. "See, Gray? Nothing to it." Then he grabs a towel and sits back down next to Kimber, who grins like a lovesick puppy and glides her hand through his wet hair while he stuffs some more chips into his mouth. I don't point out that his skin is tinged purple.

We all laugh at him. We all eat and drink and tell dumb stories like any other Fourth. It feels a bit like Scotch tape holding together a broken vase, but I can't understand why. I can't figure out why things with Luca and me are so . . . *un*–Luca and me.

But right now I don't care. I *can't* care. It's summer and this beer tastes good and my thoughts are light and airy and Eva's green bikini is ridiculously gorgeous against her dark skin and gold-flecked eyes.

Close to sunset, Janelle goes below deck to nap while Luca and Macon settle at the bow to play rummy. They've had a running game going for years, their scores somewhere in the thousands by now. Kimber fiddles with her fancy-looking camera and snaps pictures of them, the sky, the horizon, the shore. I'm about to suck it up and go talk to her about whatever the hell just to smooth out all the weirdness between us, when Eva taps my shoulder. I turn to find her grinning.

"What?" I ask.

"Come over here with me." She tilts her head toward the stern.

"Over where?"

She keeps grinning and takes my hand, weaving me through the seats near the steering wheel, around the door to the cabin, and toward the stern of the boat.

"Um, no," I say, digging in my heels.

"You don't even know what we're doing."

"Oh, yes, I do. You're about to sit on the back of the boat and probably dangle your feet over the edge, which is pretty much just asking for a shark or a humpback to come bite them off."

"A humpback?"

"Yes, Eva, a damn humpback."

She presses her lips flat, clearly trapping in a laugh. "You're a strange little bird."

"A little bird with all of my toes still attached."

"Birds don't have toes."

"Talons, then." I curl the fingers of both of my hands into claws, but she just laughs. Then she takes one of my hands and wraps it around her own back, pulling us closer together.

"I'm not afraid of your talons," she says softly.

Her eyes flick down to my lips and my mouth goes dry. The cool wind blows her hair into my face and mine into hers. We're all mixed up, and just when I think we're finally going to kiss again, she pulls back.

"Come on." She releases my hand and climbs up on padded seats that line the stern. Then, just as I knew she would, she throws her legs over them, settling on the couple feet of flat space covered with some non-stick faux-wood coating right above the propeller. A little silver ladder descends into the choppy blue abyss.

She glances at me hovering behind her and pats the spot next to her. "Here we go, little bird."

I don't fight her. Hell, as much as I hate the water, I don't even want to. She's been pretty quiet since we set sail, and there's no way I'm passing up some time alone with her, especially in the light of day. Once I'm next to her, I curl my feet underneath me and get as far away from the edge as possible. The water is choppy, and a spray of cold ocean flecks our legs.

"See?" she says. "That wasn't so hard."

"Tell me that when I'm curled into a fetal position and sucking my thumb because I spotted a fin a hundred yards away."

She laughs. "Come on, you can't say this isn't nice." She lifts her arms to the sky and throws her head back, the sun glinting off her skin and hair.

Well, *that's* nice.

"It's just so . . . endless, you know?" I say, peering over the side of the boat at the inky water. "Who knows what's going on down there?" I shudder. "Freaks me out."

She leans over the edge too. Then she links her arm with mine and sits back, pulling me with her. We settle against each other, skin to skin.

"Just pretend we're on the lighthouse, the endless sky above us," she says. "Same sort of thing, right?"

"There aren't live and curious creatures with teeth floating in the sky."

"There might be in fantasy novels."

I laugh. "So I should pretend we're in a fantasy novel?"

She shrugs. "A fantasy of sorts."

We go quiet after that, something both thick and airy hovering between us. The Atlantic tosses us this way and that, and I can't tell if my stomach is fluttering from the motion or from having Eva's body smooshed up against mine in this tiny space.

She takes one of my hands, sliding her fingers down my

amethyst-hued nails. Hers are still dark eggplant, the tips just beginning to chip.

"Why purple?" she asks.

A knot forms in my throat, a knee-jerk reaction. "Maggie didn't tell you?"

Eva shakes her head and I'm weirdly relieved Mom didn't share this with her.

"It's always been our color," I say quietly as Eva continues to smooth the pads of her thumb over each of my fingers. "Mine and Mom's. She started painting my nails purple when I was really little."

"Why?"

So I tell her about the wishing. How Mom always said that we wish on our fingertips, reaching out for what we want. Whatever that is. Mom's told me more than once that she loves purple because it's this beautiful mix of blue's calm stability and red's fierce energy. Funny how prophetic Mom was all those years ago. How wise about herself, about me, about us together.

Eva frowns a little but continues to hold my hand, rubbing circles over my nails much like she did that first day we met on the beach. The sky around us grows darker, the sun slips lower, the current slaps almost angrily against the boat. I hear Macon's frustrated groan, followed by Luca snorting a triumphant laugh and Kimber's clear voice cheering him on. Any minute the fireworks will start, filling the wide expanse behind us with impossible color.

But for the moment, it's just me and Eva, my hand in hers.

"Your freckles are more noticeable after being in the sun," she says, touching my nose with her forefinger, then tracing the little brown dots over both cheeks.

"Yeah, that happens," I say, dumbly. My heart feels huge — literally a ginormous hunk of beating muscle in my chest. I'm sure she can hear it as she scoots even closer, as close as when we lie in my bed after being on top of the lighthouse. But this feels different. Those nights are more of a comfortable intimacy, while this crackles with energy. With possibility.

"What are you doing?" I ask when her finger drifts from my cheeks, down my throat and around, her palm hot on the back of my neck. *Friends,* I say to myself. *Just friends.*

"Making a wish," she whispers, her breath fanning over my mouth. "May I?"

I barely nod before her lips press into mine. A gasp escapes my throat, but the good kind. The *finally* kind. The *not just friends* kind. My free hand reaches out to her, framing her face and pulling her as close as I can possibly get her on the end of this boat. Our mouths open, letting each other in. She tastes like beer and Eva, like wild summer nights. Her fingers dance up and down my arms, and I can't stop touching her face, gliding my hands over her hair, letting my nails drift down her neck. God, her skin. It's impossibly soft, smooth but for the goose bumps ignited by my touch. I could do this all night, wrap myself around her and never come up for air. Who the hell needs air anyway?

We break apart for a minute, and she laughs, hiding her face in the slope of my neck.

"I can't believe I just did that," she says, her words tickling my collarbone.

"What, kiss me?"

"Yes, oh my god." She stays pressed against my throat, and I sort of like her there, burrowing into me like I'm a safe space. I keep my arms around her, dipping my head so I'm leaning into her, too. And it is safe. Terrifying and safe.

"I'm glad you did," I say.

"I wasn't sure . . . I mean, after that night in the tree, we sort of fought. I wasn't sure you wanted to."

"I do. I've been waiting for that for two damn weeks."

She lifts her head. "Really?"

"Yes. In fact, I think we should do it again."

One corner of her beautiful mouth tilts into a grin. "I think so too."

So we do, this time kissing deeper, longer, harder, then softer. Her tongue traces my lower lip, her palms gliding up my thighs while my thumbs sweep over her delicate collarbone. Everything is bright and warm, the entire world turning electric under her touch. My chest feels strangely tight, but in a good way, like a deep ache that's trying to break apart.

Behind us, a series of brilliant purple and gold sparks ignite the now-black sky, like wishes blinking in and out. We both startle, our laughs touching each other's mouths. Arcing her neck, Eva stares up at the colors exploding into the sky, and she's so freaking gorgeous, I have to press my lips to her throat. Like, *have to*. She sucks in a breath and curls her arm around my shoulder, her fingertips hot on my skin.

"Come do something with me," she says, unraveling herself and reaching for the seats behind us.

"I'm pretty damn happy right here."

She jerks her head toward the ocean. "I think I just spotted a humpback."

"Oh god, let's go."

We laugh and pull each other up, keeping our hands on backs and arms as we climb over the seats and back into the boat. When the others come into view, Luca glances at us from where he's cuddled up with Kimber at the bow, a curious glint in his eyes. I smile at him. He smiles back, but it's small, and a sliver of unease cuts into all this ridiculous happy.

Eva doesn't even notice. She disappears below deck while I wander over to everyone else, wondering why she pulled us away from our little slice of paradise. More fireworks explode in the sky, so I focus on the flowery shapes, the shimmery reflections in the water.

Soon Eva's at my side again, handing me a small green bottle of Miracle Bubbles. She's holding a long, cylindrical tube of the same stuff, a huge wand slicing through its blue liquid center.

"What's this for?" I ask.

She unscrews the lid to her bubbles and pulls out the wand, a soft and wistful expression on her face. "My mom and I used to do this. Every Fourth, we'd go up to the roof of our apartment. From there we could see the fireworks over the East River, and we'd blow bubbles into the sky."

"Why?"

She smiles, a small, sort of sad bend of her lips. "You'll see."

Then she swings the wand through the air, iridescent bubbles drifting into the space in front of us. But they're more than iridescent, because at that moment a firework blasts into the sky above Cape Katie, filling the bubble with a million sparkles.

I uncap my own bottle and blow out a colony of tiny bubbles just as a gold and silver willow-shaped firework ignites. My bubbles fill and multiply the image, popping lazily, blinking out the firework one at a time. It's like viewing the whole show though water.

It's beautiful.

Eva and I continue to blow bubbles. I can feel Luca's eyes on me, but I'm not sure what he's thinking. Eva sweeps her arm through the air as she waves giant bubble after giant bubble into the sky, mingling them with my smaller ones, all of them shot through with flares of red and blue and green and purple.

The finale is just firing up, a constant *boom* echoing through the night, when I notice Eva's stopped. She's staring up at the sky, watching her last bubbles winking out, tears streaming down her face.

Capping my bubbles and placing them on the floor, I approach her slowly. I take her bubbles and cap those, too, before slipping my hand into hers. I don't say anything. I'm not sure what *to* say, and I doubt she needs words right now. I think we're just going to stand there, silent, watching the fireworks drench the black sky in rainbows while Eva cries, when she pulls away, backing up until she sinks onto the seats on the port side. Luca, Kimber, Macon, and Janelle all squirm, glancing at Eva and then me and then one another before fixing their gazes back on the sky. Because this is awkward. Sadness is awkward. Grief is awkward. A missing mother is awkward, no matter what form that missing takes. And no one likes awkward. No one knows what to do with it unless you're the person used to receiving all those averted gazes.

I walk over to Eva and sit next to her.

"God, way to ruin a good night, huh?" she says, wiping at her eyes and forcing a smile. "I'm sorry."

"You don't have to be sorry."

She nods, but she scoots a little farther from me.

"Hey," I say, pulling her knees around so her body faces me. "You're allowed to feel like this. Do you need me to leave you alone? I will, if that's what you want."

She frowns at me but doesn't move away. Then, a barely perceptible shake of her head. More tears spill over, so I frame her face in my hands, swiping her tears away. I kiss her cheeks, her eyes, the corners of her mouth. Behind me, I hear a soft "What the hell?" come out of Macon's mouth, but it's not a disgusted sort of question. I don't think. More surprised than anything, and it's followed by a *whack* sound—Janelle's smack to his shoulder. Still, I ignore them all. I keep my eyes on Eva, whose tears keep coming, but who's leaning into my touch. Finally, she exhales a shuddering breath. Her arms wrap around my waist, and she props her chin on my shoulder.

"I thought it would be good, you know? The bubbles. Like . . . I could still do something that was *ours* and it'd be sort of nice. A first step, maybe. But . . ."

Her voice fades away, her face pressed against my neck. I don't tell her it'll be okay. Maybe it won't; I don't freaking know. Our worlds are blurring, the days and nights overlapping. I hate seeing her sad. I'd do anything to make her smile right now and that thought is a relief, for so many reasons. I won't hurt her. I won't mistreat her like I may have mistreated Jay, douche that he is. And I can't help but feel that these tears—their presence in front of me—are a good thing. Maybe this will separate her from Maggie a bit. Maybe she won't *need* Maggie as much, because I'm here. I understand the missing mother. I understand that bone-deep ache too.

Weirdly, I sort of wish Emmy were here. Well, okay, maybe not *here,* because I have no idea how she'd feel about Eva wrapped in my arms right now. But I have an answer to her question. I tighten my grip on Eva, hands skating over her back as her crying calms and the wind blows her hair into my face.

*This. This is what I want.*

I lift one hand into the sky, the other still holding on to Eva. The last fireworks fizzle in between my spread fingers, the purple nails bright against the last bits of gold, like wishes come to life.

# chapter twenty-two

THE NEXT AFTERNOON, LUCA IS LEAVING LUMAC'S AS I'm walking in. Last night, after we'd returned to the pier, Luca and I parted with smiles and waves. He even attempted a halfhearted noogie, but I don't remember anything much beyond that because my entire walk home, anticipation over Eva slipping through my window and into my bed later on had covered me like a skin.

And by anticipation, I mean I was freaking the hell out. We hadn't made any plans to meet at the lighthouse or anything. She'd just cupped my chin and pressed a kiss to my forehead—*my forehead*—and then walked toward the Michaelsons' house with Macon and Janelle. What if those kisses on the ocean finally changed everything? What if she regretted them, like I had thought she regretted the tree kiss? What if she was too sad? What if she needed Maggie? What if I was too much, too little?

*What if what if what if blah blah blah.*

But, just after one a.m., my window slid open. We didn't say much, and we spent most of the first hour or so just touching—fingers idling up and down arms, palms smoothing circles over backs. We didn't even kiss for a long time, but it was all right. It's what she needed, and it felt good giving her that.

But then she needed something else. We both needed something else. It felt almost like an instinct, both of our chins tilting up at the same time and our mouths falling together. We kissed until my lips felt numb and our shirts were on the floor, until clouds blew over the moon and Eva's arms wrapped around my bare waist, her face buried in the slope of my neck as she drifted off to sleep.

"Hey," Luca says now, holding open the café door for me.

"Hello."

"*Hello?* What's this *hello* shit?"

"Huh?"

"You usually greet me with a shoulder shove or an inarticulate grunt."

I relax a little. "Sorry. Things on my mind."

He tilts his head at me. "Audition things?"

I blink at him. "Oh."

"You're still doing it, right?"

"Um—"

"Grace."

"*Luca.*"

"You can't not do it. You know that, right? Please tell me you know that."

"Of course I'm still doing the audition. Damn. I just spent

three and a half hours practicing at a freaking bookstore. Why do you care so much about my piano playing all of a sudden?"

"It's not all of a sudden. It's been years."

I look down and bite my lip, thinking about the thousand dollars he shelled out for my pre-screening video. "You're right. I'm sorry. I'm just nervous about it."

"Why? You're amazing."

I shrug. "I don't know . . . all the other students at the Boston workshop? They're not like me. They don't have my baggage."

"No one's like you, Gray. Not on the piano. And I mean that in a good way."

I nod, knotting my aching fingers together.

"Is the New York trip with Maggie still happening?" Luca asks when I don't say anything else. "You haven't talked about it much lately."

*"We,"* I say, waving my hands between us, "haven't talked about much of anything lately."

He scuffs his ratty gray Chuck Taylors against the tabby sidewalk. "Listen, Mom's making lobster bisque for dinner tonight. Why don't you come? Kimber'll be there. Maybe you guys can chat a little more."

I squint at him, but I can tell he's trying. He wants me to fit in with her, or her with me, or him with all of us. Something.

"Eva will be there too," he says when I don't answer right away. "Maybe you can talk to her, too."

I narrow my eyes at him. "Of course I would talk to Eva."

"I mean *talk to her* talk to her."

He gets my best *what the hell* look for that one.

"You still haven't told her everything about you and your mom, have you?"

I flinch. "Are you serious?"

"Are *you* serious? Yes, Gray. Maggie's not . . ." He trails off, filling his cheeks with air before letting it out slowly. "I mean, you and Eva . . . you're kissing or whatever," he finally says. "I think she needs to know."

"Do you tell all your sad stories to every girl you make out with?"

"You're not just making out with her."

"Exactly, Luca. This isn't some fling for me."

I look down, hooking my hands on my elbows, the admission making my heart hurl itself against my ribs. I feel exposed and tender, a butterfly caught in a thunderstorm.

"I know it's not," Luca says softly.

I nod, finally daring to glance his way. "Whoopie pie?" I ask.

He grins. "Always whoopie pie."

"All right. I'll see you there."

I'll do just about anything for Emmy's whoopie pies, and Luca knows it.


The temperature at dinner is about a hundred degrees of weird. The bisque is thick and creamy, and I could live on Emmy's homemade brown bread alone for the rest of my life and be totally happy, but the overall vibe? Well, let's just say I could do without a repeat.

Emmy watches Eva sip at her bisque, flicking her eyes to me, then back to Eva. She smiles and asks about Mom and piano and all that, but I can't shake the feeling that she's watching the two of us for signs of . . . what? That we made out? I'm not sure if she even knows Eva's gay.

"Mom, can we take our whoopie pies downstairs?" Luca asks when Emmy brings a platter brimming with chocolaty-creamy goodness in from the kitchen. "I told Kimber we'd play air hockey."

"Okay, that sounds fine. Go have fun." She puts the pies on small white plates and hands them out.

While Luca heads to the kitchen for a glass of milk, something he cannot live without when eating whoopie pies, Eva, Kimber, and I take our desserts and start toward the basement. Halfway down, I stop.

"I'll be right there," I tell Eva, handing her my plate. "Just want to ask Emmy something."

She tilts her head at me but nods. "Okay."

I tromp back upstairs, not sure what I actually want to say to Emmy. Everything just seems off between us. I'm not used to feeling so disconnected from her or Luca, and I really hate it. Luca knows I'm with Eva, and while I don't know if Emmy knows about me, I *do* know she'd be fine with it. When the Supreme Court legalized same-sex marriage, she baked a huge rainbow cake and sold it by the slice at LuMac's, for god's sake. Some people on the cape turned up their noses, but a lot of people loved it. So, yeah, I know Emmy will be fine with this, and I just need to hug her. Thank her for dinner. Anything to keep us feeling like us right now.

I'm rounding the corner into the kitchen when I hear Emmy's voice. It's low and laced with worry, making me stop in my tracks.

"You'll talk to Grace?" she says to Luca. "I mean really talk to her?"

"Yeah. I told you I would."

"I can do it if you need me to."

"No, I will. But she's not going to like it."

The refrigerator opens and something rattles around before it's closed. "I know, honey. I don't like it either. I wish I could give Maggie the benefit of the doubt. Everyone deserves fresh starts and second chances, but this thing with Maggie goes way beyond a few too many drinks. Under normal circumstances, I would never ask Grace to talk about her family life if she didn't want to, but . . . Eva's been through too much. I can't take that risk. Not right now."

"I don't know why Grace hasn't told her everything already."

"Oh, sweetheart," Emmy says, sighing. "Yes, you do."

"This sucks."

"You're her best friend. She knows you love her."

"It still sucks."

They fall silent, but I hear another heavy sigh. I can picture Emmy pulling her son into her arms, him towering over her and wrapping his arms around her shoulders, resting his cheek on the top of her head. I blink at the family photos lining the walls in the hallway, all the smiles and hugs and trust and predictability. Even with her lying, cheating husband off to find a new family, Emmy has always been solid. Raising her sons to be decent humans, giving them space to breathe but not so much that they floated away, unnoticed and unguarded. I've always been aware of the differences between Maggie and Emmy, between our families. How could I not? But now those differences are bright red on a white background, stark and violent. Cause for alarm. Cause for worry. Cause to protect Eva in a way Emmy wouldn't protect me. No, *couldn't*. Right? Emmy tried. She always tries. Doesn't she?

I turn and walk down the hall, closing myself into the bathroom as quietly as I can. A sob rises in my chest, blossoming into my throat until it escapes. I press my hand to my mouth to keep it in. Leaning on the tile counter, I meet my mother's eyes in the mirror. Messy hair. A little haggard from all the late nights with Eva. My heart feels ripped in two. She's my mother. The Michaelsons are my family, but she's my *mother*. And they're terrified of her. Of what she'll do or say, some mistake that she can't take back and whether or not it'll affect Eva.

But she's my *mother*.

I don't want to tell all of her sad stories. I only want to tell Eva the good ones, the ones that make me a healthily functioning human with a healthily functioning mother.

But that's not what Mom and I are.

I splash some water on my face and gulp down several breaths. I just want to go home, but I know Eva will come after me, and I don't want her around Maggie tonight. Not tonight.

Downstairs Kimber and Luca are already deep into a game of air hockey while Eva watches from the 1970s-era orange-and-brown-striped couch. Her plate is empty and she's licking her fingers.

"Damn, that's a good cookie," she says.

"*Pie,* Eva," I say, pasting on a smile and sitting down next to her. "Calling the beloved Maine whoopie pie a *cookie* will get you excommunicated around here."

"But it's like a squishy Oreo."

"And thank the gods for it, but it's *not* a squishy Oreo. It's a whoopie pie." I force myself to take a bite and then talk with my mouth full. "Repeat after me. P-I-E."

She laughs and leans into my shoulder. I want to kiss her right here, *pie*-stuffed mouth be damned. I need something to erase Luca and Emmy's conversation, the knowledge of what I'm keeping from Eva and why. Something to remind me that this—Eva and me—is still happening, still okay, still right, no matter who my mother is.

So I pull Eva's face toward me with two fingers on her chin and press my lips to hers. She smiles against my mouth and kisses me back. It's sweet and soft and perfect.

And short. Luca clears his throat loudly, jolting us apart.

"Gray!" I turn toward him slowly. He stares at me from the

air hockey table, spinning his striker in one hand. "Come play Kimber."

I stare at him for a few seconds, wondering when he's going to *talk* to me about spilling my own mother's dirty secrets. "You sure she can handle that?" I ask, something like anger bubbling just under my skin.

"Oh, bring it."

I push myself off the couch, wiping my chocolate-dusted fingers on my jeans. "Don't say I didn't warn you."

"I'm right here, guys," Kimber says, hands on her hips. "And I just kicked his ass, Grace. I can hold my own."

She's smiling, so I laugh. "Fair enough."

I take the striker from Luca, and Kimber drops the puck. We push it back and forth pretty easily at first. I take the first point, Kimber takes the next two, and then things go a little faster. And by faster, I mean harder. Soon, we're both throwing our entire bodies into the game, and my right shoulder is sore as hell. The *click-clack* of the puck echoes through the basement.

"Um," I hear Luca mumble, but I tune him out.

I slam the puck toward Kimber's side, and it collides with her fingers right next to the goal. She screams and drops her striker, clutching at her hand and glaring at me.

The nail on her middle finger is broken and bleeding.

"Damn, Gray, what the hell?" Luca says, rushing to Kimber and taking her hand in his.

"Sorry," I say. "But her finger shouldn't have been hanging over the side of the table like that. Number one rule of air hockey: Keep your fingers off the field."

"Still, you pretty much threw the puck at her."

"She was playing just as hard. I didn't *mean* to hit her finger, Luca."

"I'll get a Band-Aid," Eva says, already halfway up the stairs.

"Why are we even playing air hockey?" I ask Luca, tossing my striker onto the hockey table. It rolls over itself a couple times, clattering loudly. "Don't you want to *talk?*"

"What?" he asks. Kimber sucks on her finger.

"Don't act like you don't know what I'm talking about."

"I *don't.*"

"Here we go," Kimber mumbles.

"And what is your problem?" I ask. A little voice in my head is telling me to shut the hell up, that this isn't about Kimber at all, but I don't listen to it. I'm tired. Tired of feeling like a stain. My mother's just a person. And yeah, I do hate this friendship she has with Eva, but I hate this feeling like my mother is the human equivalent of a wrecking ball even more. I just want it to stop.

"I don't have a problem," Kimber says calmly.

"Clearly, you do. You've hated me since you and Luca first eyefucked each other."

She grimaces. "Nice, Grace. And I don't hate you."

"Well, you sure as hell don't like me."

"I think you're reckless and impulsive and dishonest. There's a difference."

"Dishonest, what the hell? Why? Because I rearranged some gnomes? So did your boyfriend. So did *you*."

"We did that for you. And don't think Luca doesn't know that you and Eva sneak around all night doing whatever the hell you want without a thought to how upset that would make Emmy if she knew."

"Kimber—" Luca says, but I cut him off.

"We're talking on top of a lighthouse, not tagging every wall on the cape."

"And riding bikes all over the place," Kimber says. "And what's with all the peanut butter?"

"Oh my god, not peanut butter," I deadpan.

Luca glares at me. "All right. Enough."

"Yeah, enough, Luca," I say as Eva tromps back down the stairs. "Just say it."

"Say what?"

"What's going on?" Eva asks, handing Kimber a Band-Aid and a tube of Neosporin.

"That you wish I were different," I say to Luca. "That you wish Maggie weren't my mother and that I would handle all of her bullshit better so you wouldn't have to deal with me."

Silence settles over all of us. My eyes sting and my chest burns. I have no idea where those words came from. They just spilled out, unconsciously rising up and filtering through all of my anger and hurt over Luca's and Emmy's worry. Now that the words are out, they feel right. It's almost a relief to have said them.

221

"Gray." Luca takes a step toward me, his eyes wide and a little watery-looking. "That's not—"

"I need to go," I say, my voice scraping against my throat. I don't know what else to do or feel. Escape is my first instinct, so I run with it and start for the stairs. "I'm really sorry about your finger, Kimber."

She doesn't respond and Luca doesn't call me back as I take the stairs two at a time.

But Eva is right behind me.

Our feet dangle over the edge of the lighthouse, our legs pressed against each other, our bodies held in by the wrought-iron railing.

It's barely ten o'clock, but Eva and I are already up here. We left Luca's and climbed the winding stairs, no hesitation or verbal agreement. We just knew this was where we needed to be. I'm not sure what Eva's thinking. My own head is full of about ten different emotions. The jar of Peter Pan we're sharing helps. Peanut butter has quickly become my number-one comfort food.

Still, a certain thought keeps popping to the surface, like those damn rodents in that Whack-A-Mole game. I smack it on the head and it disappears, only to resurface seconds later.

"What's going on, Grace?" Eva asks, interrupting my mental game. I'm amazed she's held off plugging me with questions this long. She digs a spoon into a jar, scooping a huge glob before licking it like a lollipop. It'll take her ten minutes to eat that one spoonful.

"I'm a mess, Eva," I say, my eyes fixed on where I know the ocean should be. It's just a giant swath of dark, ignited every few seconds by the lighthouse beam. "Maggie's a mess. We're just . . . we're a mess."

She reaches out and tucks a wayward strand of hair behind my ear. Her fingers tickle my cheek as they brush over the skin, and I grit my teeth to resist leaning into her touch.

"What do you mean?" she asks.

I take a breath and let it out slowly before I turn to look at her. "My mom isn't stable. I know you think she is, that she just looks at the world differently and handles things in her way, and maybe she does, but it's not *stable*. And she didn't raise me in a stable environment. Nothing about this"—I wave my hand around my face—"is stable. And it's only a matter of time before this whole thing with you and her—whatever it is, whatever you get out of it—blows up."

"Why does it have to blow up?"

"Because it always does."

She frowns, clearly confused. And she should be. I haven't told her shit and Luca's too loyal to me to tell her anything and Emmy clearly wants *me* to tell her. The worst part is that I didn't even see it, how screwed up it is to withhold all of it from Eva, not only because I like her and want her to know me, but because she *is* wrapped up in Maggie. And Maggie's a fucking hurricane.

So I tell Eva some stories. Stories of Mom's and my itinerant life, rescues from crowds of beer-soaked men at Ruby's, vodka at breakfast, and stolen money out of my jewelry box. I try to weave in some good stuff, too. The New York trip. How talented Mom is with jewelry design. The way she haggled that pastor down to a price we could afford for my piano because she knew I needed it. Because she believed in me. Still, the bad stuff is like flypaper. Everything else sticks to it.

Eva listens, her eyes on me and her half-licked spoon forgotten between her fingers.

"God, Grace," she says when I take a breath.

I shake my head and look down. "It's not that bad."

"And Luca knows all of this?"

"He knows most of it."

"And Emmy?"

I nod. "She and Mom don't get along. When I was thirteen, Mom disappeared for a few days and Emmy brought me to her house. They had a huge fight when Mom finally came home. It was bad. It's been weird between them ever since. Emmy's offered to let me live with them more than once, and she gives me money here and there, but I can't leave my own mother, can I? And who knows what sort of fucked-up stuff is in my head that I don't even know is fucked up? It's just me, the way I am."

Jay's words filter through the snarls in my head. *You never asked.* And I didn't. Not once. I didn't bat a single eyelash when I dumped him. Guys before him? Ones I mess around with or went on one date with before blowing them off? They meant nothing to me.

"No," Eva says, her curls falling into her face as she shakes her head. "You're you because of *you*."

"Eva. Our life is chaos. Please, just trust me on this."

"I'm not denying that. And it's not like I couldn't tell Maggie wasn't your average mom, but . . ." She tosses her spoon into the jar and rubs her eyes with both hands. "I wish you would've told me."

"I didn't want you to see me as some screwed-up girl. I didn't want . . . I didn't want to admit it all. It's hard enough letting Luca into all of this, and I just wanted to be me when I was with you. Just Grace."

"I get that, but—"

"And you needed it. I know I should've told you, but Maggie really seemed to help you. I didn't want to take that from you."

She doesn't answer but takes my hand in hers, playing with my nails. I notice that hers are painted freshly purple. Maybe she did them herself, but I really doubt it. The color is Mom's favorite— that same sparkly aubergine from the first time I saw Maggie and Eva together at my own kitchen table.

"Do you know the story of *Swan Lake*?" Eva asks quietly, her eyes on the ocean.

"The ballet?"

"Yeah."

"Only what I know from playing Tchaikovsky and watching *Black Swan*."

She smiles, but it's tight. "Well, this will seem totally normal to you, then."

I don't say anything, and she takes a deep breath. "We danced *Swan Lake* for our spring show last year. I was Odette. Pissed off all the white girls, but I danced the hell out of that role. Wanted it so bad, wished for it every night, just to prove to them all that I could do it. Mom wasn't even in on the casting. She said it wouldn't be fair, but the other instructors picked me anyway. In the ballet, Odette is a princess and a sorcerer curses her so that during the day, she has to fly around as a swan, and only at night can she be herself. That's how I feel now. Like there are these two sides of me — the normal me, the before-Mom-died me, and then this sad little cursed thing. I wanted to be Odette more than anything, and I got my wish."

Tears form in her eyes, and they roll down her face undeterred. I sort of love this about her, how she simply lets them happen, lets the sadness have her for a few minutes. I always fight it, always feel like I'm breaking apart when the first tears bloom in my eyes.

"Eva."

She shakes her head. "I'm fine."

"You're not."

"Okay. No, I'm not, but I want you to understand what's been going on in my head about Maggie. She's not fine either. We're both cursed with this . . . this *death* hanging over everything we do.

You know sometimes I go hours without thinking about it? About my mom? *Hours.* It doesn't seem like that should be allowed. And then I remember and I feel so guilty. Because when I forgot, I felt happy."

"Your mom would want you to be happy."

"No, I know. I just . . . it happened so fast. I woke up one morning, thinking my mom would be in the hospital for a day or two and then things would go back to normal. By that night she was in the critical care unit, machines beeping and breathing for her. I'll never forget how they sounded. How everything smelled. And then she was gone, and suddenly I was that sad little swan. The other me? Gone, too, just like that." She snaps her fingers once. "And it's like, around Maggie, I can be that sad little swan, and it feels . . . almost normal."

I inhale deeply through my nose and keep hold of her hand. Her words make sense—at least, a *sort* of sense, but they also scare me. Because the way my mother has handled her grief is anything but healthy. Part of me wonders if Mom's problems go beyond grief, beyond too much vodka and skeezy men, like Emmy said to Luca earlier. Maybe it's some chemical thing in her brain, maybe not. I don't know.

"I get that," I say. "But . . . can you see why it bothered me? Why Luca's worried? Why *I'm* worried?"

She nods, squeezing my hand tighter. "I'm sorry."

"Don't be sorry."

"Well, I am. I don't want to hurt you."

"I know."

We sit there for a while, the open air and this new clean space between us lacing us even tighter together.

"So who are you when you're with me?" I ask after a while. "When we're together at night, are you the real you? The princess?"

She smiles, bringing my hand to her lips, her breath playing over my knuckles as she speaks. "At first, yeah. But now . . . I don't know. It feels like I can be both with you. Everything. You're stable for *me*, Grace. You calm down my thoughts more than any coloring book."

I smile, relief that she thinks I'm *good* for her a palpable beat in my chest.

"I've never felt like I fit anywhere," she goes on. "With Mom, yeah, but that was it. I never felt at home in my ballet classes, even when my mom was the teacher. I loved dancing, but when someone thinks *ballerina,* they don't picture me. They sure as hell don't picture *gay.* They think *white girl,* plain and simple. Blue eyes, blond hair, stick-straight legs, with her arm looped around some lean-muscled guy's bicep. My mom always told me it would be hard to make it as a dancer. I mean, it's hard for anyone, but for a black girl?" She shakes her head. "But she never said impossible. Because she did it. She wasn't famous, but she was happy. She accomplished what she wanted. She made me believe I could do it too. I fit inside her belief, you know what I mean? And after she died, I felt like a ghost, drifting through the air, trying to land so I could dance. So I could do anything. But now . . . I don't know. These past couple of weeks have felt different. I do fit somewhere. Maybe I fit right here."

"Maybe you should move to the lighthouse." I lean back and touch the whitewashed wall. "There's room for at least one sleeping bag."

"Not *here,* the lighthouse, you silly doof." She smiles and presses a single kiss to my palm. "Here, *you.*"

"Oh." I sound all breathy, like Eva's words stole every sip of air from my lungs. "Wow, you know how to turn a girl's head."

She laughs, but then she turns serious again. "And maybe I fit with Emmy and Luca, too. I know she cares about me."

"She really does, Eva."

"Yeah. I just . . . I know she didn't mean to, but she's my guardian now, so it's like she's automatically supposed to be this replacement for my mom. And I didn't want that. I'll never want that. Emmy can't save me and I don't want her to."

"Of course not."

"But . . . I told her I'd think about dancing."

I squeeze her hand. "Yeah?

She nods, her eyes round with what can only be called fear. "I have an audition. For a dance education program."

I feel my own eyes widen. "What? Why didn't you tell me? Where? When?"

"NYU. It's not until October. It was scheduled before everything happened with my mom and I . . . I don't know."

"You're thinking of not going?"

She shrugs. "I want to. And I don't."

"Eva. You have to do it."

"Like you have to do yours?"

I blink at her. I never told her how conflicted I feel about my own audition, my own future. I guess I didn't have to.

Scooting closer, I lace our fingers together. "We shouldn't have to feel guilty about being happy. Should we?"

"I don't want to."

"Do you feel guilty when you're with me?"

She rests her head on my shoulder, and her voice goes soft around the edges. "Sometimes, yeah. But not because of you. It's just weird feeling happy about anything. But my mom would've loved you. Or maybe she *does* love you."

"Do you believe in heaven? Or . . . I don't know. Life after death?"

She lifts her head, gaze fixed on the ocean. "It's a nice thought. But, honestly? Not really. Still, I think I believe in *something,* because it doesn't feel like Mom's just . . . nothing, you know? It feels like she's still here. Or maybe it's just here." She taps on her chest a few times. Even when her hand stills, she keeps it settled over her heart, her eyes on the black ocean pressed against the black sky.

The briny wind clings to us, tossing our hair together, our scents, our breaths. I take the hand she has against her chest and link it with mine, transferring it to just above my own heart. I squeeze and she squeezes back. As it turns out, I'm starting to suspect that I can commit to someone, I can fall in love. At least I think I can, because I don't believe someone incapable of love could feel as terrified and relieved and excited as I feel right now just sitting here, holding Eva's hand.

"I want you to know something," I say to her as I pick up my own spoon and take a bite of peanut butter.

"What?"

A million butterflies zing through my stomach, but I need her to know because Jay never knew anything.

"You're . . . you're really important to me," I say, forcing my eyes on hers. "More important than any guy I've ever been with."

She tilts her head at me, a smile flashing across her mouth, there and then gone. "Because I'm a girl?"

I shake my head. I know that's not it. I mean, I love that she's a girl. I love her smooth skin and the soft curves under my fingertips when we kiss, the way my mouth can slide from her lips to her neck with nothing to slow me down, but that's only her body. I liked Jay's body too, how his arms seemed to swallow me, the way he smelled, the flat plane of his chest where I would lay my head, that little V where his hips met his pelvis. I like it all in different ways and for different reasons. But those are just details for my hands and eyes. This—this pull toward Eva—has nothing to do with what I can see or smell or touch. It's something more, almost animal and instinctual, buried so deep inside my chest, I feel it like blood flowing through my veins.

I'm not sure how to say all this. It's all so overwhelming. Suddenly I feel shy, unsure, a fourteen-year-old me wondering if I can really take another girl's hand.

"Hey." Eva squeezes my fingers and a small smile curls over my mouth — I already am holding her hand.

So I tell her the truth. "You're important to me because you're Eva."

Her smile widens. She grabs the neckline of my T-shirt and pulls me closer and closer until our mouths collide.

# chapter twenty-three

T HE NEXT MORNING, I'M JOLTED AWAKE AT GOD KNOWS what time. I don't have to work today, which means I can avoid Luca, and I sure as hell don't want to wade through Chopin after staying up with Eva until nearly three a.m. the night before. I'd planned to sleep and sleep and then sleep some more.

Hurricane Maggie has other plans.

She blasts into my room, mascara streaks running down her cheeks, but her eyes are still rimmed in black, which makes me think she hasn't washed her face in a couple days. I rub my own eyes, wondering if sleep is just clouding my vision. Nope. Her face is a mess, her hair stringy and greasy-looking, and her white tank top has a smear of something that looks like raspberry jam. She looks like absolute crap.

"Get up," she says, throwing my covers back.

"What's going on?"

"We have to go." She opens my closet and digs around, emerging with the empty boxes she unpacked only a couple weeks ago.

"What? Why?" I slide off the bed, but I feel paralyzed as I watch her open my drawers and start throwing clothes in the boxes. This is all too familiar. The last time we lived with one of her boyfriends, she lasted three weeks and we hightailed it out of there in the middle of the night. I thought she'd last at least a month this time, especially since it's pretty clear Pete isn't a bad guy. Poor judgment, maybe, but not a bad guy.

"We just do," she says, pulling the sheets off my bed. "I'm not going to stay here another minute with someone who doesn't trust me."

"Just hang on a second." I grab her hand to stop her. "What happened?"

"Pete's a misogynistic ass, that's what happened, and I—"

"Maggie." Pete's form fills my doorway, but he backs up a little when he sees me in nothing but a camisole and sleep shorts. "Sorry, Grace."

I wave him off, more concerned about what the eff is going on than what I'm wearing.

"I didn't say you had to leave," Pete says from halfway in the hall.

"Yes, you did," Mom says. She keeps tossing my stuff into boxes.

"No. I said things between us won't work if you keep taking my money."

My heart plummets. "What? Mom, why—"

"I'm not having this discussion in front of my daughter," Mom says, glaring daggers at Pete.

"I think she needs to know why you're dragging her away from yet another home."

"This isn't a home," Mom spits out. "This is a prison."

Pete's face grows increasingly red, a sure sign he's getting more and more pissed. "You took a grand from the safe in my closet, Maggie. A *grand*. I gave you that combination to store your own valuables, not steal mine. Did you expect me not to notice? Or to say it was fine? Whatever you need for your little project or birthday party or whatever that is you were up all night decorating for?" He throws a hand toward the living room.

"What?" I say. "A thousand dollars? Jesus Christ, Mom. For a party?"

She finally stops whirring around. "It's important."

"It always *is*," I say, a bite to my tone that makes her flinch. I push past her, and Pete moves out of my way as I all but stomp into the hall.

And come to a very abrupt halt.

The living room is decked out in all different shades of purple. A cluster of lavender and periwinkle and violet balloons surrounds the light fixture over the table. Little poms made out of tissue paper cover the floor and counter. Purple napkins fan out over the table, and a centerpiece of gorgeous roses blooms majestically from the center.

*Purple* roses.

A tray of amethyst-colored macarons sits near the stove. Mom's apple muffins, dyed purple. Purple, purple, everywhere. On the kitchen counter, there's a roll of foiled wrapping paper the color of grape jelly, a small white box next to it. I walk over, approaching even though there's a loud voice in my head screaming at me to stop. But it's like a car accident on the side of the road, I can't stop rubbernecking. I flip the top off the box. Inside, it's exactly what I expected. The necklace. My necklace. No, *Eva's* necklace. Three triangular pieces of that beautiful aqua sea glass wrapped up in copper.

I turn my back on the necklace and blink a few times, hoping the scene is different every time I open my eyes, but it never is. On my last attempt, I catch a swath of lilac stretching from one side of the living room windows to the other.

*Happy birthday, Eva. We love you.*

"Happy birthday, Eva. We love you," I whisper, staring at the banner.

"Gracie." Mom comes up behind me and puts her hand on my back. I barely feel it.

"Happy birthday, *Eva*. We *love* you?"

"It was going to be a surprise," Mom says.

"Well, *I'm* definitely surprised. I didn't even know it was . . ." I whirl to face her. Because maybe that's it. Maybe she screwed up Eva's birthday too, and that's why I didn't even know about this.

She's throwing this whole shindig for Eva, and it's the wrong day. It has to be. The thought settles in, filling me with this sort of sweet, cool relief, but then it turns acidic. Because how effed up is that? Hoping my mother once again can't keep dates straight in her head. Hoping she's wrong, messed up, flighty, and flaky, because if she *isn't*, what does that mean? That she remembers for Eva, but not for me? That my girlfriend didn't tell me about her own birthday?

And all this—all this *purple*—was bought with Pete's money. Was stolen.

"Is her birthday today?" I ask.

Mom nods. "And I know you two are close. I wanted to talk to you about helping me get her here. Maybe Luca and Emmy too. It was going to be a quiet thing. You know, after your dad died, I didn't celebrate my birthday for years. Just pretended it was any other day . . ."

Her voice drifts off as she runs her eyes over the beautiful world she's made. It does look lovely. All the shades of color. My mother is creative and organized and driven when she decides to be.

"But," she says, sighing, "it won't happen now because Pete has his panties in a wad."

"Come on, Maggie," Pete says from the hallway. "That's not fair. You can't tell me this is how normal relationships are supposed to go. You don't steal."

"For the millionth time, I wasn't stealing—"

"Call it whatever you want, sugar. You took my money without asking." He glances at me, his expression softening. "I'm sorry, Grace. Y'all can stay here until you find a place. Long as it takes. But me and your mother . . . it's not going to work."

I nod, grateful for the stay of execution, but Mom's having none of it.

"Oh, no," she says, waving her arms around before snatching up the box with the necklace in it and stuffing it into her pocket. "We're leaving today. This minute, in fact. Grace, go finish packing."

"What? Where the hell are we going to go?"

"Just do it, baby."

Pete runs a hand over the back of his neck. "This is ridiculous. Grace, you can stay here if you need to, all right?"

I start to say something, but Mom explodes. "Don't you dare try to take my daughter away from me!"

"Maggie, for god's sake. That's not what I'm doing. But you can't keep hauling that poor girl all over the cape. It's not good for her."

"I know what's good for my daughter. She's been *fine* for seventeen years, and she'll be *fine* today, too."

Her words cut through me like a jagged piece of ice.

*I know what's good for my daughter.*

*She's been fine for seventeen years.*

*She'll be fine.*

Is that really how she sees our existence? Doing me good? *Fine?*

238

I glance around at all the beautiful decorations, the roses, all of it for Eva, and probably on the right day, too. Eva didn't tell me. She didn't tell anyone, most likely. But my mom thinks she can fix it. Make it something memorable and good and maybe even therapeutic.

She's trying to make sure Eva is fine.

And that's when it really hits me. I've thought it all before, the shadow of a truth I never allowed to really take root. I've brushed it off, excused it, said *yes* to the next duplex, tolerated the next boyfriend, but now it's glaring. It's in Pete's worried expression. It's in Mom's overreaction and overconfidence. It's in every single one of those purple roses.

*I am not fine.*

# chapter twenty-four

W E END UP AT THE LUCKY LOBSTER MOTEL, Cape Katie's cheapest accommodation for tourists who plan on spending as little time as possible indoors. We've stayed here a couple of times before in between one shitty apartment or duplex and the next.

Mom checks us into a room with two double beds. The carpet is a dingy coral color, the wallpaper a faded seagrass motif, and the bedspreads are a dull gray. I'm pretty sure they used to be bright blue. The whole room smells like a mix of cigarette smoke and Comet.

I toss my suitcase onto one of the beds. The rest of my stuff is still at the lighthouse. Mom told Pete we'd come back for everything in the next week, but right now she wanted *to get the hell away from your ugly face.* Direct quote. I don't even ask what she's going to do with all that party stuff. I don't want to know.

Jay came into my room while I packed some essentials. He didn't say anything, just handed me my music books and watched me. What the hell was there to say? Again, I had felt the need to apologize. Who knows, maybe that thousand dollars was for Jay's football equipment come fall. Maybe it was for food or SAT prep courses or something for the lighthouse. And Mom just took it.

When I finished packing, I couldn't even look at him. But when I went to pass by him, he stopped with a hand on my arm, there and then gone. "I'm sorry," he said.

I lifted my gaze to his. I wasn't sure what he was apologizing for, but it felt like it was for more than what had happened with our parents.

"Me too," I said, and I was. Not because that whole Tumblr fiasco was okay. It wasn't. But because I really was sorry for hurting him. For never *asking*. For generally not giving a shit.

Now I look around my new home for the unforeseeable future. Again. I feel a sob rise up in my throat, a longing for my room at the lighthouse, that room I hated so much when Mom first tossed me in there. But it's the room where Eva and I became *us*. I almost wish I had taken Pete up on his offer and stayed. But Mom needed me. She's going to spin the hell out because of this thing with Pete. How could I say no? How could I leave her?

How *can* I leave her?

I sink down onto the bed while Mom flits throughout the room, unpacking her toiletries onto the chipped bathroom counter, humming like nothing even happened. She cracks open a beer, one of several she no doubt lifted from Pete's fridge on the way out the door.

*I'm not fine.*

*How can I leave her?*

*I'm not fine.*

*How can I leave her?*

On the scratchy bedspread, I tap out Schumann's *Fantasie.*

It seems fitting, this piano piece that probably could've landed me a scholarship but won't. Because Mom will never change. And I'll never feel okay about leaving her the way she is, so unstable, so lonely and desperate for . . . for what? I don't even know anymore. The New York trip is just that—a trip. And then we'll come back home and go on with our lives.

"I need some air," I say, standing up.

"Now?" Mom turns, glancing out the window. "It looks like rain."

"I won't melt."

"I'd rather you stayed in today, baby." She laces her fingers together, wringing them into a knot. "I'm so upset, I don't know what to do with myself."

I take a step toward her, because I don't really know what to do with myself either.

"Oh, shit, Eva's birthday." She presses her hands to her cheeks. "I need to call her." She grabs her ratty pleather purse and digs out her ancient flip phone.

I take a step back.

I'm already out the door by the time I hear her say Eva's name into the phone.

· · ·

By the time I reach the pier, the rain has soaked through my black *Star Wars* T-shirt. It's one of Luca's, and I think it used to be Macon's. It's so worn and thin, it feels like it might disintegrate against my skin.

I want to call him. I want my best friend with me, right here, right now. But I leave my phone in my pocket, turned off. Because he'll just say *I told you so,* and, yeah, while he did *tell me so,* I don't want to hear it.

*Emmaline* bobs on the water between several other boats, a little haven of safety. I step on board and open the compartment next to the steering wheel, finding the keys that open the door leading to the cabin below deck. I walk down the short set of stairs and into the darkened room. A strand of white lights encircles the space, hanging on thumbtacks, and I plug them in under the tiny two-seater table. A soft glow fills the cabin. There's a set of bunk beds near the back, beds I've slept on so many times, I've lost count. I drag myself to the top bunk and collapse onto the mattress, still soaking wet. Underneath me, the navy-blue comforter is soft and well-used, and my fingers fly over its surface easily.

Tapping, tapping, tapping.

Tapping out my *Fantasie.*

# chapter twenty-five

T HE MATTRESS SHAKES AND I JOLT AWAKE, SITTING UP
and hitting my head on the low ceiling.

"Ow!" I yell, my hands flying to my head.

"God, I'm sorry! I didn't mean to scare you."

I rub my eyes once, twice, then crack them open to find Eva's
face peering over the edge of the bed. Her feet are propped on the
lower bunk, hands holding on to the top mattress.

"Hey," she says softly.

I release a breath and flop back down onto the bed, my head
pounding. Outside the little window, the sky is ink-dark and star-
less, rain pattering softly on *Emmaline*'s roof.

"Grace," Eva says, "I didn't know about the party."

"Is today really your birthday?"

A pause. A deep breath. "Yes."

"Eighteenth?"

"Seventeen. Mom homeschooled me during junior high, and I
skipped a grade when I got to high school."

"Why didn't you tell me?"

Another beat. "Will you come down here, please?"

"Why?"

"Because I want to see your face, and I'm five-nine and the thought of folding myself into the top bunk makes me feel like I need to breathe into a paper bag."

I release a single bark of a laugh, but oblige her and climb down.

"You're all wet," she says, running her hands over my shoulders when I reach the floor.

"And possibly concussed," I say, rubbing my head.

She opens the built-in drawers below the bottom bunk and finds a dry T-shirt.

It's one of mine, left here years ago, and features the cast of *My Little Pony*.

It's purple.

"This isn't really my color," I mutter as she pulls my arms up, followed by my soaked T-shirt. Then she slides the dry one over my head and settles it around my hips.

Tossing the wet shirt into the miniature kitchen sink, she leads me to the green-and-yellow-striped love seat on the other side of the room. Settling into one corner, she pulls on my hand until I follow, but I sit in the other corner. Still, our legs brush, our hands inches apart.

"I didn't tell you because I didn't tell anyone," she says. "Emmy knew because she was friends with my mom and also because she had to sign a bunch of forms about the guardianship, but I asked her not to do anything for it. I didn't want to celebrate. Your mom only knew because she point-blank asked me when my birthday was, and it didn't feel right to lie. I had no idea she was going to plan that party."

The rain continues to fall, chopping up the Atlantic and tugging *Emmaline* this way and that. Eva's not telling me anything I didn't suspect already. Still. Today is her birthday. Mom got the date right and ordered her a bunch of purple roses.

"Did you know she stole a thousand dollars from Pete to buy everything?"

Eva's mouth drops open. "What? No."

"Did you know she left Pete because he dared to be a little irritated about the whole theft thing, and now I'm living in a motel room with about five seconds of hot water and crusty sheets for god knows how long?"

Her jaw drops even further, if that's even possible. "Oh my god, Grace. Maggie just told me about the party and that she'd have to postpone it. When she called, she sounded fine and said she wanted to take me out for my birthday anyway. Just dinner or whatever."

"Did you go?"

She frowns. "Yeah, I did. But not because of my birthday. I wanted to talk to her, tell her I didn't think we should spend as much time together. I didn't know what had happened. If I had, I wouldn't have—"

"Where'd she take you?"

"Just . . . just the Crab Trap."

"I hope it was a good meal. Although you should probably stop by the lighthouse and thank Pete for the fried shrimp and garlic biscuits."

She rubs both hands over her face. "Grace, I left right when we got there. Luca called me and asked me if I knew where you were. He's been calling you."

"I turned my phone off."

"I know. When I told him I didn't know, I asked Maggie."

"Oh?" I laugh, a bitter, sharp thing that hurts my throat. "And what did Maggie say?"

"She said she didn't know, but she didn't seem worried—"

"Of course she didn't."

"—but *I* was worried, so I told her I wanted to go find you."

"Well, here I am." I stand up and pace the tiny space, energy and anger and I don't even know what making my fingertips tingle. "God, do you want the truth, Eva? The real truth? Because this is it. Do you see it now? Why this is something I never, ever want to have to talk about? Do you see what she does? She takes these beautiful motherly gestures and fucks them up. She steals money for a party. She forgets her own daughter's birthday. She thinks I'm *fine* and that she's mother of the year just because she's still here. She moves me from place to place to place, thinking it's good for me. It's an adventure. It's normal. Well, it's not. It's *not* and this"—I wave my arms around—"this thing that just happened with Pete is going to spiral down and down and down. It does every single time she breaks up with someone. She gets mad and then she leaves and then she acts like she's fine for about ten damn minutes and then she switches from beer to vodka or gin or something clear or I don't even know what the hell it is, and—"

"Grace." Eva stands up and tries to stop me, but I keep moving, circling the room like a wild animal.

"—and before you know it, I'm sitting at a bar at Ruby's, fending off forty-year-old assholes running their hand up my arm while Maggie dances the night away. Until it's not fun anymore and then it's all: *Gracie! Gracie! Save me!*"

"Hey, come on, sit down."

I stop pacing and look at her. I take a step closer and closer until we're chest to chest. Almost like it's an instinct, her hands come to rest on my hips, and she pulls me even closer.

"I didn't ask you last night, Eva," I say, and she frowns. "I didn't want to ask this. I didn't want Luca and Emmy to be right, but they are. So please. Please promise me you'll stop hanging out with her. It's not a jealousy thing. It's not because I'm pissed about the attention she's giving you. It's because you're going to get hurt. You probably shouldn't be with me, either, but you can't be with her. Just . . . go back to Emmy's and talk to her, or don't, but Maggie's not good for you. *I'm* not good for you. *Please*—"

"Hey, hey, hey," Eva whispers, and her hands come up to wipe away tears I didn't even know had started falling. Big, fat tears too. Tears full of days and hours and years of the same old bullshit. The same old *Grace is fine* bullshit.

"Please," I whisper again. "Promise me."

"Okay," Eva says. "Okay, I promise."

I exhale the world onto her shoulder, sinking against her. "Thank you."

"But I'm not leaving you or going back to Emmy's right now."

"Eva—"

"No, Grace. I know you think you're all messed up, but who isn't? I'll stay away from Maggie and do whatever you need me to do to help you with all this, but you're not her. You're *you* and there's no way in hell I'm staying away from you."

The relief is palpable. She pulls me even closer, her arms curling around my waist, one hand drifting up to rest on the back of my neck. She presses her lips to my temple, whispering things I can't even decipher into my ear, but her voice is low and soft and feels like a hot bath after a day in the snow.

And for the first time in a long time—for this moment, at least —I am fine.

Eva calls Luca to update him on what's going on. He asks to talk to me, but I decline. I just want to live in this world—both huge and tiny at the same time—for a little while longer. Just Eva and me. Luca says we can stay the night on *Emmaline,* that he'll explain everything to Emmy, and that there should be some things to eat in the cupboard in the little kitchen.

We find a box of macaroni and cheese and a pan. Eva boils the noodles while I root around for anything sweet, but only come up with a half-eaten jar of peanut butter, which is sort of perfect when I think about it. After Eva squirts bright orange cheese goo all over the noodles, we eat out of plastic *Star Wars* bowls on the couch.

"I need to tell you something," Eva says as I grab the jar of Jif from the table and hand her a spoon.

"What?"

She inhales deeply, twirling her spoon between her long fingers. "Maggie asked me if I wanted to live with you guys."

"What?" I nearly choke. We don't even have a house. "She asked you this today?"

"No, no. A few days ago. She knew how much Emmy was driving me up the wall and asked if I'd feel more comfortable with her." She shrugs. "Emmy said no."

My throat aches, but I swallow it down. This is an ugly twist—Mom asking Eva to live with us after she nearly had a stroke when Emmy asked the same thing concerning me a few years ago. "That's what you were fighting about on the Fourth, isn't it?"

She nods. "I know it was stupid, but it made sense at the time, in my head. I guess I wanted to feel like I belonged somewhere again, had some control. Maggie made me think . . . I don't know what."

"Yeah," I say quietly. "She's really good at making people think *I don't know what*."

"I'm sorry."

"It's not your fault."

"And I thought I'd get more time with you."

I can only nod and put the peanut butter on the floor, my appetite sapped. Restlessness simmers under my skin. I flex my hands, then ball them up, tuck my legs underneath me only to unfold them again, and let them hang off the edge of the couch. Next to me, Eva is watching me, her own tension and helplessness as thick as the peanut butter I couldn't eat.

Then she inhales deeply before letting her breath out in a slow, steady stream. She gets up off the couch and turns to face me.

"What are you—?"

But my question dies as she lifts her arms into the air. They rise up from the sides of her body, her fingertips meeting over her head. She stands so her heels are touching, her feet turned out and toes facing opposite directions.

And then she dances. It's nothing like the kind of dancing I saw on top of that table at the bonfire. This is ballet, pure and graceful, method and freedom.

I have no names for the way her arms arc gracefully through the air. There's not much room in the tiny cabin, but even her wrists turn her hands in a beautiful sort of dance of their own. Everything about her is lovely. The muscles in her legs flex as she lifts herself up onto her bare toes, as she moves in the little space afforded her. She makes the most of it, transforming her body into a work of art.

And her face.

It's tear-streaked and smiling.

When she finally comes down, her arms floating back to her sides like feathers, I can't stay sitting. I'm on my feet before I'm even aware of it, my hands on her face, my forehead against hers.

"That . . ." I say. "You." It's all I can get out. She sniffs a little and trembles in my arms, but she's still smiling. It's tiny, but it's there. "Thank you."

She nods. "I'm trying to be brave like you."

"Like me?"

She pulls back to look at me. "Like you."

We look at each other for a few seconds, and then I back up, holding out my hand. "Come on."

"Where?"

I don't answer, just hold out my hand until she takes it. Walking her back to the beds, I give her a gentle push onto the lower bunk. Then I lie down next to her, tangling my legs with hers, pressing my palm against her lower back and pulling her closer. She does the same, wrapping me up with her hands and arms and legs.

I release my lungs, breathing out all the birthdays and purples, necklaces and tips stolen out of my jewelry box.

And when I take a breath in, it's all Eva. Her soft jasmine scent, the silky slide of her skin, the way her mouth is slightly parted like it's waiting for me. We stay like that for a long time. Long enough for everything in me to loosen, relax, think clearly. Feel clearly. Eva's patient. She doesn't talk or ask me questions. Doesn't make a move to kiss me. She simply trails her hand over my face, my hair, my shoulders, and my back while we watch each other and my eyelids grow heavy.

Eventually I fall asleep. I'm not sure how long I've been out when a crack of thunder wakes me. I startle in the bed, but Eva's arms are there, tightening around me.

"Hi," I say.

"Hi."

"Did you sleep?"

"A little, I think."

I nuzzle closer to her, everything about this moment so warm and perfect, scattering every dark thought and fear and worry.

"Was I really your first kiss?" I ask, my lips brushing over Eva's mouth.

She smiles, gliding a finger down my cheek. "Yep. I had *so* many other offers, but I was waiting for a blond girl with freckles on her nose. I had to have a blond girl with freckles on her nose."

"Redheads can't be trusted."

"Not a bit."

I smile, but it fades quickly along with our silly jokes. She fits herself even closer against me, our bodies perfectly aligned.

"Totally worth the wait," she whispers against my mouth.

It's that word that wakes me completely and undoes something in me. *Worth.* Suddenly, everything about this moment feels urgent. Desperate. I can't even respond with words. There's no time, because I have to cover her mouth with mine. Like, if I don't kiss her right here, right now, I might die. Just stop breathing and dissolve. She opens her lips to me, touching my tongue with hers, and I can breathe again.

The boat bobs underneath us, a gentle sway pushing us together. My fingers curl around the hem of her shirt, pulling it up so I can touch her skin, sweep my thumbs over the firm planes of her stomach. Goose bumps break out below my touch, and I smile against her mouth. Soon, she's reaching out too, her hands on my bare waist. My stomach isn't nearly as toned as hers, and when her fingers brush the skin there, I suck in.

"This okay?" she asks, pulling back for a minute.

I relax. "Yeah. Is it okay for you?"

She smiles and we kiss until I'm dizzy, until my entire body aches and all I want is more. More her. More us.

I lift her shirt over her head, revealing a Tiffany-blue bra with a little swath of lace over the top of each cup. She's so beautiful, I can barely see straight. I meet her half-lidded gaze and she nods, gliding her finger up my rib cage. I dip my head to the slope of her collarbone, tasting the hollow of her throat, sliding down to press a kiss to her sternum. My hand drifts up, over her bra and her small, soft breasts. Her breath catches and she arches a little into my touch.

"Lift up," I say, and she does. I unhook her bra and slide it down her arms.

"You too." She grins and pulls at my purple shirt. "It's only fair." I tear it off, my bra following quickly. Our skin presses together.

Curves and planes, light and dark, an amazing sort of sameness mingling with all the differences.

She releases a long breath, or maybe I do, because being together like this is such a relief. I glide my fingertips up her thigh. She huffs out a gaspy laugh, so I do it again and soon we're both breathing heavily but sort of laughing at the same time, and the whole thing is just so *right*, it feels almost wrong.

The thought intensifies my touch, which encourages hers, and soon there's no more talking. She rolls over so she's hovering above me, her fingertips light, her mouth warm, a glint of wonder in her eyes. I'm totally aflame. That's the only word for it. Red and crackling and hot. As she touches her mouth to mine again, her hand drifts south and flicks the button of my denim shorts free.

"Okay?" she asks, pausing.

I can only nod, and the zipper *zurps* downward.

"I want to take care of you, Grace," she whispers, her voice trembling a little.

"You are. We don't have to do anything else for that to be true."

She inhales a shaky breath. "I know."

"You're nervous. We can stop—"

"I don't want to stop. I . . . I know I'm not experienced with this stuff, but I want to be with you. I want to take care of you *this* way too." She holds my gaze, her teeth pressing over her lower lip. "Can I try?"

All I can do is nod, my throat tight with tears—the best tears that have ever threatened to fall. I feel totally undone. Again. Something knotted and hard and perpetually pissed off and nervous unravels inside me.

She slides off my shorts. When she starts to lie down, I hook my finger under the hem of her own shorts, tugging a little. Her brows lift and I tug a little harder until she laughs and wiggles them down her legs. They get caught on one ankle and she shakes her foot, sending them flying across the tiny room.

"Oh my god," she says, lining up her body next to mine and pressing her mouth against my shoulder. "Are we really doing this?"

"I think so," I say, huffing a laugh. Eva actually giggles, which just makes me laugh harder.

But soon the laughter fades, our shaky breaths the only sound remaining. Her fingers glide over my skin and down my stomach and between my legs, over my underwear. I inhale sharply, my entire body igniting in a way it never has before. I've experienced this plenty of times with Jay and a couple other guys, plenty of times alone, but nothing can compare with this, with her.

I bury my hands in her curls, holding on as her fingers slip inside my underwear and touch me. Her mouth is on my neck, then my lips, but not for long because I can't breathe, can't share breath. She presses her face to my hair, lips against my ear. My stomach tightens in all the best ways, and soon I'm touching her, too. Our hips seem to reach for each other, hungry for contact, for movement and feeling. It's not long before I can't tell the earth from the sky, can't even remember my own damn name.

There's only her. Only this.

Soon my world goes white, every nerve in my body firing down to the very tips of my fingers. Her touch slows and stills, but mine remains with her until she tenses and shudders against me too, my name a ragged whisper on her lips. We stay pressed together, both of us trying to get air into our lungs again.

"Wow" is all I can get out.

She laughs. "Yeah?"

"Um, yes."

She presses her face to my neck. "I was worried I didn't know what I was doing."

"You knew enough."

"You did too."

"Oh, I know."

She bites down on my shoulder a little.

"Hey, now!" I say, arcing away from her, but pulling her with me because our legs are tangled together.

"That was a big wow for me, too," she says quietly when we've settled again.

"First time in a girl's pants?" I ask teasingly. "And first time with a girl in *your* pants. Lots of girls in pants going on here."

She laughs and props herself on her elbow. "I really can't believe that just happened."

My stomach does a little anxious flip. "Like, *good* can't believe it?"

"Yes," she says, sliding her mouth over mine. "So good."

Later we curl up side by side on the bed, still naked and happy, and eat peanut butter right out of the jar.

"Happy birthday," I whisper into her ear.

And I know I mean it.

# chapter twenty-six

TWO DAYS LATER, LUCA FINDS ME AT THE BOOK NOOK. I've been sitting here for a good half-hour, staring at the keys, the music, my hands. Not playing. Every now and then, Patrick clears his throat dramatically. Eva's nestled in one of the upholstered chairs by the front window watching YouTube videos of this famous ballet dancer Misty Copeland. She gets up every five damn minutes and wanders around the store, tossing me a smile like she's casually browsing instead of making sure I'm still alive.

This goes on and on until Luca's shaggy head appears in the storage room doorway. I watch him as he hovers, my eyes never leaving his.

"Hey," he says, sitting down next to me on the piano bench.

"Hey."

"Not playing much today?" He gestures toward my still-closed music books.

"I can play without them."

"Yeah, but you're not. And you never play without them for important pieces. Aren't these important pieces?" He flicks the edge of my Schumann book.

"Did you come to harass me about the audition or talk?"

"Don't you know me at all? Both."

He grins and nudges my shoulder and I nudge back, and that's when I know we'll be okay. We'll always be okay.

"I'm sorry, Gray."

"About which part?"

"All of it. It's been hard, adjusting to Eva in the house. Not because we don't want her there. It's just . . . Mom's always trying to help her, you know? And, I'm sorry, but Maggie—"

"I know."

"I'm sorry."

"You said that already."

"Because I mean it. I wish things were different. For you, for Eva."

"I would never let Eva get hurt, Luca."

"I know you wouldn't mean to. But you don't see clearly when it comes to Maggie. You know you don't. And she's your mom, so I don't blame you for that. But look at what's going on, Gray. You're living in a crappy motel room. Again."

I look away, embarrassment filling me up like wet concrete poured into a pothole. My throat starts to ache, threatening tears. "You know what's weird?"

"The way Patrick keeps peeking through the door? He's freaking me out."

I laugh and wipe at my eyes. "He feels very invested in my playing. If I'm quiet for too long, he clears his throat or just point-blank lectures me about how *practice makes perfect.*"

"Or he heard you're living at the Lucky Lobster and he's rubbernecking."

"Or he heard I'm living at the Lucky Lobster."

God, it sounds so awful when I say it out loud. Like Wes Anderson got really depressed and this is the movie he made.

"What's weird, Gray?" Luca asks.

I take a deep breath and glance toward Eva on the chair. Her eyes are on her phone's screen, probably watching leaps and pirouettes or whatever you call them. She looks beautiful just sitting there. She looks sad, too, and I know she misses more than her mom.

"I just . . . it's so easy with Eva," I say.

Luca tilts his head. "And that's weird?"

"A little? I don't know. I feel *happy.*"

Luca frowns. "You mean, you've never felt happy before now? God, I *am* a shitty friend."

I laugh. "No, you're not. It's just different with Eva. You and Emmy have always made me feel . . . hopeful. Safe." I look down, sliding my finger over middle C. "I know I'm too much sometimes."

"Hey." He nudges my shoulder until I look at him. "You're not too much. At least, no more than me or Eva or whoever the hell. You're just . . ."

I lean against his shoulder. He leans back.

"I'm just what?" I ask.

He sighs. "You're just a kid who's had to be a grownup way too many times."

Tears spring into my eyes, but I squeeze them back. "Being a grownup sucks."

He laughs and wraps an arm around my shoulder. "It *looks* like it sucks. Let's never get old."

"Neverland, here we come."

"I've always wanted to wear a leaf shirt and tights."

"Will Kimber be your happy thought?"

He grins and waggles his eyebrows. "Well, I know who yours will be."

I flap my hands and lift up a little like I'm about to take flight right there. Soon we're laughing and Luca's trying to noogie me to keep my butt on the piano bench.

"How long are you going to be in the motel?" he asks after the laughter dissolves.

"Not sure. Mom's looking for a place." At least, I think she is. I haven't seen her much, to be honest. I've spent most of my time at work or here, practicing. When I went to sleep last night, she'd been AWOL all day. I set my alarm to wake me up every hour, and around three, I lifted my head to see her small form curled up on the bed, reeking of cigarettes and beer. Most likely, she's been hanging out at

Ruby's, but I don't have the energy to fight her on it. At least she's not asking me to go, which is both a relief and worrisome.

"Come to dinner tonight," Luca says. "Eva's got to work and I know she's your girl and all, but some you-and-me time wouldn't hurt, you know? Mom said she'd make whatever you want. She hates that you feel like this. We don't wish *you* were different, Gray. We really don't."

I smile and nod, relieved as hell that Emmy wants me there.

"Pizza fries?" I ask.

"Pizza fries."

I lean my head on his shoulder, and he swings an arm around me.

"I think you're good for her," he says. "For Eva. She's happy —well, *happier*. And I think she's good for you, too. I just wanted you to know that."

"Thanks. I mean it."

Suddenly, he shoves me upright and flicks open my music book in one motion. "Now get your ass to work."

I plant my fingers on the keys and smile like I'm posing for a picture. He ruffles my hair, and I start the beginning of *Fantasie* as he leaves.

But as soon as he's out the door, my fingers go still.


Luca and I are in the middle of the most epic pizza-fry war in our history when my phone rings. I have about five overlapping strings of cheese stretching from the plate to my mouth. Luca has only three, which means for the first time in years, I'm winning. My mouth is full of fries and pepperoni. Emmy sits on the couch in the living room and plans out a fall menu for LuMac's, mumbling that we're going to choke to death, but she's got a little smile on her face.

When I first got there, Emmy gulped me into her arms and held me for what seemed like hours, so I know Luca must've filled her in on everything that's happened and what's going on between Eva and me. It felt so damn good to prop my chin on her shoulder, I let her hug me for as long as she wanted.

"You know I love you to pieces," she whispered in my ear. "And I love Eva to pieces, but I worry about you both. Put the two of you together and double the worry. Do you understand what I'm saying?" I could only nod against her shoulder. We didn't say anything about Maggie. What *was* there to say?

Turns out, Emmy refused to feed me a meal consisting solely of pizza fries, so she made roasted chicken with mashed potatoes and green beans, which was a little slice of freaking heaven after two days of vending-machine food and LuMac's doughnuts. But she's nothing if not a total softy, so she cooked me up a batch of pizza fries too. Now it's nine o'clock at night, my stomach is close to popping from the home-cooked meal, and I'm stuffing fried potatoes covered in cheese and processed meat into my mouth in Luca's kitchen.

And I love every minute of it. Because I'm laughing and Luca's laughing, and I think he and Emmy both knew I needed this.

My phone trills in my bag, and Luca points a finger at me that says, *Don't you dare answer that.*

I ignore him, chewing rapidly and, unfortunately, breaking my victorious strands of cheese. Grabbing a napkin, I wipe my face while I dig my phone out of my bag's depths. Only one person would be calling me right now, and I say a few silent prayers to the gods that she's not stranded at Ruby's or some guy's apartment a town away.

But it's not Mom.

It's Eva, and the second I see her name, a little flare of happiness ignites in my stomach, despite all the food in there right now.

"Hey," I say after I swipe my finger over the screen. "I thought you were at work."

Nothing for a split second, but I think I hear her sniffle or something.

"Eva?"

"Yeah. Hey."

Her words flow out on an exhale, and her voice sounds small. Small and tired and scared. Immediately, my hackles are up, and I'm out of my chair and walking toward the front door.

"What's wrong?" I ask. "Are you okay?"

"What's going on?" Luca's out of his seat too, following me. I shake my head at him and hold up my forefinger.

"Um," Eva says, her voice shaking. "I'm . . . I'm at the hospital."

"What? Why?"

"I'm okay. Just a bump on my head, but—"

"Just a bump on your head? What the hell happened?"

Luca disappears from my view, and I hear him call for Emmy. On the phone, Eva doesn't answer me, but I hear her labored breathing and some beeping in the background.

Hospital noises.

"Grace, please come. I'm so sorry, but please come. They won't let me leave and it's too . . ." She takes a deep breath before going on. "I can't be here alone. I can't breathe. They're about to call Emmy, but I had to call you first—"

"Okay. It's okay, I'm coming, but tell me what happened. Did you get hurt at work?"

"I left work early."

"Why?"

Another pause. Another attempted deep breath. "I was . . . I was with Maggie."

The floor feels like it falls out from under me. My knees sort of buckle, but I grab the front door's knob, keeping myself upright. "What?"

"She called me and she was really upset and I was worried, so I went with her."

"Where?"

"To that place, Ruby's? She just wanted to dance, I guess. After a while, I convinced her it was time to go and she said she was fine to drive, but—"

"You got in a car accident?"

"Yeah. I didn't know she was that drunk or I wouldn't have—"

"Is she okay?" My voice is quiet. A pinprick. A wish.

"She . . . I think she hurt her arm. Maybe it's just a sprain. They won't tell me anything, but she was conscious when the ambulance came. She wasn't going super fast, and the airbags came out when she ran into a tree."

I can't even respond. I don't have any words and I feel myself crumpling, folding in on myself, disintegrating, right there in Luca's entryway. A million emotions war for dominance, and I can't see straight. My vision is blurring, and I can't tell if the world is going wonky or if I'm about to cry. I can't feel my face, my hands, my heart.

*I want my father.*

That's all I can think. I don't even know where the thought comes from, but something in me, something small and scared and exhausted, rises up and grasps onto that single need.

*I want my father.*

I'm about to scream or cry or something when I feel the phone slip from my hands. I expect a crash to the floor, but instead I hear Emmy's calm voice. She's talking to Eva on my phone, getting details, telling her to breathe, telling her we'll be right there. Luca comes up behind me and wraps both arms around my shoulders, pulling my back to his chest.

Emmy ends the call and hands me my phone. Her keys are

already out and her jaw is clenched tight, tears gathering in her eyes. But they don't fall. She holds them in and opens the front door, gesturing us outside.

*I should say I'm sorry,* I think vaguely. I should've been there. I should never have left Maggie alone. I should've told Eva about everything sooner. I should've taken Mom's keys, her phone so she couldn't call Eva, should never have started that first piano lesson with Mr. Wheeler all those years ago, because maybe that's it. Piano is pulling me away from her. Eva is pulling me away. Luca. New York. The world.

*Fantasie.*

In the car, Luca buckles me into the back seat. I should probably apologize for that. For the dot of pizza sauce still on his chin. Near the hospital in Sugar Lake, we seem to hit every red light. I'm sorry for that, too.

I'm about to say it all, an apologetic vomit, but then Luca reaches behind him from the front seat and grabs my hand. He doesn't say anything. Doesn't say it's okay. We both know it's not. He just squeezes my fingers and I squeeze back, and I keep squeezing until the car comes to a stop at the emergency room entrance.

# chapter twenty-seven

AT THE HOSPITAL, EMMY IS A FORCE. SHE BLASTS INTO the waiting room, ponytail flying, purse slapping against her hip, Luca and me trying to keep up. I let her talk to the nurse behind the counter, a young guy in bright orange scrubs that make me think of inmates in a prison. She talks calmly, evenly, with that tone she used to use whenever Luca and I jumped on his bed when we were kids, catapulting ourselves off and crashing to the floor over and over again.

Mom's name comes out of Emmy's mouth, and she gestures toward me. Should I wave? Raise my hand? I feel totally numb, like I got pumped full of some prescription painkiller on the way here.

"This way," she says after talking a bit more with the nurse, whose name tag reads Bryce.

"Gray?"

I snap my eyes to Luca, who's starting toward the double doors that lead into the patient rooms with Emmy. I blink at him, trying to make this whole scene make sense. When I don't move, he frowns and starts walking back toward me.

"You okay?"

I don't answer him, just grab his hand and follow Emmy, who's blazing a trail, her flip-flops squeaking over the tile floor.

We get to Eva's room first. It's not really a room, just one of those pleather examining tables behind a sea-foam-green curtain. A nurse in blue scrubs with little sunshines all over them is fitting a butterfly bandage over a cut on her forehead, just over her left eyebrow.

"Oh my god," Emmy says, eyeing some bloody gauze and what looks like a huge pair of tweezers on the metal tray next to the table.

"I'm fine," Eva says weakly. Her eyes go to mine, but I skirt my gaze away.

"Fine, my ass," Emmy says, popping her hands on her hips.

"Whoa," Luca says. Even I blanch a little. Emmy never swears.

"She really is fine," the nurse says with a smile, but it quickly fades as she looks between Emmy and Eva, a confused pucker between her brows. "Are you . . . I'm sorry, are you Eva's mother?"

Silence fills the room until Eva inhales a choked sob, one hand covering her mouth to hold it in.

"No. I'm Emmy Michaelson," Emmy says quietly, firmly. "I'm Eva's guardian."

"Oh." The nurse swings her head around, staring at all of us, her brown ponytail bobbing. "Well, that explains how different you two look from each other!"

Emmy just stares at the woman.

The nurse clears her throat and pastes on a professional smile. "I just brought Eva up from some tests. No concussion, just a cut on her head from some glass. Not too deep, though. The doctor will release her shortly."

"Fine. Thank you," Emmy says.

"Can I go now?" Eva says, barely a whisper. She's staring at her lap, her shoulders rising and falling with deep desperate breaths. "Please. I want to go home. I want to go *now*."

"Soon, honey," Emmy says, brushing a curl out of Eva's face as the nurse cleans up the dirty bandages. Eva tangles her fingers with Emmy's, gripping tight. "I'll go find the doctor and ask, okay?"

Eva nods and releases Emmy's hand. My own hands tingle, needing to touch her, hold her, press a kiss to that ugly butterfly bandage with the little peek of red seeping out the side, the harsh crimson burn on her neck from her seat belt.

But I don't.

Suddenly, my fingertips feel heavy—too dark purple, too *Maggie,* a hurricane waiting to make landfall.

So instead, I walk out of the room, ask a nurse heading down the hall where Mom is. She asks my name. I tell her and she spits out a number.

Luca doesn't follow me to her room. Neither does Emmy.

It's just me, just us, Maggie and Grace, blasting through the world and breaking shit on our way through.

Mom's in a real room at the end of the hall. She's lying on a bed, clad in a hospital gown, a blue blanket over her legs. Her left arm is in a brace, and there are a few other scratches here and there, including a large bandage near her right temple, but she's awake.

"Baby," she says, smiling through droopy eyes.

I don't return her greeting, but sit on the edge of the bed and gesture to her arm. "Is it broken?"

"No, just a sprain. But they're keeping me overnight because I bumped my head pretty bad. Hit the door or something."

All I can think about is how the hell we're going to pay for all this. For that tube in the crook of her elbow. For that bandage on her head. For that sling on her arm. It's not like we have health insurance. We've *never* had health insurance. As a kid, I got all my shots at the county health department.

Emmy took me.

"And I have to talk to the *police*," Mom says, spitting out the last word like it's a swear. "It's absolutely ridiculous."

"Why is it ridiculous?"

"It was just a little accident. They're making it into this huge deal."

I rub at my eyes, hoping this isn't really happening, that I'm not actually seeing her annoyed expression or hearing her flippant tone get rolling on her *just* parade again. "You were drunk, Mom. You had a minor in the car."

"Oh, Eva's fine."

"Eva's freaking out!"

Suddenly I'm standing. And yelling. Loudly enough to draw attention.

"Everything all right?" a deep voice asks from the doorway.

It's Bryce.

"Yes, thank you," Mom says.

"No, *Bryce,* it's not."

"*Gracie,*" Mom hisses. Then she smiles at Bryce. "We're fine."

He frowns but nods, eyeing me warily as he leaves.

"For god's sake, Grace."

"What were you thinking? How could you drive with Eva in the car?"

"Baby—"

"Why did you even call her to go with you to Ruby's? Do you know how screwed up that is? Taking a kid to that dump? She could've been hurt, worse than she already is."

"You were always fine."

"Was I? Do you know how many nasty guys hit on me? Tried to buy me drinks? Handed me drinks already made? Did you know some asshole followed me to the bathroom one time? I had to pretend I was about to puke just to get him to leave me alone."

Mom's eyes widen. "You never told me that."

"I did!"

"I would've remembered that, baby. Did he touch you?"

"You *wouldn't* have remembered. Even if you had, you probably would've said he was *just* being friendly. And no, he didn't touch me. I learned how to fend off that kind of miscreant at a really young age, so thanks for that, I guess."

I pace the room, so fucking angry and sad. So fucking over it.

"You know what?" Mom says, sitting up a little, her chin thrust out like it does when she gets mad. "I don't like this attitude of yours lately. Everything I do seems to piss you off, and I'm a little tired of it. I think we need a fresh start."

"What does that mean?"

"It means as soon as I get out of here and settle this with the police, we're leaving. Away from Cape Katie. I'm tired of all the small-town mealy-mouthed crap here anyway. Everyone is always in everyone's business. We need something bigger. Portland maybe. Some place where there will be more opportunities for you to find a job after you graduate next year."

"After I grad—"

But the words die on my tongue. I stare at her. She watches me, her annoyance melting into something hopeful, something needy and desperate, that same look that's always simmering just underneath every other look, even when she's telling me her grand plans for a trip to New York. That *It's you and me forever* kind of look.

Before I can say anything, two uniformed police officers knock on the door. They look bored and tired and ask if I could please give them a few minutes with Mrs. Glasser.

I barely hear them. Barely register their scruffy faces and badges. I just nod, still trying to wrap my mind around Mom's words.

"Go back to the motel and get our things together, all right?" Mom calls, and I drift out the door. "The car's totaled, but I'll figure it out when I get back in the morning."

I don't say okay. Nothing is okay. But as I walk down the hall, I know I'm going back to a dank motel room to pack up all of our belongings. There's nothing to else to do.

Maggie and Grace, together forever.

I sit in the waiting room. Around me, everyone is coughing and hacking and sneezing and bleeding, and it's a general cesspool of humanity, but I barely notice any of it. My nose burns from the bleachy and medicine-y odors wafting through the air. I'm not sure how long I'm there, blinking heavily at CNN on the TV, before Emmy comes out with her arm around an exhausted-looking Eva, Luca trailing behind them and carrying Eva's bag.

"Are you coming with us now, Grace?" Emmy asks, digging through her bag for her keys. "Or do you need to stay?"

"Yes," I say, standing. "I mean, no. I'd like to go now. If that's okay."

She pulls her keys out of her purse and takes a deep breath. I'm not sure what I expect from her. Whatever it is, what I get is a weary smile and a whispered "Of course, honey." She hasn't looked at me once. Just takes Eva's arm and guides her out the door, Eva's gaze on me the whole time.

Tears pool in my eyes, but I can't let them fall. Not yet.

Luca's hand slips into mine. "Mom's just freaked out, Gray. This whole thing shook her up. Remember when Macon was sixteen and got in that fender-bender? Barely a dent on the car, the airbags didn't even deploy, and Macon didn't have a scratch on him. She still she took him to the emergency room."

"She's mad."

"She's mad at Maggie. Not you."

I don't say anything. Luca squeezes my hand, but I pull away and walk outside into the silvery drizzle.

The drive back to Cape Katie is silent. Nothing but a few soft drops of rain on the windshield, the wipers *swip-swapp*ing every few seconds. No one asks about Maggie. I don't offer any information.

It's like we're both already long gone.

# chapter twenty-eight

*AFTER YOU GRADUATE . . .*
*After you graduate . . .*
*After you graduate . . .*

By the time Emmy pulls up to the Lucky Lobster, Mom's words have already rolled through my head about a million times. They're so loud, her voice so tinny in my mind, I barely hear Luca telling me to wait when I toss the car door open and get out.

I'm halfway to the stairs leading up to our crappy entrance-on-the-outside motel room when I hear the door of Emmy's Accord squeak open again.

"—let me do it," Eva's voice says. "I'll be right back . . . No, I'm okay."

I walk faster.

I don't want to talk to her. If I do, I'll cry or scream or try to kiss her, and I can't do anything of those things.

"Grace?"

The stairs are in front of me. They're right there with their

277

tarnished handrail and paint-chipped wood. All I have to do is take them two at a time and our room is the second on the right. Safety.

"Grace."

But I can't take the steps two at a time. Her voice stops me, holds me, turns me around.

"What?" I try to say it forcefully, angrily, even meanly, but it comes out a cracked whisper.

Now, *she's* right there. Right in front of me. She smells like Band-Aids and smoke.

"Grace."

"Please stop saying my name." I finally lift my eyes to hers, to that cut on her head, to her red-rimmed eyes haunted by another hospital hours away. The rain falls softly, tiny sparkling diamonds on our skin.

"Is Maggie okay?"

I blink at her. I didn't expect that question. It seems like a simple one because, yes, my mother is okay. Bumps and bruises, that's all. But I can't say yes. I can't answer it, because in that moment, with a thin mist of rain coming down on us, Eva's eye makeup smudged and her hair a mess, I don't know the answer.

"You promised me," I say quietly.

She looks down, but not before I see a fresh wave of tears fill her eyes. "I know."

"You promised me, Eva. And you . . . you got hurt." *And it's my fault.* Instinctively, my hand comes up and swipes away one tear from her cheek before I force my arm back to my side.

"I'm sorry," she says again, stepping closer, but I step back. "She called and I told her I was at work, but she was so set on going to Ruby's tonight."

"She's always so set on doing whatever's in her head, Eva."

"I know. Or maybe I don't. I don't know, but I could tell she was in a bad place, so I went with her. I was worried."

"Why didn't you call *me?*"

She presses her eyes closed. "Things were already so awful with you and her. I didn't want to make it worse. You were so sad and angry. I was trying to help. I thought I was helping."

"You promised me." I say it again because it's my only point, really. Her own reasons make a sort of sense, and I can't argue with her. Don't have the energy to. "You *promised* me and then we . . . we spent that night on *Emmaline* and barely two days later you broke that promise."

"I wasn't trying to. I was—"

"I'm tired, Eva." And I'm almost shocked by how much my voice sounds it. "I'm tired of broken promises. And this"—I wave my hands between us—"it's just one more thing I have to worry about. And I can't . . . I can't be the person you need me to be anyway."

"Don't say that," Eva says.

She tries to take my hand, but I wrench it back. I'm so sick of this. No one is safe with Maggie, and, by extension, no one is safe with me. Not even *me*. But this is my life. I'm used to it, stuck in it, for better or worse, and I'm sick of wishing for it to change. Sick of feeling happy only for all of it to go to crap. Even if I did leave for school, I'd never feel okay about it, never feel *right.*

Because it's Maggie.

It'll always be Maggie. Not because that's what I want, but because it's all I have. It's all that's mine, all there's room for.

Maybe Mom's right.

Maybe we have outgrown this town, our lives here. Or maybe we never fit in at all.

*Just* a home.

*Just* a girl.

"I have to go," I say. I start to turn away, but she hooks her hand around my elbow and whirls me back around.

"Are you for real?" Eva asks, tears sparking her eyes again. But underneath that, there's a flare of anger. And I know she's finally seen it. Too much. Not enough. Whatever. She's finally sick of it all too. "You're actually mad at me?"

I just stare at her because I don't know *what* I am.

"I really was trying to help," Eva says, taking a step back. "Yeah, your mom's a mess, Grace. But she's still *here.* She's alive and breathing, and you get to call her *Mom* every single day. But fine. Go tell yourself whatever you want about us, about who you are, about what you think is your fault."

She wipes rain and tears from her eyes, her face all hard edges and determination. She looks at me, waiting for me to say something. Comfort her, yell at her, I don't know. Just *something.* But I can only watch her. Watch us unravel.

Eva's expression goes soft and slack, realization spilling over her face like a sunrise.

Love isn't enough.

It never is.

If it were, Eva would still have her mom. I'd have a house I've lived in for years and a sober mother with a normal job whose eyes would light up every time her daughter sat down at the piano.

"Maybe you're right," Eva says. Her eyes are on mine, but they don't see me. They look through me, like what she's about to say has already been said. Because it has, at least in my head. "Maybe this isn't a good idea, you and me. Maybe you really can't love me the way I want you to. Maybe I can't either."

And then she turns away from me, her arms wrapped around her middle as she runs back toward the car, a curtain of rain cutting us off from each other. I watch her go, my sad little swan, while my lungs try to pull in enough air.

Then I push myself up the steps, two at a time. I think I hear Emmy call out to me. I think I hear Luca yell my name.

I know I hear someone choke on a sob.

I think that someone is me.

But I keep taking those stairs, two by two, until I can't hear anything anymore.

The rain comes down in sheets as I pack. There's not much. A lot of my stuff is still at Pete's. I'm not sure what Mom's planning to do about all that, but right now I can't think about it. I can't think about anything, about any*one;* the only thing that distracts me is running through piano pieces in my head, and that only makes me think about what Mom said in the hospital.

*After you graduate . . .*

My finger pauses in mid-zip on my suitcase. She never really believed I'd go to New York. When my audition invitation letter came, it was still a far-off dream, too far away to be real for either one of us. I don't know what she was thinking when she made those hostel reservations. Maybe it really was just a bribe to keep me from freaking out over moving to the lighthouse. Whatever it was, that excitement has long since fizzled out, replaced by a mourning girl and purple balloons and necklaces and a new start in Portland.

Because this is Maggie we're talking about.

I sink onto the bed. Back in April, before she said anything about a girls' trip to the city, I'm the one who asked her to go with me to New York. I begged her, never even considered taking Luca with me. Maybe deep down, I knew this would happen. I knew we'd never make it. Hell, I think I counted on it, too scared to actually make the decision to leave her. Too scared to risk reading *not good enough* in a rejection letter printed on college letterhead. It was self-sabotage at its finest.

The realization settles over me like one of those April snows we sometimes get. Surprising and expected all at once. Ice-cold when you're ready for warmth. My fingers dig into my eyes, pressing so hard until I see fireworks of color. I let myself fall back onto the mattress. My phone buzzes loudly from inside my bag. Could be Mom. Could be Luca or Eva. Could be Jay-freaking-Lanier for all I know. Whoever it is, I've got nothing left for them.

# chapter twenty-nine

"Gracie, let's get moving."

I blink.

Once.

Twice.

"Baby. Get up, now."

The room comes into focus. It's still dark out, the lobster lamp on the bedside table coating the faded room in a salmon glow. The cheap alarm clock flickers 4:13 a.m.

I sit up on the bed and push my hair out of my eyes. Mom whirs around the room, throwing the toothpaste into her toiletry bag and grabbing bras down from where they're hanging on the shower curtain rod.

"Mom? Why are you home so early?"

"I'm fine. Just get moving."

I swing my legs off the bed, still clad in my jeans from yesterday. Ugh, I feel like death. Probably look like death too. Mom doesn't look like she's got both feet in the land of the living either.

She's dressed in what I can only assume are her going-out clothes from last night—a pair of black skinny jeans and a sparkly red tank top that's now sporting a tear at the hem. Her arm is in a navy-blue brace, and she keeps muttering "fucking arm" under her breath.

"What happened with the cops?" I ask, digging my phone out of my bag. Eleven missed calls. All from Luca.

Except one.

I stare at her name, but then Mom's voice cuts off my thoughts.

"Nothing. I mean, I have a court date for the ticket or whatever, but it's not for weeks. I'll come back for it."

*Ticket or whatever.* Translation: DUI. Not like it's her first.

"Gracie, we've got to go." She brushes her hair out of her face, her usually messy ponytail messier than ever. "Get my suitcase out from under the bed, will you?"

I watch her for a few seconds. Usually, I'd say *okay.* Usually, I'd say *yes.* But this time, she's asking me to leave the only town I've ever known. She's asking me to leave Luca and Emmy. She's asking me to finish high school in some strange new city, only to rope myself to retail jobs or waitressing for the rest of my life so she can steal my tips out of my *Wizard of Oz* jewelry box.

This time her whims are riding on the tails of a car accident that totaled our car and hurt my girlfriend, and her every movement right now has this tone of panic to it that's setting me on edge. Or *more* on edge. I'm already hanging off a cliff here.

"Gracie!" Mom snaps. "Suitcase. Now. We're catching the six a.m. bus."

"Why are we in such a hurry?" I ask as I reach under the bed and grab her suitcase handle. It slides reluctantly over the carpet, and I wonder what Mom's stuffed in there to give the appearance of a clean room. Her soldering iron, maybe. That thing's heavy as hell.

"I'm just ready to get out of here," she says. "And I have an old friend in Portland I want to look up."

"An old friend."

"Yes, Gracie, Jesus Christ. I do have friends outside of this hick town."

If she does, it's news to me. The only *friends* she could possibly have that don't live in Cape Katie are skeezes she hooked up with at Ruby's.

"What about our stuff at Pete's?" I ask.

"He'll mail it to us! Now, for god's sake, enough questions and open that up for me."

To buy myself some time and try to figure out what the hell to do, I slowly unzip her suitcase. I flip the top open and suck in a breath when I see it's not full of her soldering iron or jewelry materials or old magazines.

It's full of bottles. Five of them. All Grey Goose vodka. Some of them blueberry flavored, some of them lemon, but all of them empty.

*Is Maggie okay?*

*After you graduate . . .*

"Oh, shit," Mom whispers.

I glance up to see her frozen in front of me.

"I forgot those were in there."

"You forgot . . ." But my voice trails off, shock replacing coherent thought. Standing up, I back away from the suitcase. All the liquor she drained in what had to have been the past couple of days, because she definitely didn't flee Pete's with a bag full of empty bottles. My back collides with the wall, but my eyes stay on those bottles. They almost look pretty, the geese flying free over the soft colors on the label.

"We'll just leave them on the bed," Mom says. She kneels down and starts emptying the suitcase onto the mattress, one-armed and one bottle at a time. They clink together roughly, so hard I'm amazed they don't shatter. "Housekeeping will take care of it."

For some reason, all I can think about are those bubbles Eva and I blew aboard *Emmaline,* the two of us viewing the world through tiny slivers of color. It was beautiful.

But it wasn't real.

Each bubble eventually burst.

Each firework fizzled out.

Each lens got stripped away, and each girl saw the world like it was, all nakedness and reality and live action.

Where *love* gets all mixed up with *duty* and *scared* and *lonely* and *no way out.*

But escape comes in more than one form, I guess, because I help my mother pack. A voice whispers in the back of my mind, asking me what I want. What I need. What I should do. I don't know any of the answers. So I keep loading up my mother's suitcase with her things, good things like toothbrushes and clean underwear. If I don't, who will? If I leave her now—if I leave her *ever* —how many more bottles will pile up in the next hotel room?

An hour later I get on a bus with my mother.


Portland is huge and beautiful. Cobblestone sidewalks under my feet, Portland Harbor shimmering under the afternoon sun just behind the red and blue buildings and steepled churches. If it weren't for this knot of dread in my stomach, it would feel exciting, but it's hard to get pumped up about anything when you're not sure where you'll be sleeping that night. When you can't get your mind off a pile of empty bottles abandoned on an unmade hotel bed.

We wander the downtown area for a while, hauling our suitcases behind us, their wheels bumping into tourists and over cobblestones. Mom's eyes peel through the streets. For what, I'm not quite sure. A watering hole, most likely. I follow her, numb and obedient like a puppy that's been kicked in the side one too many times, relieved to still have *something*.

"What'd I tell you, baby?" Mom asks, her eyes sparkling as she lifts her hand to shade them from the low-hanging sun. "Isn't this lovely?"

"Yeah" I hear a voice say. It takes me a couple seconds to realize it's mine, the raspy, passionless tone so foreign in my ears. I glance at Mom to see if she's noticed and barely react when it's clear she's found a new love, a new city, an entirely new world to throw herself into and around and before. Something almost manic glints in her eyes, in the slight curve of her mouth. Something wild and free. It would be completely captivating if it didn't look all wrong on her face, a mask she shouldn't be wearing.

"So who's this friend you want to meet up with?" I ask.

She waves a hand as we cross the street on a Do Not Walk sign. Cars honk and drivers yell, but she keeps sashaying along, wearing her torn shirt like it's a brand-new Chanel. "I'll call him later."

*Him.* Fucking great.

Mom checks us into a Holiday Inn in the Portland Arts district. I breathe a sigh of relief when she opens the door and we're greeted by two double beds, a fresh linen scent, and sparkling white tile in the bathroom.

I don't know how she's paying for it—how *I'm* paying for it —but for now, I don't care. I need a hot shower, a soft blanket, a room in which I can close my eyes and make believe it's a home.

Mom showers while I lie on the bed, listening to my phone *not* buzzing in my bag. It hasn't made a sound in hours, which means everyone's done calling to check on me for now. Or maybe forever. Just like that, I'm gone and it's as if the world didn't even notice. With the realization comes a weird sort of relief, like I've been waiting for this to happen, to simply give in and become a little Maggie, letting the wave roll over and under me until there's no more me. No more Grace.

It's easier like this.

No one to love.

No one to lose.

"Good god, you look morose lying there," Mom says, standing at the bathroom mirror. She's all gussied up, a slim black dress hugging her hips. Her hair is clean and falls in gentle waves. It's not shiny or even healthy-looking, but it's not a mess, so that's something. Her face is done up too, soft mascara around her eyes and an elegant rose-colored hue to her mouth. She looks pretty. She looks like my mom should look all the time, and I can't help but smile at her reflection.

"Cheer up," she says. "It's a brand-new day, baby." She kisses the air, then pushes up her boobs a little more. "I'm meeting my friend, all right? Don't wait up. I left a few bucks on the sink here if you get hungry."

She motions to the couple of dollars lying on the counter—literally, *two* dollars. And just like that, all that beauty in the mirror goes foggy and drippy, a gorgeous painting neglected and ruined by the rain.

"Fine," I deadpan, and flip on the TV. I don't say goodbye as she flounces out the door.


Later, I take Mom's two dollars and walk a block to the Walgreens. With that and my last five bucks, I buy a Dr. Pepper, a small bag of Sun Chips, and fresh bottle of nail polish remover. I eat my meager dinner on the walk back to the hotel. Once inside my room, I unroll a few sheets of toilet paper and remove every trace of purple polish from my fingers. When they're clean, I dig my favorite shade of violet out of my toiletry bag, but I don't open it. Instead, I stare at my naked nails, bare and tinted faintly pink from so many years of color.

*Why purple?* Eva had asked that night we sat together on the back of *Emmaline,* lost in each other, in possibility, in hope.

*It's always been our color,* I had answered, but that wasn't really why. For years I wrapped myself in this purple, made my silly wishes, telling myself it's what linked Mom and me, and I was so desperate for that connection, it was enough. But really, it was the opposite. These fingers, these nails wrapped in color, they were my way out. My *hope.* My wishes for who Mom *should* be, who I'll be for her, for myself.

I wore that color as the ultimate wish.

And I'm finally done wishing.

Nails bare and free, I toss my bottle of Violet Glow into the trash and then run a bath. I'm not sure how long I lie in the hot water, but there are clean washcloths and a tiny bottle of bubble bath that smells like spearmint and rosemary and a beautiful girl's face framed in dark curls floating in and out of my head. I miss her so much, it hurts to breathe, my lungs rebelling against me. I can't close my eyes without seeing her, so I force them open. But I can't keep them open without seeing some part of me she touched, some part of me I loved because she loved it too. So I close my eyes again and just let her face bloom in my mind while my skin prunes and softens. When the water gets cool, I let it out and run more, hoping if I get it hot enough, it'll scald that girl from my mind, her memory from my fingertips.

# chapter thirty

I WAKE TO THE SOUND OF A DOOR SLAMMING OPEN AGAINST a wall. At least, I think that's what it is. The bath water is long cold and my neck aches when I sit up, so I know I've been in here for a while. Another loud bang, this time the door slamming shut. This room is separated from the bathroom sink and main bedroom, only the tub and toilet inside. Out of habit, I had closed the door when I got in the bath, so I can't see whatever the hell it is Mom's doing. I hear a giggle and then a low rumble.

It's that low rumble that makes me freeze, my hand under the too-cool water and on the drain plug, ready to pull it up and wash everything empty.

Because that low rumble is definitely not my mother's girlish voice.

As quietly as I can, I get out of the tub and wrap myself in a white towel. My hand grips the doorknob, every nerve in my body alert and listening. No more voices. Just rustling, a thumping noise like the lamp on the nightstand got a little hip bump, a long exhalation followed by the squeak of mattress springs.

"The hell is she doing?" I whisper to the door. To no one.

My naked nails curl around the knob even tighter as more sounds filter under the door. Breathy moans. Breathy giggles. A breathy "Aw, yeah, baby" drenched in a male tone.

I'm not sure what makes me open the door. Even as I'm doing it, there's a voice in my head telling me to go back in the bathroom, huddle in the tub, and wait it out. She's done this before, brought guys home, but even in the worst apartments, I've always had my own room, a lock on the door, a Luca to call and ask if I could stay over. Here I'm trapped like a rat in a cage, hitting a food-pellet bar over and over and over that never, ever yields any nourishment.

*Is Maggie okay?*

*After you graduate . . .*

Eyes fixed on my colorless nails, I throw the door open and finally answer that question, the supposition.

*No.*

The bedroom is dark, the only light a white-blue flicker from the TV I left on mute. They're on the bed farthest from me. Bile rises up in my throat as I see my suspicions confirmed—my mother on her hands and knees, her dress up around her hips, some guy I've never seen before wrapped around her from behind. Her *friend*, no doubt. He grunts and smacks her butt a little with the palm of his hand, and my face burns red. All I can see is his back, his jeans around his ankles, and his long button-up shirt covering most of the rest of him, thank god. But with that little slap, something ignites in my gut. Something that lights up my veins, so hot I can almost feel it slithering right under my skin. There's something cold under there too. Something childlike and lost and tired.

Something reaching for a new wish.

Eerily calm, I pick up the TV remote from where I left it on the white duvet cover and hurl it at his blond head. It makes contact exactly where I intended, cracking him on the back of his skull. The sound echoes through the room, and he cries out, his hands leaving my mother's hips and flying to his head.

"What the fuck?" he screams, and staggering forward a little, bracing himself with one hand on the mattress.

Mom scurries out from under him, yanking her dress down to cover herself. "What happened? Tom, are you—"

Her voice dies when she sees me standing there, hair dripping, clad in nothing but a skimpy white towel.

"Grace."

I don't acknowledge her. Instead, I direct my attention to the dude now sitting on Mom's bed. He's breathing hard and rubbing at what is probably a quickly forming knot on the back of his head. His pants are still down, *everything* on display for the entire universe to see.

"Get out," I say.

"Gracie—"

"Get. Out," I say again. Tom—or whoever the hell—blinks at me, like he's trying to figure out if I'm real. "Or I'll call the cops and tell them you exposed yourself to a minor."

"Grace!" Mom gasps, like my threat is what's *oh so shocking* about this situation. But not Tom. In the TV's light, I see his expression fall, and he quickly yanks his pants up with one hand and grabs his boots, scattered by the door, with the other.

"Call you later," he mumbles as he stumbles out the door.

"Wait. Tom—"

But he's gone, hightailing it down the hotel's hallway. The door clicks shut behind him, filling the room with a ringing silence. Mom stares at me, agape. I stare back, but it's more of a cool observation than shock. I feel so completely *unshocked,* and I shouldn't be, you know? I should be completely flabbergasted.

"Margaret Grace, what in the ever-loving hell are you—?"

"Just stop," I say, my voice thin and cold like a razored slip of sheet metal.

She pops her hands on her hips, her mascara smeared into black half-moons under her eyes. "What has gotten into you?"

*Wishes,* I think. I hold one hand out in front of me, the other still gripping at my towel. My nails are bare, but I can still see it. A few flecks of leftover purple.

"God, I can't wait for you to grow up," Mom says, heading toward the sink behind me. She's shaking it off, ready to wash up and hit the sack, no doubt. No big deal. Just another day in the life of Maggie and Grace.

My hands start to shake as I hear the faucet turn on, water rushing, Mom's sigh loud enough to drown it all out. A million lights are coming to life inside me, their force and glow and color almost too much.

Or just enough.

*Maybe you really can't love me the way I want you to.*

Eva's words come back, latching on to every single little light, turning them inside out and outside in.

*But I can,* I say back to her now, wishing I were still standing with her in that crappy motel parking lot in the rain. I'd do everything differently. I *can* love Eva the way she deserves, the way *I* deserve. I can have what I need. Maybe even what I want.

"Mom," I say softly.

The word stops her. She stiffens, bent over the sink, her hands full of water. She lets it splash back into the bowl and flips the faucet off. Then she turns around to face me, a stony expression just underneath that fuzzy gaze caused by whatever she drank tonight.

"Grace, it was *just*—"

"Don't you dare." Unbidden, tears well up, and this time I let them come. They feel right; they feel *good.* It seems so easy now, just to cry about it. Just to feel pissed off and cheated, to love my mother this damn much, but love myself a little more because I *need* to. I have to.

"Don't you dare," I say again through a clogged throat. "It's not *just* sex or *just* some guy. It never has been. It's not *just* a town. It's not *just* music. It's not *just* a birthday. It's not *just* a little vodka or *just* some bar or *just* some new drafty duplex's address. It's not *just* my life. And you know it."

She flinches like I smacked her. Maybe I did. Everything burns —my chest, my eyes, the palms of my hands. My fingertips tingle with certain wishes dying out, others coming to life.

"Don't you dare talk to me like that, Gracie. I'm your mother."

"Then act like it! Fucking act like it, for *once* in your life."

"What is wrong with you?"

"Really? Are you serious? Look at what just happened! You brought a guy back to our hotel room to screw with your teenage daughter twenty feet away, naked in a bathtub."

She frowns but has the decency to blush. "I didn't know you were here."

"Where else would I be? You left me alone with two dollars in a city I don't know."

"Grace—"

"Please just tell me you realize how fucked up this is."

"I don't know what you're saying."

"Mom." I take step toward her, my voice so soft it pulls up more tears. Her eyes are on mine, genuine confusion underneath genuine embarrassment. I'm not sure which one is stronger. "Two days ago, you drove drunk with Eva in the car."

"Eva is fine—"

"And then you ran her into a tree. You hurt her, after everything she's already dealing with. She's not fine. And then you pulled me away from everyone who ever mattered to me. And then tonight with Tom or whoever the hell that was. And then, and then, and then. Where does it stop? How many bottles in the suitcase next time? How long until some boyfriend you bring home looks at me and—"

"I would never put you in that position," Mom says, her hands pressed to her heart.

"You have, Mom. You *do*."

She folds her arms and shakes her head.

"Mom. This is not okay. I am not fine. You are not okay."

"Why do you keep doing that?" she asks, her voice small and low.

"What . . . calling you Mom?"

She nods.

"Because that's who I need you to be."

She heaves a choked sob and closes the distance between us, taking my hands in hers and gripping them tight. The fingers half covered by her brace are cold. "I am fine, baby. We're going to be fine. We always are."

"No," I say, so calmly it almost scares me. But it enlivens me too, fear of becoming this woman in front of me—of irreparably *losing* this woman in front of me—trumping the fear of ending this whole charade. "Look at our lives. You're not okay. *I am not okay.* I love you so much, and I want to help you—I do, but I *can't* anymore. And I'm done making excuses for you. For what happened tonight. For the countless nights before this one."

She squeezes her eyes shut like a little kid refusing to hear reason. "You are *fine*. Eva. Is. Fine."

"No, she's not! And that's not the point! Do you even hear yourself? Do you hear what you're saying about me? About the girl I might love?"

She startles and my words sizzle between us for a few seconds. "The girl you might . . . I'm sorry, what did you say?"

I can't help but snort a laugh at her total cluelessness, but in that tiny moment, I know the truth. And it warms my blood in every good and shocking way. I'm not going to be a girl who doesn't ask her boyfriend of six months where the hell his mother is. Not anymore. I'm not going to wake up one day and realize I don't know my own daughter because *I* never asked, never listened. I'm not going to push people away because deep down I'm incapable of caring about them. And I'm not going to push them away because I *do* care about them. I'm going to love—love boldly *and* carefully.

Starting with myself.

"Not 'might,'" I say, taking a deep breath. "I do love her."

She blinks like a hundred times. "Like, *love* love?"

"Yes."

"Oh. Well." She keeps on blinking. "So, does this mean you're a lesb—?"

"Oh my god, really?" I stare at her. Sure, years ago I told her that I liked girls and, yeah, she blew it off. But I guess somewhere deep inside I'd hoped she still knew. She could tell, because I'm her daughter and she's my mother and I belong to her, no matter what.

But when it comes to Maggie, hope is a sad, silly thing.

"No, I am not a lesbian," I say. "And if you'd ever paid one bit of attention to *anything*, you'd know that."

"What are you talking about?"

"I'm bisexual. Okay? Do I need to spell it out for you or are you going to wave your manicured hand and say, *Well, sure, who isn't?*"

"I don't understand."

My lower lip jumps all over the place and my throat aches. Never has anything my mother has said been more on point than those three little words. They hit like a punch in the gut, real and raw and oxygen-sucking.

"I know that," I say softly. "You never have and I'm done."

She drops my hands and backs up. "You're *done?*"

I bridge the distance between us again, but I don't touch her. "I can't live this life with you anymore. It's not who I am, and it shouldn't be who you *want* me to be. You should *want* college for me. You should be shoving me out the door; you should—"

Her mouth falls open, horrified, and it stops me for split second, something habitual and protective unlacing inside me, but I tie it back up.

"I'm not going to get a job after I graduate," I say quietly. Resolutely. "*You* need to get a job and let me do what I need to do, what's best for *me*, what I want. Mother"—I gesture toward her and then tap my finger on my own chest—"and daughter, like we should be. And you need to *deal* with things for once in your life. Pay Pete back—"

"I am not paying that asshole back."

I let her have that one because as usual she's missing the point. So I step even closer and link our hands, our fingers, dark purple on stripped bare. I press my forehead to hers.

"I want you to get some help," I say. "Real. Help."

She jerks back from me, and her eyes go hard. "You're *my* daughter. You can't tell me what I need. And what do you mean 'real help'? Are you talking about one of those treatment centers where everyone sits around and talks about their feelings and pretends they can actually get better? That life won't continue to shit all over them?"

Her words slice through me.

*Pretend they can actually get better.*

She knows. She knows she's sick. She knows she needs help. She's probably known for years. She just won't try.

"Yes," I say, my voice thick. "I'm talking about one of those places, but I do believe you can get better."

She jerks away from me. "I don't need that kind of help. Couldn't afford it anyway. I just need my daughter. That's it."

I shake my head. "No. I'm sorry, Mom. You don't *need* me. You *want* me with you, to clean you up, keep you out of trouble, whatever. There's a difference. But that's not what I need. And you can get a loan for the rehab. I'll send you money now, get a job when I get to New York and send you money next year too. Anything."

"What the hell? *New York?*"

I press my eyes closed, swallow down the hurt I still feel at her surprise over my future, over the future she seemed to really believe in once upon a time. The hurt I'll probably always feel. "Either way, Mom. Whatever you decide to do, I'm going back to Cape Katie tonight."

"What? You belong with me. You're really going to leave me? I can't do this alone." Tears spill down her cheeks now. She digs her fingers into her eyes. Her nails are immaculately purple, even after the car accident. Not one chip. She takes a few heaving breaths, and her voice is clogged and small when she speaks again. "I *never* planned to do this alone."

And I know she's not just talking about me coming with her anymore. In this moment, I see her for who she is, who I maybe should've seen sooner but didn't know how to deal with, didn't know what it meant for me. My mother, a woman who planned a life with the man she loved. A woman who lost that man in a blink. A woman who was left alone and sad to raise a little girl who could never fill that void, no matter how hard she tried. And maybe it's more than just grief and too many vodka bottles. Maybe she's sick in a way that has nothing to do with situations or loss. I don't know. Whatever it is, she's still facing it alone, desperate for her kid to act more like a partner.

"Do you remember what you used to say about wishes?" I ask her, stepping closer.

She lifts her head to look at me.

"How we wish on our fingertips?" I take her good arm and press my hand against her palm. Our fingers are the same length now. And after all these years, I realize she's right. The stars won't help me. No one will, not really. No one *can*.

No one except me.

"Of course I remember that, baby," she whispers, increasing the pressure between our hands.

"This is my wish, Mom. You need help. And I need to let you go." And then I pull my hand back from hers slowly, widening the space between us.

I spent my last dollars on junk food and acetone. I sit on a bench on Spring Street, staring at my phone, trying to get up the nerve to call Luca, Eva, Emmy. Even Macon. But I can't seem to get my fingers to tap their names. Can't seem to stop my eyes from leaking, my heart from pounding, my mind from screaming out in simultaneous relief and anger and hurt.

After I asked Mom to get help—after I made my wish, for better or worse—Mom escaped to the shower, speechless, and I knew I had to leave right then. I didn't know if I'd have the strength to stay if I'd waited for her to get out.

And now, I know if I don't call someone, I'll go back to that hotel. I'll try to fix it. Fix her, and I can't. Only she can do that.

I stare at my phone, flipping between the names of the only people in the world who love me.

There are a few more missed calls from Luca and Eva. Even Emmy called once, but now it's the middle of the night and everything's quiet, allowing doubt upon doubt about what I've just done to pile up. It's hard to wade through them. Where will I live? Luca and Emmy are the obvious choice, but do they even want me? Emmy's got Eva now, a brand-new girl to take care of. Will I be too much? It's all too overwhelming. I'm too tired, too sad, too desperate to see Eva, and too terrified she'll turn me away.

But I need to go home.

So I tap on a different name and press the phone to my ear.

An hour later Jay's peeling-paint Jeep pulls up to the corner of Spring and Pleasant Streets. He doesn't say anything as I round the front of his car, open the back door, and toss my suitcase onto the back seat before climbing in next to him. He just stares straight ahead, waiting until I'm buckled to start driving.

"Thanks for coming," I say as he pulls onto I-295.

"Sure," he says.

Some band I've never heard croons out of his iPod, and he turns the volume up. That's fine. I don't want to talk either.

He doesn't say a word until we pull up outside of Luca's house. It's the middle of the night, I've just left my mother in a hotel room in Portland, and now I'm sitting in my ex-boyfriend's car, staring at the darkened windows of Macon's old room and wondering if my girlfriend is still my girlfriend.

It's almost enough to make me laugh.

Almost.

"You going to tell me what the hell happened?" Jay asks, his hands still wrapped around the steering wheel.

"Is that your subtle way of *asking?*"

"Is that your subtle way of saying no?"

We stare at each other for a moment, and then I laugh. I laugh long and loud, tears springing into my eyes, and I'm not sure if they're from actual laughter or exhaustion or sadness or what.

"Did we fight like this when we were together?" I ask, wiping under my eyes.

"Hell, yeah, we did. It was hot."

"Jesus, you're such an ass," I say, but I laugh through the words and Jay grins.

"So," he says. "You and Eva, huh?"

My eyes widen. "Where did you hear that?"

He shrugs. "I saw her in LuMac's yesterday looking like someone killed her kitten. I asked Michaelson if she was okay. He asked if I knew where you were. And then I remembered how you used to stare at that Daisy Lowe poster in my room a little too intensely."

My stomach flip-flops. My heart flip-flops. Everything flip-flops. This is the first time someone I didn't already trust implicitly —or trust implicitly by proxy, like Kimber—has found out about Eva and me. It's terrifying. My fingers tighten on my bag, my whole body flushing cold and then hot. I brace myself for a jeer, a mean joke, a slur, even anger—I *did* sleep with the guy—but Jay just narrows his eyes at me. He's even smiling a little.

"I put two and two together," he says quietly, gently.

I feel myself relax, breath audibly whooshing out of my tight lungs. "Well, aren't you the little mathematician."

He gives me a withering look, and I hold up my hands.

"Sorry. Yes. Me and Eva." I hope. I *wish*. My eyes drift toward her window again.

"That's cool," he says, nodding. And I don't know if it actually is cool to him—he's a teenage dude, and it doesn't seem all that unlikely that he might get weird or maybe a little judgey or, hell, even excited when a girl who used to like him now likes a girl—but for now, I'm happy to take him at his word.

"What, no threesome jokes?" I ask.

"Oh, I've already made plenty in my head, trust me."

I laugh. "I have no doubt."

"You still think I'm hot, right?"

"Oh my god."

He laughs, but it fades quickly. "For real, though. You all right?"

I bite my lip, rolling his question over and over again in my head. "I think I will be."

"Okay, then."

"Okay."

"See you 'round?"

I nod. "Yeah. Thanks, Jay."

And then I get out of his car and he drives away. I'm left staring at a dark house—*my* house, for all intents and purposes—and it feels just like coming home.

. . .

Emmy answers the door dressed in a tank top and a pair of blue-and-yellow-plaid pajama bottoms, her hair a sleep-tossed mess. She takes one look at my tear-ruined face and the suitcase in my hand before she releases a long sigh, like she's been holding that breath for years. Maybe she has. Maybe we all have. Then she smiles a sad smile—part relief, part heartbreak—and pulls me into her arms.

# chapter thirty-one

THERE'S NO SIGN OF EVA, BUT LUCA MUST HAVE HEARD my soft knock. He comes into the living room just a few seconds after Emmy lets me in, clad in green pajama bottoms and a LuMac's T-shirt.

"Where the hell have you been?" he asks, but he doesn't wait for an answer before he yanks me into a hug and gives me a soft noogie.

"I'm sorry," I say into his shirt. Then I lift my head and meet Emmy's gaze. "How's Eva? Is she okay?"

Emmy nods. "Physically, yes."

"I'm really so sorr—"

She holds up her hand. "Don't. You and Eva might have some things you need to work out between you, but nothing about that car accident was your fault. Do you understand me?"

I press my eyes closed and take a deep breath before I nod.

She steps closer. "Do you *understand* me?"

I keep my eyes open. "Yes."

"All right."

Emmy gets me a glass of water and some tissues, and the three of us settle on the couch. I rest my head on Emmy's shoulder, and Luca's head rests against mine. We're like a little domino train half tipped over.

And then I tell them everything that happened with Mom.

"Is she going to stay in Portland?" Luca asks when I'm finished.

"I don't know," I say, my voice cracking on the last word.

Emmy sighs, squeezing me closer to her side. "You're exhausted. We're all exhausted. Let's go to back to bed and get a little more rest. We'll see everything clearer in the morning."

Even so, we sit in silence for a little while longer, the mini grandfather clock that's older than Macon *tick-tocking* on the mantle the only sound. Well, that and my sniffling. I can't seem to stop the damn river leaking out of my eyes.

Then Luca turns his head and gently bites my arm.

"Ow!" I shake him off and he laughs, which makes me laugh a little.

Emmy reaches across me to slap his shoulder.

"Sorry, sorry," he says. "I just wanted some damn smiles up in here."

"There's a time and a place," Emmy says, standing up. "Grace, I'll get some blankets for the couch. Hope that's okay. Eva took over Macon's old room."

"That's fine," I say, my eyes darting down the hallway leading to the bedrooms.

"Unless my chivalrous son would like to give up his bed for you," Emmy says.

"Hell, no," Luca says, yawning.

She whacks his shoulder again.

"I'm kidding! Take my bed, fine, fine."

I laugh. I've always loved Emmy and Luca's playful dynamic, and the fact that they maintain it even when the shit goes down makes me love them even more.

After Luca changes the sheets on his bed—thank god—he smacks a kiss on my forehead and stumbles back to the couch.

I've just brushed my teeth—something I neglected to do last night—and settled under the R2-D2 sheets when Emmy comes in with an extra pillow. She hands it to me, then sits on the side of the bed, spinning the silver-and-rose-gold ring on her middle finger. Luca and Macon gave it to her for her birthday a few years ago.

"Think you'll be able to sleep?" she asks.

"I don't know. I hope so."

She nods, patting the pillow in my lap and standing. She takes a step toward the door, but then stops and turns. She cups my chin. "You're a brave girl, Gracie. Braver than me. I'm sorry that I ever made you doubt that you belong here. That we're on your side. I lost my friend and I gained a daughter, and, I'll admit, I was overwhelmed and worried about Eva spending so much time with Maggie. But, honey, I've always been worried about you, too. I couldn't simply take you away from your own mother, though you know how much I wanted to. But Eva, well, I thought I could control whether or not *she* got hurt. She's my responsibility. Does that make sense?"

I nod, my throat thick as a damn tree trunk.

"Maggie loves you, Grace," Emmy goes on, sliding her hand up to cup my cheek. "Things haven't always been easy or even friendly between her and me, but I know she loves you more than life. No matter what happens, she'll always be your mom and you'll always be her girl. But you're my girl too. As much or as little as *you* need to be. Okay?"

And this time, when I say *okay*, it doesn't feel like a duty. It feels like letting go.

I know the Michaelson house inside and out. I know Luca's and Macon's double beds are situated on the shared wall between their rooms. When they were younger and Macon still lived here, they would tap out Morse code at night—or their own indecipherable version of it—staying up way too late telling secrets through little knocks on the drywall.

I press my hand against this wall, knowing Eva's sleeping on the other side, probably conked out from exhaustion and painkillers. Even in the barely burgeoning dawn, I can see the smooth, natural hue of my nails, so foreign and familiar at once.

*I wish.*

Shoving the covers back, I tiptoe across the room and crack open the door. I wait for an alarm blast, half expecting Emmy to have set up some sort of obstacle course to prevent me from sneaking out. I know she knows about Eva and me, and I assume she would view my slipping into her ward's bed about the same way she'd view Kimber snuggling up with Luca in the middle of the night. As in total mom freak-out.

Considering Maggie wouldn't bat an eye, the thought sort of makes me smile. Still, freak-out or no, I need this. Eva needs this. At least, I hope she does.

Hearing nothing but a silent house, I slip from Luca's room and into Macon's in a few quick motions, wincing as the door clicks shut a little louder than I intended.

The room hasn't changed much since Eva moved in. Emmy used this for extra storage after Macon moved out, and there are still remnants of its former purpose. Books stacked along a wall. Boxes full of Macon's old soccer trophies in one corner. But there are traces of Eva, too, if only a few. A picture of a woman I assume is her mother on the dresser. A wide smile like Eva's, hair in a bun, arms stretched to the sky and her toes raised up on pointe. There's another picture next to that one. It's Eva and she's dancing too, body flexed into the same position as her mother's. I run my fingers over both frames. Side by side, their mirrored bodies are beautiful, almost sad, almost haunting. I can't decide which effect is stronger.

On the bed, Eva is curled up under a handmade quilt, facing the wall. I slide in beside her, breathing out a sigh of relief just to be this close to her, to smell her jasmine scent, to feel her warmth. I lie there, not touching her, for a while. I listen to her breathe, thanking every wish I've ever sent floating into the sky that she's safe, that *I'm* safe, and that I'm here next to her.

She rolls over and releases this cute little moan that makes me almost smile. I watch her sleep, drinking in all the details of her face that I love so much. I could watch her for hours, her gentle breaths, the soft flutter of her lashes against her cheek, everything that makes her Eva and takes her through the minutes, through the world. Then, suddenly, she's not sleeping. Her eyes are open and on mine. She puts a hand on my face, letting it drift down my jaw and neck to press against my chest where my heart thrums underneath.

"You're back," she says. "Thank god, you're back."

"I'm back."

"Maggie?"

I press my eyes closed and shake my head, all the explanation I can manage right now.

"I was so worried about you," she says, her palm still hot against my skin.

"I'm sorry," I say. I feel like I've been apologizing for the last hour, but the word fits on my tongue just right.

"For what?"

That is the question. *For what?* There is some fault to bear, but there's also a lot of fault to go around. Hell, maybe no one's really at fault. So I just say, "For everything," because it's true. Sometimes you say you're sorry because you fucked up. Sometimes you just say it because *everything* is fucked up.

She curls her hands together against her chest. "I'm sorry too. I shouldn't have said what I did the other night."

"No, you were right. My mom *is* here. But you have to understand that it's never felt like that. It's never felt like I had my mother —at least, not my mother like she should've been."

"I know. I'm so sorry."

I reach out and touch her, just two fingers pressed against her cheek. I'm relieved as hell that she lets me, that she's warm and soft. "It doesn't mean what happened to you, to your mom, sucks any less."

She nods, her tears building and spilling over, a beautiful sort of release. Like always, she doesn't fight it. She just lets it all wash, run, stomp through her.

She *is* like Maggie in that way, I guess. In a good way.

"I missed you," she says through a shaky breath.

"You did?"

In answer, her hand slides around the back of my neck. My eyes flutter closed as she pulls gently, moves forward gently, until our foreheads touch. Then our noses. Then our lips. We fit together like two puzzle pieces. She sighs into my mouth. Or maybe I sigh into hers. Either way, we get all mixed up, and it's perfect and wild, a desperate holding on.

"I don't want this to be all we are," she says against my mouth.

"What do you mean?" I ask.

"Me, the girl whose mom died when she should've lived. You, the girl whose mom can't seem to be a mom. We can't be like that

315

Hattie girl, the one who jumped off the lighthouse a hundred years ago and now that's all she's known for. We have to be more than that."

"We will be. We *are*."

"Can I tell you something?"

"Anything."

She inhales deeply. "I'm . . . I'm still a dancer."

The smile on my face is immediate and huge, even through my leftover tears. "You are."

"And you're a pianist."

"I am. Always."

"And we're more than that."

"You and me," I whisper, "we're sandy spoons and fireworks, lighthouses and wishes and peanut butter."

She smiles and kisses me again.

And I know it's all true. I know we'll be okay. I know we'll be more, for ourselves and together.

Even after loss.

Even after saying goodbye.

Eva and me, two motherless girls finding a new home.

# chapter thirty-two

Here's the thing about wishes: They're always changing on you. They're either dying out or they're realized, and then they're not wishes anymore. They're only truly alive in their anticipation. When I was a wide-eyed little girl, I used to kiss my fingertips and wish I was as beautiful and spirited as my mother. A few years after that, I wished for quick and graceful fingers over the piano keys. Those wishes turned into silent tears at night when my mother brought home some strange guy and all I wanted was for the two of us to go away somewhere together and never talk to another living soul.

I wanted us to run away.

Then, years later, I wished for freedom. I wished for my own life. I wished for the courage to really mean that wish for my own life. I wished for normal days and family dinners and New York City concert halls.

I wished for a sad and beautiful girl to smile at me.

To love me.

I wished against all other wishes to become someone who could love her well.

So many of those wishes have come true. *Are* coming true. It's such a strange feeling, standing on Luca's porch right now, watching him load our overnight bags into his truck, bound for New York so I can audition for Manhattan School of Music tomorrow morning.

So I can play *Fantasie* and bring a wish to life.

Eva comes up behind me and circles both of her arms around my waist, her cheek pressed against mine.

"You ready?"

I don't answer at first because, honestly, I don't know. I never thought I'd get here. And in those moments when I allowed myself to believe New York was a real possibility, I never imagined I'd be doing this without Mom.

But I am.

Because she's not with me.

It's been a little over two weeks since I left her in Portland, since the night I made my wish and said goodbye. The morning after, I called her phone no less than a hundred times, but it always went to her voicemail, and because her box is always full, there was nothing else to do but hang up.

Since then, I've spent most of my time with Eva. I've cried a lot, which pissed me off because I'm not used to crying, but dammit if it didn't feel good. Eva cried a lot too. We'd climb to the top of the lighthouse in the middle of the night, the key Pete gave me when I went by to apologize for everything that happened and get the rest of my stuff safe in my pocket, and we'd trade stories. Good stories. Happy stories of happy mothers during happier times.

Still, I wasn't *un*happy.

A weird thing I'm learning about grief—grief in all its forms—is that you can feel almost everything once. You'd think all those tears, all that laughter, all that deep sadness and even deeper hope would still the lungs and stop the heart.

But no. It's sort of the opposite.

And that's the funny thing about wishes—only when one comes true do you realize the full scope of that wish. What you really wanted. The beauty of it. The complexity.

The cost.

I cover Eva's hands with mine. "Yeah, I think I'm ready."

She presses a kiss to my temple, and I turn, resting my fingers on her slim hips. "Are *you* ready?" I ask.

Her eyes dim a little, but she smiles. Eva's coming with me to New York. In a few months, we'll all pile in Luca's truck again for her audition at NYU. About a week ago, I sat with her on the floor of Macon's old room while she got out her pointe shoes for the first time since her mom died. They were ripped and dirty and smelled like resin.

"Wow, those are so old," I had said, and she laughed.

"They're actually pretty new. We have to break them in when we first get them. Run razors over the bottoms, rip the satin, burn the tips." She ran a finger along a shiny ribbon, a sad smile on her face.

"I want to see you dance again."

She lifted her eyes to mine. For a few seconds she just looked at me, but then she leaned forward and kissed me. A few days later, I went with her to her first dance class at the studio in Sugar Lake, and I watched her come alive again.

"I'm ready for more," she says now, her voice a soft whisper.

I run my hand down her face and cup her jaw. "Something more than a sad little swan."

She leans into my touch, a single tear blooming and spilling over. We both let it fall. "Yeah. Something more than that."

Luca slams the bed cover on his truck closed and takes out his phone. I know he's texting Kimber that we're about to leave to pick her up. She's coming with us, much to my chagrin, but she makes Luca happy, so I know she and I will find a middle ground somewhere.

Emmy comes out the front door, Macon and a waddling Janelle behind her. They all hug me, wish me luck, say all the right things a family should say. Still, it's not the same, and a knot forms in my throat so huge, I'm not sure I'll ever swallow again. Emmy must read something in my expression, because she cups my face in her hands and kisses my forehead.

"Is this what you want, Gracie?" she asks, peering into my watery eyes.

"Yes." No hesitation. I know this is what I'm supposed to do, what I want to do, but it's still hard as hell. Because getting what you want always means giving up something else.

Emmy nods knowingly. She runs her thumbs over my cheeks and winks before enveloping Eva in a hug.

True to form, Luca gives me a noogie as I pass him to get into his truck. I slap his butt and he yelps. He's just started the engine when a brown UPS truck pulls up behind us, blocking the driveway.

"Dammit," Luca says.

"Oh, chill, it'll only take a second," Eva says from the back seat, but I'm sort of with Luca on this one. My entire body feels like it's lit on fire. Like, if I don't go *now*, I never will. Or something will happen to prevent this whole thing. Luca's truck will break down before we even get off the cape. Manhattan School of Music will call and cancel. New York City will sink into the Atlantic. All of these thoughts are totally stupid and paranoid, but, hey, my butt's in the car, so I'm already way ahead of where I'd ever thought I'd be.

We watch Emmy walk over to the driver and sign for a package a little smaller than a shoebox. She tells him thanks but frowns down at the package. When she lifts her eyes, they land right on me.

The truck rumbles away and Luca's just about to throw the

truck into reverse when Emmy walks over and knocks on my window. I roll it down.

"Is that for me?" I ask, even though I can't possibly imagine why it would be. But Emmy nods and holds up the package.

There's my name right above the Michaelsons' address. My full name.

*Margaret Grace Glasser.*

Written in a chicken-scratch handwriting I'd recognize anywhere.

Suddenly I'm standing in the driveway, the box in my hands. I don't remember getting out of the truck, but Eva's right there next to me, Luca on my other side, his finger trailing over the return address label.

No name.

At least, not a person's.

*Mountainside Behavioral Health Center. Portland, Maine.*

I feel Eva's hand press into my lower back as I tear the package open. The tape is stubborn and I'm pretty sure I get a paper cut on my thumb, but I barely feel it. I keep tearing until all I see are balls of white tissue paper.

Carefully, I sift through them until my hand collides with another box. I lift it out. It's a simple white box, square and light. Luca holds the ripped-to-shreds UPS package while I remove the lid and blink at the contents, hardly believing my eyes.

It's a necklace.

Triangles of aqua sea glass, edged in rusty red copper. At first, I'm confused. I angle the box in Luca's hand to check my name, wondering for a split second if this was meant for Eva instead of me because I know Mom never got around to giving it to her. But no. It's my name. And looking closer at the necklace, I can tell it's not the same one Maggie made for Eva. The glass is lighter, more blue than green. I remember Eva's had a little smear of copper on one of the triangles, but this one is nearly flawless, the copper applied expertly around each cool edge.

Hot and cold.

Calm serenity rimmed with fiery energy.

*Us.*

There's no note, but that's not too surprising. The necklace speaks for itself. The return address speaks for itself.

She granted my wish.

She's getting help. She's still my mom and I'm still her daughter and we're still us, somewhere under everything we've been through.

"That's beautiful," Eva says. "Did she make that?"

I can only nod, the tears blurring my vision.

"Want me to help you put it on?"

She takes the necklace out of the box, and I lift my hair so she can circle the delicate chain around my neck. Her hands linger on my throat as the cool glass settles on my chest, just above my sternum.

I look down at the necklace. It's not a lot. Such a small thing, really. But it's something. A start. A hand reaching out. A change. Maybe it'll all go to shit again. Maybe real healing for Mom and me will take a few rounds of falling apart and coming back together. I don't know. Time will tell, I guess.

For now, I can breathe. I know where she is and that she's safe, and I can *breathe.* I can go to New York with her necklace pressed against my heart and play out my *Fantasie.*

No, I never thought I'd be doing this without my mother.

I never really thought I'd be doing this at all.

And I sure as hell never thought I'd be doing it with Eva's hand in mine.

I would never *think* any of it, all this missing and sadness mingling with happiness and relief.

But that's the funny thing about wishes.

# acknowledgments

In many ways, I feel like this is the book I was always going to write. Teen me needed this book, even though she didn't know it at the time. Adult me? I still need this book for a lot of different reasons, and it makes me immeasurably happy that it has found its way into your hands. So, first, I must thank you, dear reader. For persevering, for believing in yourself and in me, and for sharing in Grace and Eva's journey because of and regardless of what their story might mean to you. You are not alone.

Many thanks to my agent, Rebecca Podos, whose unfailing faith in me carries me through many freak-outs and worries. Your editorial eye, humor, friendship, and unparalleled GIF game are a daily inspiration. You championed Grace and Eva before they were even Grace and Eva, and I'm forever grateful.

Thank you to my editor, Elizabeth Bewley, who took a chance on this little book and gave me the freedom to say what I needed to say through Grace and Eva. I'm so grateful for the support you've given my girls. Thank you for giving me room to mess up and for being ready with encouragement as I journeyed through this story. Your insights made this book all that I hoped it could be.

Thanks to everyone at Houghton Mifflin Harcourt for your faith and support. Thank you, Erin DeWitt, for your amazing eye and copyediting skills, and thanks to Lisa Vega and the design team for the gorgeous cover. It captures the feel of this book and these girls so beautifully. Nicole Sclama and Alexandra Primiani, thank you for always being so supportive and enthusiastic. I'm so glad to have you all in my corner!

Endless thanks to my critique-group girls: Lauren Thoman, Paige Crutcher, and Sarah Brown. This book would not be what it is without your early reads and insights and passion. *I* would not be who I am without your friendship and humor and support. I'm so happy to have discovered pizza fries with you ladies.

To my beta readers and first readers, Dahlia Adler, Anna-Marie McLemore, Tristina Wright, Jenn Fitzpatrick, Nita Tyndall, Sara Taylor Woods, and Tehlor Kinney, thank you so much for giving your time, your thoughts, and your excitement to this book. Because of you, I am overwhelmingly thrilled to put this story into the hands of readers who may need it. I can't thank you enough for talking Grace and Eva through with me. I can't thank you enough for talking *me* through with me. I adore you all.

Thanks to Destiny Cole and your constant support and insights on this book. So happy to continue on this journey with you.

Thank you, Ami Allen-Vath, for the last minute-fact checks and enthusiasm. I'm so thankful to have you in my life. Love you, girl.

Thanks to Tess Sharpe, for your enthusiasm and excitement over this book. I found myself inside the pages of *Far From You* for the first time, and it means so much to me to be able to share this book with you.

Thanks to Sarah Crowe, for sharing part of your story with me.

To my Nashville community of amazing people: Courtney Stevens, Lauren Thoman, Paige Crutcher, Sarah Brown, Victoria Schwab, Carla Schooler, Christa Lafontaine, Kristin Tubb, Erica Rogers, Alisha Klapheke, Rae Ann Parker, Kathryn Ormsbee, and Jeff Zentner, I am in constant awe of your friendship and support. I could not ask for better friends, and if I *could,* I'd ask for each and every one of you ten times over.

Jen Gaska, you continue to amaze me with your love and friendship, your faith in me, and your infectious optimism. Thank you for being my pal and for being a safe space.

Becky Albertalli, who is probably the kindest person I know. Thank you for your friendship and constant support for my writing.

Thank you to Parnassus Books and Stephanie Appell for being the best indie bookstore and advocate for children's books a writer could hope for. I am so proud to call this store home.

Dahlia Adler, for her tireless book-and-young-adult advocacy and all the work she does over at LGBTQReads.com.

Thank you to all the bloggers who have shown interest, lent support, and worked to help my little book find the readers who need it.

Thank you to all the Blakes, Herrings, Cowns, Stricklands, Popes, Timmons, and Todds, for loving me the way only a family can.

Benjamin and William, my beautiful boys, thank you for helping me love just as freely and wildly as you do.

Thank you, Craig, for being my partner, for loving me where I am and encouraging me to follow my dreams.